CRACKER

TO SAY I LOVE YOU

D1471081

CRACKER

TO SAY I LOVE YOU

Molly Brown

First published in Great Britain in 1994 by
Virgin Books
an imprint of Virgin Publishing Ltd
332 Ladbroke Grove
London W10 5AH

Cracker © Granada Television and Jimmy McGovern

Text copyright © Molly Brown 1994
from a screenplay by Jimmy McGovern

Cover photographs © Granada Television

The moral right of Molly Brown to be identified as the Author
of this Work has been asserted by her in accordance with the
Copyright Designs and Patents Act 1988.

ISBN 0 86369 827 1

Typeset by Galleon Typesetting, Ipswich
Printed and bound in Great Britain by
Cox & Wyman Ltd, Reading, Berks

To Brandon, with thanks for all the tea.
Thanks also to Shirley Dennis for
her invaluable help.

PROLOGUE

She was lying on a mattress in one corner of the floor, wearing nothing but a kimono, watching Richard and Judy doing a make-over on some fat suburban housewife, when the knock came at the door. She switched off the telly and froze, listening.

'Open up, love. I know you're in there.'

She huddled beneath the duvet, shivering at the sound of his smooth, deep voice. He was a handsome bastard with flash clothes and gold rings, called himself a businessman. 'Don't worry, love,' he'd told her that night down the pub. 'I'll help you out, no problem.' He took the money out of his wallet right there and then. She took him for an easy mark, just another guy who'd had a few too many drinks, trying to impress her. She'd only just moved back to Manchester from Sheffield then, didn't realise who he was, what she was getting herself into.

'You're being stupid, love,' the voice said. 'You're being bloody stupid.'

She took a deep breath, gathering her courage, and walked down the hallway to the door. She ran her fingers through her long black hair, combing a couple of stray curls back from her forehead as she forced her face into an expression of nonchalance. 'Yeah?' she said, opening the door just a crack.

A hand shoved the door back; she stepped out of the way.

'Took your time.'

'I was asleep,' she said.

He strode into the flat, closing the door behind him. Thirtyish, thick brown hair, built like a boxer. Wearing a

1

skintight black tee shirt beneath his white linen suit. 'Time you got up then.' He pointed to an envelope on the floor. She bent down to pick it up. He grabbed it from her, ripping it open. He took the cheque from inside it, carefully placing it in his inside jacket pocket. He let the torn envelope drop onto the floor. 'Get dressed,' he told her.

She walked back down the hall, took some clothes from a rail, and stepped behind the curtain that separated her bed from the rest of the room.

'Maybe you shouldn't get dressed after all,' he said, pulling the curtain to one side.

'Just give me a minute,' she said. 'You'll get your sodding money. Right?'

He raised one eyebrow, laughing as she pulled the curtain back across.

He escorted her along the balcony and down the stairs, gripping her firmly by the arm. On the opposite side of the forecourt, a narrow passageway led through to the street and a small parade of shops. He opened the door to the newsagent's and pushed her through. There was a sub-post office at the back of the shop; he stood behind her in the queue, shoving her towards the counter when she finally reached the front.

He handed her back her giro, standing close by her side while the man behind the counter pushed the money through the slot beneath his window. She reached to pick it up; he wrenched it from her hand, counting it carefully before he stuffed it into his bulging wallet. 'Bloody peanuts, that's all I'm getting from you,' he said, walking away from the counter. 'Hardly worth my time. You'll have to do better than this, love. I've been patient with you so far, but now I'm warning you my patience is wearing bloody thin. You're not even making a dent in the bleedin' interest.'

' 'Ey, come on,' she said, following him outside. 'Give us back a couple of quid at least.'

'Ha!'

'But you've left me with nothing! How am I supposed to eat?'

'Get a bleedin' job,' he told her, walking away.

'At least lend us a couple of fags then,' she pleaded, hurrying along beside him.

'Never touch 'em,' he snorted. 'Bloody filthy habit.'

She stopped dead in the middle of the pavement, curling her hands into fists. Heartless bastard.

He kept walking, never once glancing back.

A car moved slowly down a side street, hugging the kerb. The passenger-side window rolled down. 'You workin', love?' a voice called out.

She stopped walking, bent down to see the driver, didn't like what she saw. She shook her head.

'You sure?' the man persisted. He reached over to open the passenger-side door. 'I'm a nice bloke really, once you get to know me.'

Pay the bastard off, she told herself, there's only one way to get shot of him: take anyone who comes along, and pay the bastard off.

She walked towards the car, smiling.

It was dark when she headed back to the flat. It had been raining on and off all day, a chilly, spattering rain that made her shiver. She walked up the five badly-lit flights of stairs, littered with cans and bottles and needles and condoms, then along the concrete balcony, past a seemingly endless line of windows and doors. Lights were on in most of the flats; the people behind the doors carried on as always, living out their dull little lives. She could hear their music and their television programmes, smell their cooking, see their shadows moving behind net curtains. She didn't know any of them. Never spoke to any of them. Didn't want to.

As she closed her front door behind her, she thought she could hear someone screaming. She walked down the hall towards the living room, and crossed over to the window.

3

She thought she saw someone lying on the pavement, but she couldn't be sure. It was a long way down and it was dark. She opened the window slightly, heard glass breaking in the distance.

She shrugged and closed the window; there was nothing to see.

She unzipped her short leather skirt, let it fall to the floor. Pulled her jumper off over her head, threw it onto a chair. Kicked off her boots and made her way to the bathroom, unfastening her bra as she walked.

She sat on the edge of the tub as it filled with water, thinking of words to describe it. Hot, she thought. Wet.

These were easy words, obvious words. She wanted something more evocative. Liquid, she thought. Soothing. Yielding. Lapping.

She ran a hand across the surface of the water, making little waves. Lapping, she thought again; she liked the sound of lapping. Then a picture came into her head: a dog with its head down a toilet bowl, its slimy pink tongue lapping at the water. It made her feel ill. She clamped her eyelids shut, rubbing at the picture behind them with her knuckles. Scraping it out. She decided she didn't like the sound of *lapping* after all; would never use it again.

She got into the bath, watching the steam rise and condense into trembling droplets on the walls and ceiling. She slid down into the water, immersing her long black hair, imagining how she would describe the man in the car to her sister. 'Big nose,' she would say, 'pock-marked, spongy flesh. Crooked teeth. Had the bloody nerve to quibble about price!'

She imagined herself going over every detail for her sister's benefit. She imagined her sister in a white cotton dress, sitting on a hard wooden chair, back straight, knees pressed firmly together, hands folded across her lap, listening dutifully. Dark brown hair tied back in a big red bow, neat fringe cut straight across her forehead, a slightly bored expression on her face.

4

She imagined herself going on to describe the others, the techniques she had learned to get it over with quickly. She imagined her sister looking at her disapprovingly, then she imagined spitting in her perfect face.

Late morning sun streamed through the window, its harsh light emphasising the cracks in the wall, the balls of hair and dust on the floor. Making everything in the flat look cheap and ugly.

She rocked back and forth on the mattress, shivering. She squeezed her eyes shut, trying to remember what had made her wake up sobbing like that, but it was gone. The dream was gone. All she remembered was a voice, telling her to do *something*, but she couldn't remember what. She reached for her cigarettes and lit one, leaning back against the wall, forcing herself to relax.

She eventually got up and made herself a cup of coffee. Took it back into the living room and sat down on the sofa to count the previous day's takings. She put twenty aside for herself, put the rest in an envelope, then got dressed.

The shop window display consisted of about a dozen secondhand videos and television sets, covered in a fine layer of dust. The door was open; she took a cautious step inside.

The shop interior was cluttered and dim and forbidding. Rows of metal shelving held every sort of electrical equipment, all of it second-hand. A number of leather coats and jackets hung from a clothing rail. A glass display case held a selection of jewellery: mostly wedding rings. She'd heard he always gave you a choice; you could either take the ring off yourself, or let him take it off for you. And he always made it clear the former choice would be the wiser, if you didn't care to lose your finger as well.

'Yeah? Who's there?' a man's voice called harshly.

She took another step forward, saw him sitting at a desk in the rear corner.

'Ah, it's you,' he said, leaning back in his chair. 'What do you want?'

She walked over to the desk and threw the envelope down in front of him.

He smiled, his gaze travelling slowly along the length of her body, taking in her black-stockinged legs, her short tight skirt, her clingy low-cut top. Mentally undressing her, an ironic half-smile on his lips.

She clenched her hands into fists, fully aware of what he was doing. 'I've brought you your sodding money,' she said.

'Did you? Where did you get it?'

He was taunting her, relishing the idea of how low he'd brought her, what she'd had to do for him. And now he wanted to hear about it; he wanted every detail. He wanted a description. She wasn't about to describe anything for him. 'Borrowed it off my parents,' she said.

'Should have thought of that a long time ago, shouldn't you?' He turned his attention to the envelope sitting on his desk. Picked it up, ripped it open, counted the notes inside. He reached into the top desk drawer for a notebook, found her name, jotted down the amount.

'That's it,' she said. 'We're finished.'

He looked at her as if she had to be joking. 'Where do you get an idea like that?'

'I've paid you,' she said. 'I've paid back every penny.'

'All you've paid is a bit of back interest, love. And about bloody time, too.'

The air in the shop was warm and stagnant; it was difficult to breathe. 'What do you mean, back interest?' she said. 'I've been paying you bloody interest every week!'

He shook his head. 'I told you before it wasn't enough. I told you before you weren't even making a dent. Interest on the full amount owing is compounded daily, love,' he explained with exaggerated patience. 'That means interest on the previous day's interest, understand? I've been lenient with you. Extremely lenient, considering how much you owe me.' He pushed the notebook across the desk towards her, letting her see the amount pencilled in after her name. It was thousands. Thousands. How could that be? It wasn't possible, it just wasn't possible.

She felt sick and dizzy; she could never come up with that kind of money. Never. She grabbed onto the edge of his desk to steady herself, felt his hand touch hers. She looked from the hand to his face and saw that he was laughing at her.

'If I were you,' he said, 'I'd get out and start earning.'

ONE

Doctor Edward Fitzgerald sat behind a cluttered desk in a cluttered room on the second floor of an ageing, slightly dilapidated building within easy walking distance of the university. The ceiling-high shelves that leaned against one wall bowed beneath the weight of dusty books stored two or three deep. A long table ran along the length of the wall beneath the window, holding a stack of file folders, a model ship he'd built when he was twelve years old, and even more books.

He glanced down at his notes before addressing the cadaverously thin young woman seated across from him in his office. There were dark circles beneath her pale blue eyes; her shoulder-length blonde hair hung from a centre parting, almost completely obscuring her hollow-cheeked face. She wore black leather trousers and a matching waistcoat with a white silk blouse and a pair of platform shoes. According to his notes, her name was Sarah Heller and she was twenty-seven years old; worked her way up from a copywriter to vice president of one of the biggest ad agencies in the Northwest. Hardly the typical profile of an anorexic. 'How tall are you, Sarah?'

'Five-six.'

'And how much do you weigh?'

'At eight-fifteen this morning, I was six-stone two.'

He glanced at his watch. 'That was almost forty-five minutes ago. What do you weigh now?'

'I don't know. Have you got scales?'

He shook his head. 'How many times a day do you weigh yourself?'

'Every chance I get.'

'You eat one grape, you weigh yourself. You drink a glass of water, you step on scales. You go to the toilet, you weigh yourself before and after.'

The woman sighed. 'That's about right.'

He reached for the pack of cigarettes on his desk. 'You like a cigarette? I'm not a medical doctor, you know. I won't shout at you about cancer.'

'No thank you.'

He held a cigarette to his mouth and lit it. 'Must seem strange to you – referring an anorexic to a person like me.'

'A psychologist?'

'Not just anorexic,' he said, 'but sarcastic with it. No, I was referring to my . . . general body shape. I am hardly a slender reed. But . . .' he took a gulp of coffee from a polystyrene cup, 'Doctor Peterson is a friend of mine; I've known him a long time. And if it's any consolation, he's always shouting at me to *lose* some weight. Surprising, isn't it?' He leaned back in his chair, crossing his arms across his ample stomach. 'You know I get up in the morning and I stumble into the bathroom . . . and you know what I see when I look in the mirror?'

She shook her head, regarding him warily.

'Mel Gibson.'

'Do you really?' she asked drily.

'Tell me, Sarah, what do *you* see when you look in the mirror?' He tapped his fingers lightly on the desk, waiting for her reply. 'Hmm?'

She didn't answer him.

'Maybe you don't want to say it because you don't want to hurt my feelings?'

She looked puzzled. 'What don't I want to say?'

'You don't want to say that when you look in the mirror, you see someone fat like me.'

'I don't want to say that because it isn't true.'

It was his turn to look puzzled.

'I know what you're trying to get at, Doctor Fitzgerald.'

9

'Fitz,' he interrupted.

'Sorry?'

'Everyone calls me Fitz. Just Fitz. Now you were saying?'

'I was saying I know what you're thinking. I've read all the articles, I've seen it on *Panorama*. You're thinking I have a distorted body image, that I am a thin person who looks in the mirror and sees someone fat looking back. Well, you're wrong. I look in the mirror and I see myself exactly as I am.'

Fitz leaned forward, his voice earnest. 'Then surely you must see that you are dying.'

She shrugged.

'Don't just shrug at me,' Fitz said angrily. 'You are killing yourself! That is not conjecture, not pseudo-scientific mumbo-jumbo, that is a fact. All anyone has to do is take one look at you to know that you are dying! Jesus wept, you make me furious, you know that? You make me bloody furious!'

She raised her eyebrows, surprised. 'I thought you were supposed to take notes and make soothing noises. Isn't that what psychologists do? I didn't think they were supposed to yell at people!'

'Well, this one yells, Sarah,' Fitz said, standing up and walking towards her. 'This one yells when he sees an intelligent, attractive person wilfully destroying herself! Sarah, if someone does not get through to you – and I mean soon – you are going to die.' He stood towering over her, his massive frame shaking with emotion. 'I'm talking death, Sarah! I'm talking the end of everything! The end of hope. And you're colluding with it! That's what really upsets me, Sarah. That's what really gets to me. I will not stand by and watch someone knowingly destroy themselves. Knowingly! That's the part I can't accept. You know what you're doing Sarah. You're not stupid. You know.'

'You're right,' she said. 'I know what is happening to me, what I'm doing to myself. But that doesn't mean I can stop, or that I even want to. For nearly a year now, I have been watching myself disappear. Watching my flesh shrink, my bones become more prominent, my eyes become larger in relation to the rest of my face. But I still get up and go to work every day, I still function. I'm still breathing. My heart is still beating. It's like a fascinating experiment, to see how far I can go, how much my body can stand.'

'A fascinating experiment!' Fitz repeated, incredulous. 'It's bloody killing you!'

'You know what the Chinese say?'

Fitz shook his head. 'No, what do they say, the Chinese?'

'You can appreciate the beauty of the tiger, even as it leaps to devour you.'

He leaned back against his desk, crossing his arms. 'I've never heard such bullshit in my life,' he said, disgusted.

Detective Sergeant James Beck walked past Piccadilly Gardens towards the Arndale Centre, scanning the faces of everyone he passed coming the other way. Mid-thirties, medium height, thinning brown hair, bushy moustache, wearing a suit. Most people he passed didn't even give him a second glance. Most people – civilians – walked with their eyes cast slightly downwards, too embarrassed to let their eyes meet with a stranger's. They weren't the ones he was interested in.

He'd learned a long time ago how to spot a villain: look for the guy who's looking for you. When you're in plain clothes, ordinary people going about their ordinary business don't even see you, you're just another faceless person in the crowd. But to the villain, you stand out a mile because you're *law* and they can smell it. It doesn't matter what a copper's wearing, it's the eyes that give it away. Cop's eyes. Always watching, always taking it all in. Let them see you, Beck always told himself, it doesn't matter. Let them know you are the law, and they always give themselves away.

A crowded street has its own cycles, its own natural rhythm; people walking in one direction stay on one side of the pavement, those going the opposite way stay on the other. It happens automatically. He saw the movements of people in the street as currents in a flowing stream; his objective was to search out signs of disturbance in the flow. Ripples of movement, shapes beginning to form. And then he saw it: a narrow triangle, pushing its way upstream. He nodded to the man walking beside him, indicating the approaching shape with a slight movement of his eyes.

Detective Sergeant George Giggs nodded back, noting the three men at the front, shoving and jostling their way through a throng of shoppers and briefcase-carrying commuters all heading the other way. Two other men followed closely behind. A woman with a large bag slung over her shoulder brought up the rear.

A young man in a nondescript sweatshirt, jeans and trainers stood in the doorway of a chip shop across the street, watching the crowd with the same unwavering intensity as Giggs and Beck. The lookout. He hadn't spotted Giggs and Beck yet. So far, Giggs was just another man in a suit, dark-haired, round-faced, mid to late thirties – might have been a sales rep. Giggs reached into his pocket, radioing the two unmarked cars that waited around the corner.

The lookout's sweeping gaze moved up and down the road, took in a man speaking into something that might have been a mobile phone, but could just as easily be a radio. He raised one hand to signal the alarm before he vanished from the doorway, blending in with the crowd.

The gang scattered, doing an abrupt about-face to move with the flow. 'Let's go!' Beck shouted.

He pushed his way through the press of bodies, eyes on the five heads bobbing up and down, maddeningly just out of reach. Two unmarked cars screeched to a halt at the top of the street; a number of officers jumped out, blocking the relentless surge of pedestrians, cutting off any means of escape. One of the bobbing heads broke through the crowd, knocked a woman holding a baby off her feet as he pushed

12

her aside. The woman's head hit the pavement. The baby seemed unhurt but was screaming hysterically. The man, young, in trainers and a shell suit, ran out into the middle of the road.

Beck leapt off the kerb and tackled the runner, twisting his arms behind him, pinning him to the ground with a knee on his back. 'There's a bus coming!' the man beneath him screamed.

Beck looked up, saw a double-decker barrelling towards them. 'So there is,' he said.

'Let go of me, you crazy piece of shite!'

'No.'

Detective Sergeant Jane Penhaligon heard the report of an incident outside the Arndale Centre over her car radio. She picked up the handpiece. 'Penhaligon here. I'm heading east on Chapel Street. ETA Arndale Centre, three minutes. Over.'

A voice came back over the radio. 'Control to Penhaligon.'

She recognised the voice immediately. David Bilborough, Detective Chief Inspector. Her boss. Young, ambitious, infuriating. 'Yes, sir.'

'Scratch that previous destination. We've had a report of a burglary at number three-three Vale Road, that's three-three Vale Road. Seems the victim is a bit of an old dear, possibly a bit confused. There's an officer at the scene already, but it seems this one could use a woman's touch. Over.'

Penhaligon gritted her teeth. Three minutes from the scene of an incident in progress, and Bilborough sends her to the other side of town because he thinks the case needs *a woman's touch*.

'DS Penhaligon, did you receive me? Acknowledge please. Over.'

'Yes, sir. Am on my way to three three ... that's thurree thurree,' she repeated, sarcastically exaggerating the pronunciation, 'Vale Road. ETA ... When I get there!' She had a sudden, horrible realisation. Her application for promotion would have to be approved by none other than Bilborough. For God's sake, keep your nose clean, she scolded herself, whatever you do, don't piss the man off. 'ETA ten minutes,' she corrected herself quickly. 'Over.'

Fitz lit another cigarette before he picked up the phone on his desk and dialled his wife's office.

'Salford Project,' a woman's voice answered. That was Lise, the receptionist.

'Hi, Lise. It's Fitz. Can I talk to Judith, please?'

'She's in a meeting,' Lise answered quickly.

'Oh yeah?' Fitz said, rubbing his forehead. She was lying. 'Could you ask her to come to the phone for just a moment? It's very important.'

'I'm sorry, Fitz. She's not in the office.'

'You just said she was in a meeting.'

'The meeting is out of the office,' Lise said. 'She's meeting a . . .' There was just a moment's hesitation; he visualised her staring up at the ceiling while she groped around for something to say. '. . . Development committee. At the town hall.'

'What time do you expect her back, then?'

'Don't know, Fitz. She could be out all day.'

'Just tell her I phoned then.'

'I will.' *Click.*

He pressed the redial button on the phone.

'Salford Project,' Lise said brightly.

'Hi there,' Fitz said, putting on an exaggerated American accent, straight out of a Hollywood B-movie. 'May I speak to Judith Fitzgerald, please?'

'I'll see if she's available. Who may I say is calling?'

'Jason Buckhurst of Buckhurst Enterprises,' he said, 'calling from Ohio, USA.'

'Just a moment, sir. Putting you through.'

Another woman's voice came on the line. 'Judith Fitzgerald speaking. How may I help you?'

'Judith, don't hang up.'

'Fitz!' she said angrily. 'I should have known it was you! Jason Buckhurst indeed. Just what do you think you're playing at?'

'If I'd said it was me, they wouldn't have put me through.'

'Has it ever occurred to you Fitz, that there just may be a reason why they won't put you through? That maybe they've been told not to put you through?'

'Judith, please. I want to see you.'

'But I don't want to see you, Fitz. If you insist on destroying yourself, I don't want to be there to watch it.'

'I am not destroying myself.'

'Oh but you are. You bloody well are. With the drinking . . .'

'I haven't had a drink in weeks, Judith,' he interrupted. 'Weeks.'

'. . . And the gambling. Especially the gambling. That is exactly what you are doing: destroying yourself. And you know what is the worst part of it, Fitz? The part that I just can't take?'

'What?'

'The fact that you know exactly what you're doing. You know what you're doing, but you go ahead and do it anyway, like it doesn't really matter. Like it's all just some bloody academic puzzle, some bloody game. That's the part I just can't take.'

Fitz sighed and scratched his head. 'Well, Judith, you know what the Chinese say . . .'

'Fitz, I don't have time for this. I'm at work.'

'Then let's meet,' he insisted. 'Come home. Or I'll come to see you at your father's.'

'No, Fitz. If I agree to meet you at all - and I'm only saying *if* - it has to be on neutral ground.'

'Neutral ground?' he repeated. 'What do you mean, neutral ground? We're not at war, Judith! *I'm* not, at any rate.'

'I have to go.'

'All right, all right,' he said. 'Just don't hang up yet! Please not yet! We'll meet anywhere you want – how about a restaurant? A nice crowded restaurant? Is that neutral enough for you?'

Thirty-three Vale Road was a terraced two-up, two-down cottage with a small, lovingly-tended front garden, bordered with pink roses in full bloom. Penhaligon radioed in her arrival, then got out of the car. She spent half a minute taking in her surroundings, the house, the quiet street, looking for anything unusual, anything that might be important later.

Tall, wearing a crisp dark grey jacket and matching skirt, with only the slightest hint of make-up on her sharp, pale features, she pulled her long auburn hair back into a ponytail, securing it with an elastic band. Nothing must be allowed to detract from her air of competent, detached professionalism, and that included her unruly mop of pre-Raphaelite red curls. Her hair, unfortunately, was almost as difficult to control as her resentment of DCI Bilborough and his condescending attitude.

She walked up to the cottage door, adopting her confident, meet-the-public persona. A uniformed PC answered her knock. She knew him; his name was Smith.

'What's the problem here?' she asked him.

'Well, Miss,' PC Smith said as she stepped into the narrow hallway, made even narrower by the peeling chocolate brown paper on the walls. 'The lady who lives here is a Miss Knight. Insists she had a burglary sometime between three and four yesterday afternoon, while she was out at the shops . . .'

'Why did she wait so long to report it?' Penhaligon interrupted.

'Says she didn't realise she'd been burgled until this morning.'

Penhalion's eyes narrowed slightly. 'Any damage? Signs of forced entry?'

16

The PC shook his head. 'No, Miss. I've checked everything.'

'So what's missing?'

'A ring, Miss.'

'A ring,' she repeated, sighing. 'Where is this Miss Knight? I'd better talk to her.'

PC Smith opened the door into a small, cluttered lounge that looked as if it hadn't been redecorated since the early 1950s. 'Through here, Miss.'

A tiny woman leapt up from a thickly padded chair next to the grate. Penhaligon guessed the woman must be in her late seventies or early eighties, but her eyes were bright and alert and her movements were quick and light as a butterfly's. She was about four foot eight with silver hair tied into a small round bun at the nape of her neck. She wore a floral print dress, lace-up shoes, thick stockings, and a white shawl draped across her shoulders. 'Hello, my dear,' the elderly woman said as she fluttered across the room to clasp Penhaligon by the hand. 'Thank you so much for coming.'

'Miss Knight, Detective Sergeant Penhaligon,' PC Smith said, handling the introductions.

'Detective Sergeant?' the old woman repeated, a look of wide-eyed amazement on her face. She gave Penhaligon's hand a little squeeze. 'Your family must be very proud of you, dear.'

Penhaligon carefully pulled her hand away. She reached into her bag and took out a notebook and pen. 'Now, how can I help you, Miss Knight?'

'I've been burgled,' the old woman said, looking up at her. 'They must have been watching me for weeks, maybe months.'

'Who has been watching you?'

'Why, the burglars, of course.'

'The burglars have been watching you,' Penhaligon repeated, exchanging a bemused glance with the uniformed PC. 'Do you have any idea who these burglars are?'

'Oh no,' the old woman said. 'But that is what they do,

17

isn't it? I believe they call it "casing the joint".'

Jane Penhaligon was beginning to feel a slight throbbing in her temples. Promotion or not, she was going to murder Bilborough. 'Do you mind if I sit down?'

'Oh, I've been terribly remiss,' the old lady apologised. 'Please make yourself comfortable. Shall I pour you a cup of tea, dear? You look like you could use one.'

'No thank you,' Penhaligon said, sinking down onto the sofa.

'And what about you, young man?' the old lady asked PC Smith. 'Can I tempt you with a cup of tea?'

'Yes, please,' he said. 'Two sugars.'

Penhaligon shot him a glance.

'On second thought, maybe not,' he said.

'No, no,' the old lady insisted. 'It's no trouble at all, I assure you. I'll only be a moment.'

Penhaligon got up and followed her into the kitchen.

'This won't take long,' Miss Knight said, lighting the ancient hob beneath the kettle with a match. 'And you must have a scone. I baked them myself.'

'No, please,' Penhaligon said, switching off the hob. 'I don't want any tea, I don't want any scones. I just need to ask you a few questions.'

'Of course, dear. Ask me anything you want.'

'Why do you think you were burgled? Look ...' She walked over to the back door. 'This door hasn't been touched. And the windows, they've all got locks on them, all perfectly intact. And there's nothing missing, is there?'

'My ring is missing,' the old lady insisted. 'It's very old; it belonged to my grandmother. She gave it to my mother, who passed it on to me. I've had it since I was nineteen.'

'When did you last see this ring?'

'Yesterday morning. I wore it to my bridge club, at the pensioners' centre.'

'Could you have lost the ring while you were out?'

'No! I definitely had it when I came home!'

'And when was that?'

18

'About twelve.'

'And you went to the shops in the afternoon, between three and four?'

The old lady nodded.

'Couldn't you have lost it at the shops?' Penhaligon asked her gently.

'No, I definitely wasn't wearing it when I left to do the shopping.'

'Then it's somewhere in the house,' Penhaligon told her.

'But it isn't,' the old woman insisted. 'I've looked everywhere. I'm telling you, someone stole it!' The old woman started trembling. Her eyes filled with tears. 'My grandmother's ring,' she said.

Penhaligon looked up at the ceiling, cursing her luck. She put a hand on the old lady's quivering shoulder; the woman felt so thin and fragile. 'Look, Miss Knight, please don't cry. OK?'

'I'm sorry, dear. I'm sorry.' The old woman's voice was quavering, there were tears rolling down her cheeks.

'Miss Knight, I promise you. We are going to find your ring. OK? So please stop crying. If you will just stop crying, I swear I will find your ring! All right?'

Penhaligon and PC Smith had the old lady retrace her movements from the moment she came home from the bridge club until she went out again at three. The old lady had been everywhere; in three hours she'd managed to cover every square inch of every room.

They lifted the rugs, stuck their hands down the back of the sofa, looked under the bed, sifted through the rubbish, even poked down the drains. No sign of the ring.

'I'm sorry,' PC Smith apologised. 'I know it meant a lot to you.'

The old lady sat huddled in a chair. 'It's all right. You tried. I'm grateful that you tried.'

Penhaligon leaned against the patterned living room wall, thinking there had to be something they had missed. Something obvious. She remembered her first look at the house, how she'd tried to take it all in. Then she remembered the beautifully tended roses. 'Miss Knight, did you do any gardening yesterday?'

The old woman scratched her head. 'I might have. This time of year, I'm almost always doing something in the garden.'

PC Smith rushed out the front door to check the bushes.

'With all those roses,' Penhaligon said, 'you'd wear gloves to protect you from the thorns. Where are they?'

The gardening gloves were hanging from a hook in the shed. The ring was stuck down the third finger of the left hand. 'You're a genius,' Miss Knight exclaimed. 'A true detective! Better than Poirot! I'm going to write a letter to your station, thanking them for sending you.'

Penhaligon visualised herself back at the station, writing up her report: *Went to investigate a reported burglary. Spent one hour searching for missing property. Said property eventually recovered inside a gardening glove. Case solved!*

'I'd rather you didn't,' she said.

TWO

Detective Chief Inspector David Bilborough sat behind his desk, looking up at Detective Sergeant Beck, standing before him with arms held stiffly down at his sides. He and Beck went back a long way, had worked together for years. Beck was a good, efficient copper, but he could also be a major headache.

Bilborough was painfully aware of the fact that a lot of people in the force resented him for moving up so fast so young. A lot of people were looking out for any screw-up, major or minor, anything they could pounce on as evidence he wasn't really up to the job. And once again, Jimmy Beck had given them the ammunition they needed. 'You have to admit it, Jimmy. You went too far this time.'

'The bus stopped in plenty of time, Boss. The driver hit the brakes with feet to spare.'

'That's not the point, Jimmy! The point is you held a suspect pinned to the ground directly in the path of an oncoming vehicle. That is the point! There are witnesses, Jimmy. There are scores of witnesses to this fact.'

'Those same witnesses will tell you if you ask them that that scumbag knocked down a woman holding a baby, and that woman is now in hospital with a suspected concussion and it's just by some miracle of luck that that baby wasn't seriously injured or even bloody killed! They'll tell you that, Boss, if you only bloody ask them! And in my book, Boss, someone who would knock a baby to the ground is less than scum!'

Bilborough leaned back in his chair, shaking his head. 'This was supposed to be a simple operation, to pick up a gang of dips. And now it's turned into some kind of bloody circus, with you in the centre ring! It's going to be in all the papers: copper holds suspect under wheels of bus. That awful Parsons woman from PR has been onto me already, talking about bloody damage limitation!'

'I'm sorry, Boss, but I don't see the problem. We brought in the bodies, didn't we? We got them all! And every single one of them has got form as long as your arm! And we got the bloody evidence as well, didn't we? Cheque books, charge cards, thousands in cash . . .'

'All right, Jimmy,' Bilborough said tiredly. 'Point made. That's enough.'

'We've got at least a dozen victims downstairs making statements, didn't even know they were victims 'til Giggsy found their wallets . . .'

'Point made, Jimmy! That's enough.'

'Yes, sir.'

That was the trouble with Beck: he got results. He went completely over the top, he put everybody's backs up, but he was completely dedicated to the job, and nine times out of ten, he got results. 'Just show a little restraint in future, will you? At least in front of the bloody public!'

'Of course, sir. Is that all, sir? I still have suspects to interview.'

'Giggsy can handle the interviews.'

'With the greatest respect, sir . . .' Beck began.

Bilborough recognised the ritual recitation: *With the greatest respect, sir . . .* (translation: *Bollocks*), which invariably preceded an argument with a superior officer. Bilborough didn't feel up to another argument with Jimmy Beck just now, there were too many other things on his mind. 'You've got a report to write,' he said, cutting Beck off. He gestured towards the rows of desks in the incident room, visible through the clear glass wall of his office. 'Go write it.'

Jane Penhaligon walked up the two flights of stairs to her desk at Anson Road Station and sank down into her chair.

Bilborough wasn't in his office. That was a relief; she wasn't in the mood to face him just yet. The senior officers' incident room was empty except for her and Beck, off in the far corner, typing something with two fingers. He didn't acknowledge her presence.

She took her notebook from her bag and placed it on the desk in front of her. Paperwork, she thought, sighing to herself, now comes the bloody paperwork. She needed a cup of coffee first. She got up and walked over to the pot, found it contained an inch-thick layer of black sludge. 'I'll make the coffee, shall I?' she said out loud. No-one answered her.

She carried the pot to the nearest ladies' room, back down the two flights of stairs. She washed it out and filled it with water, then headed back up the stairs to the incident room. Bilborough was back in his office; he waved to her from behind the glass wall at the top end of the room. She put the pot down on the nearest desk.

'Yes, sir,' she said, stepping through the door into his office.

He commented on the fact that she'd been gone quite some time; she told him she'd gone to thirty-three Vale Road, as instructed. He asked her how it had gone, and she told him. He reminded her to write a report and she told him she was about to do exactly that.

'All right, then,' he said. 'That's all.'

She went back into the incident room and picked up the pot once again. She felt like she'd been carrying the damn thing around with her forever, and she still wasn't any closer to getting a cup of coffee. *Where have you been, Penhaligon? What did you do? How are you getting along? Don't forget your paperwork.* Why couldn't Bilborough just leave her alone and let her get on with the job? She knew what she was doing, if he'd just let her get on with it.

A phone was ringing on one of the desks. 'I'll get that, shall I?' she said sarcastically.

Beck didn't even lift his head.

She put the pot back down and walked across to the ringing phone. 'Penhaligon.'

'Jane,' a woman's voice said. 'It's Emma. How have you been keeping? I haven't seen you in ages.'

'I'm OK, Emma.'

'You must come round for a meal. I keep telling George to ask you.'

Penhaligon shrugged, realising it was a pointless gesture; Emma couldn't see her. 'I've been busy, Emma.'

'That's no excuse. We'll make a date soon, OK?'

'OK.'

'Is George around?'

'I don't know,' Penhaligon told her. 'Just a minute.' She yelled across the room to Beck, 'You know where Giggsy is?'

'Interviewing a suspect,' Beck shouted back.

'He's busy downstairs, Emma. Is it anything important?'

'No, just ask him to phone home when he gets a chance. And let me know when you're coming round, OK? You're always welcome, Jane, you know that.'

Detective Sergeant George Giggs walked out of Interview Room 2 and headed towards the front door of the station, loosening his tie. It had been hot in that windowless room, and he needed some air.

The desk sergeant leaned forward confidentially as Giggs walked past. 'Hey, Giggsy.'

Giggs walked up to the desk. 'Yeah, Tom.'

The desk sergeant nodded towards a blonde WPC talking to a couple of uniforms at the bottom of the stairs. 'So what do you think? Is that her natural hair colour, Giggsy?'

Giggs looked back towards the stairs, eyes widening in appreciation. 'I don't know,' he said, nudging the desk sergeant across the counter, 'but I wouldn't mind finding out, know what I mean?'

THREE

She stared at herself in the mirror for a long time, hating what she saw. Ugly. She felt so ugly.

She pulled her long black hair back from her face, twisting it into plaits and tying it with black ribbon. She carefully circled her eyes with a line of black kohl then applied three coats of black mascara, making her lashes look long and spidery. She painted her lips and nails a deep shade of red.

She was starting to feel better already.

She put on a black lycra miniskirt, sleeveless black top, matching waistcoat. Black fishnet tights, black ankle boots, silver earrings and bangles. The finishing touch was the string of satin tied around her neck, like a choker.

She threw on a mid-calf length leather coat – also black – and slammed the door behind her, making her way along the concrete balcony to the badly-lit stairs, then down and down until she finally emerged at ground level.

Kids had smashed most of the streetlamps; the Manchester night was as dark as her clothes. She became invisible, blending into the shadows as sirens wailed in the distance.

Something inside her thrilled to this feeling of invisibility – of being one with the darkness. In the dark, she could forget who she was and where she came from; she could be anyone she wanted to be. She strode forward confidently, heels clacking on the pavement, head held high and proud. She was bad news, a dangerous woman; a Hollywood *femme fatale*, living out her own private *film noir* on the litter-strewn pavements of Moss Side.

Something was going to happen tonight, she could feel it.

Something important. Something good.

She could hear music coming from a pub, just up ahead. Orchestral music, all strings and horns, loud and overblown – the sort of thing her mother might listen to. It was an old Tom Jones song, something that had been a hit years before she was even born. And then she heard a voice: '*I, I who have nothing. I, I who have no-one, adore you, and want you so . . .*'

She went inside, following the voice. Walking past the chattering crowd at the bar, the pinging, flashing fruit machines, a man who appeared to be sound asleep. The voice drew her on, leading her into a small back room, divided from the front by an arch. There, she joined about half-a-dozen people watching the singer.

He was young, in cheap baggy jeans, yellow tee shirt and green hooded jacket. He had a mop of light brown hair that looked like it had been cut with a pudding bowl over his head, a pushed-in face with narrow, slanting eyes and a nose that had obviously been broken more than once. But for that moment – swaying and gesturing in the glare of a single spotlight on a tiny stage, singing along with a karaoke machine as if his heart would break: '*I'm just a no-one, with nothing to give you, but . . . Oh, I love you . . .*' – he was a star. And he knew it; she could tell that he knew it.

She glanced around; in the few seconds she had been standing there, his audience had nearly tripled.

'*He, he buys you diamonds. Bright, sparkling diamonds. But believe me, dear, when I say that he can give you the world but he'll never love you the way I love you . . .*'

He sang those words as if he really meant them, as if no-one could ever love anyone the way he could.

'*He can take you any place that he wants. To fancy clubs and restaurants.*'

More and more people came into the back room. The crowd was with him. Loving him. Even the people at the front bar had stopped talking. And he was revelling in it; eyes flashing, lips curling into a smile.

'*But I can only watch you with* . . .' he tapped his nose with one finger '. . . *my nose pressed up against the windowpa-a-a-ane* . . .' He pounded at his chest, he tossed the microphone playfully from hand to hand, the audience whistled and cheered. '*I, I who have nothing* . . .'

Someone was murdering an old sixties' song in the back room. She found him standing with his elbows on the bar, arms crossed, staring straight ahead. Next to the half-empty lager in front of him sat a small "silver" cup, made of tin. He was alone.

She took a long pull on her cigarette, exhaled it slowly, and walked up beside him. He didn't notice her at first; she moved a little closer. Just enough to get his attention.

He turned his head briefly, saw her, and turned away again. Startled. He was shy; she liked that. She leaned in a little further, brought her face around in front of his. She tilted her head towards the little cup. 'Did you win?'

He shook his head, lifting the cup so she could see the inscription on the plastic marble-look base.

'Second?'

He shrugged and nodded, trying to look her in the eyes, even trying to smile. But he couldn't maintain it; an instant later he was staring down at the bar.

He was obviously uncomfortable; she guessed he didn't have much experience with women. She liked that, too. It gave her the upper hand, put her in control. What a change that would be: to be the one in control.

She leaned in a little closer; her face was open and smiling and friendly. Eyes wide and sparkling, lips slightly parted. Nothing to put him off; nothing threatening. 'I'm Tina.' She waited, still smiling, for his response.

He bit his lip and looked around the room.

Something was wrong. He was supposed to tell her his name, maybe ask her if she came here often, not look away as if he was panic-stricken. She shrugged and laughed nervously, deliberately keeping the smile on her face. Keeping it light. 'Can't get a word in edgeways, can I?'

He turned to her with a look of despair. Then he seemed to come to some kind of decision. He took a long, deep breath, and straightened his back as if he was bracing himself. Finally he pursed his lips, partially baring his teeth, and made a sound like a rush of escaping air.

Tina's smile faded; she struggled to keep her face impassive. What was he doing?

His face contorted as if he was in agony; he closed his eyes, throwing his head forward with every exhalation: 'Sh . . . Sh . . . Sh . . .'

And then she realised he was trying to tell her his name.

'Sh . . .' He gave up, exasperated.

She took a guess. 'Sean?'

He looked relieved. And then embarrassed. 'Yeah,' he said.

'Hi, Sean.'

'Hi.'

'I like the way you sing.'

'Th-th . . .'

She said the word for him: 'Thanks.' She took a pack of cigarettes from her bag, offering him one. 'No need to thank me,' she said. 'No need to thank anyone.'

He tilted his head towards the collection of bottles and glasses behind the bar. 'D . . .' He threw up his hands.

'Do I want a drink?'

He nodded, smiling shyly.

'Dry cider,' she said.

He reached into his pocket and pulled out a handful of coins, mostly ten-pence pieces. He was as skint as she was. She watched him pile his little stack of coins on the bar top, trying to catch the barmaid's eye, then came to a decision of her own. 'I have a better idea,' she said. 'Come round to my place for a coffee.'

He looked as if he couldn't quite believe what he was hearing.

'I don't live far,' she said. She started to walk towards the door; he hesitated. She turned to look back at him, smiling. He stepped away from the bar to follow her into the street.

'Do you go to karaokes often?' she asked him, carefully stepping around some shattered glass.

'Y-y-y . . .' He sighed and shrugged.

'I like karaokes,' Tina said. She turned at the corner, leading Sean past a row of derelict buildings with boarded-up windows. A fire blazed inside a metal rubbish bin, tended by a man in a woolly hat. He shouted something at them as they walked by. 'You can go on your own,' she continued, ignoring the man, '. . . maybe pretend you're one of the singers. Or go with one of them.'

Sean grunted in reply.

'Just over here.' She pointed to a passage between two pillars.

Sean seemed to hang back as he followed her up the steps and along the concrete walkway that led to her front door, as if he was keeping a distance between them. She could sense that he was nervous. She'd soon do something about that. 'Come in,' she said, unlocking the door.

She led him down the narrow hallway, past the bathroom and the kitchen, into the living room.

She moved around the room self-consciously, switching on lights – little table lamps with plastic shades, draped with scarves to soften the glow. She slipped off her coat, tossing it across a chair, and turned to face him. She saw him take in his surroundings – pink walls covered in posters for films and bands and even a Yin-Yang symbol of the Tao, a sofa, a couple of chairs, some half-burned candles on a low table, a curtain draped across the corner where she slept – and then she saw him looking at her.

She moved across the room, positioned herself in front of him, eyes searching his face. There was something different about him, about the way he looked at her. Not the same as other men, not the same at all. He looked so vulnerable. As if he'd been hurt one too many times.

His lips moved; he was trying to tell her something. He

held out the cup he'd won that evening, pushing it towards her.

'For me?'

He nodded, blushing.

'Thanks,' Tina said, genuinely touched. He'd said more with that simple action than most men could say in a thousand words.

She took the cup from Sean's hand and placed it on a shelf next to her *Badlands* poster: the nearest thing she had to a place of honour. 'Coffee?' She had to ask him that, it was supposed to be the reason she'd asked him back: to have a cup of coffee.

He nodded, silently mouthing the word: 'Yes.'

She picked up a couple of mugs from a table and took them into the kitchen.

Sean glanced around the room and saw a photo album sitting on the table. He picked it up and sat down on the arm of a chair, flicking through page after page of what he assumed were family photos. Most of them seemed to be pictures of a dark-haired little girl – that had to be Tina. But she was never alone, there was always someone else in the photo with her – someone slightly taller than her, whose face and body had been scratched out, leaving only the ragged outline of some anonymous figure, forever looming at the young girl's side.

He looked up and saw Tina standing in the kitchen doorway, watching him. He froze, caught in the act. She didn't like him touching her things, she was going to ask him to leave. He closed the album and braced himself.

'Sugar?' she said. That was all. She just wanted to know if he'd like sugar in his coffee.

'Y-y-y . . . yeah,' he said, relieved.

She came back a moment later, put the steaming mugs back on the table. Sat down across from him, studying him. He sipped nervously at the coffee, waiting for her to speak.

'You live around here, Sean?'

He nodded. 'Y-y . . . yeah.' He said it again, relieved he

could get the word out: 'Yeah.'

'Where?'

He wished she hadn't asked that. He took a deep breath.

'H . . .' He stopped, took another. 'H . . .'

'Hostel,' she said. 'You live in a hostel?'

He closed his eyes. 'Yeah.'

He felt a cool, dry hand on his cheek; he opened his eyes and saw her standing over him, eyes boring into his face. 'A winding metal staircase,' she said. 'Makes you think of a snake, coiled to strike. A long corridor lined with numbered doors. Each leads into a narrow cubicle with partition walls as thin as cardboard; they don't reach the ceiling. Stand on a chair, you can see into the next cubicle. There's always someone coughing, always someone shouting, always someone lurking in the hall outside your door.' Her lips curled into an ironic smile. 'And some idiot social worker tells you you're lucky to be there.'

He gazed at her open-mouthed; it was as if she'd seen right inside his head.

'Describing things,' she said. 'It's something I used to do when I was little. Hardly ever do it now, don't like to. I have this dream sometimes . . . it's more like a nightmare, really. Someone's locked me in this room full of bizarre, misshapen objects and they won't let me out until I've described every one of them.' She laughed, embarrassed by her admission. 'Stupid, yeah?'

'B-b-but . . . h-h-h . . .'

'How did I know what to describe?'

He nodded.

'Stayed in a place just like it a couple of nights once,' she explained. 'They thought they were doing me a favour; getting me off the streets. I left two days later because I couldn't stand the stink.' A look of understanding passed between them. 'Don't go back there tonight.'

She stood up and walked around the room, switching off the lamps and lighting candles. She took more candles from a drawer; soon there were lit candles everywhere, arranged

31

in random patterns across the floor, the tabletop, the shelves. Filling the air with the scent of jasmine. She slipped a cassette into the tape deck: The Cocteau Twins.

Sean followed her to the mattress behind the curtain, sitting tentatively on the edge. She knelt down in front of him, taking his head in both hands. He took a deep breath and closed his eyes. She leaned forward, pressing her open lips against his mouth, lightly at first, then harder. Her hands slid down his back, pulling him towards her.

He could feel his heart pounding, his breath coming in ragged gasps. He threw his arms around her, clinging to her in a kind of desperation.

She rolled onto her back, moaning softly.

FOUR

Fitz shifted forward uncomfortably as a party of six squeezed past behind him. He was trying to push his chair back to its original position when a uniformed waiter suddenly appeared at his shoulder. 'Drink, sir?'

'Er . . . Coke. On second thought, make that a Diet Coke. You know the stuff, don't you? Brown, fizzy, full of E numbers. Favourite drink of the pussy-whipped.'

'Yes sir.'

The waiter gone, and the party of six gone, he simultaneously pushed his chair back and the table forward, until at last he could breathe. Jesus wept! How did they expect a man to eat in a place where you couldn't inhale without bashing your stomach against the bloody table? And where the hell was he supposed to put his feet? He shifted sideways, thrusting one massive leg into the aisle just as the waiter returned, balancing a glass of Diet Coke in the middle of a little silver tray. The waiter stepped over the leg without missing a beat.

'You've done this before.'

The waiter placed the drink on the table. 'Sorry sir?'

'Nothing.' He held a cigarette to his mouth and lit it. Judith couldn't object to that, could she? The gambling she'd mentioned, the drinking she'd mentioned, but he didn't recall her ever saying: 'Stop that smoking or I'll leave you', so he figured he was on safe ground with that one. Dying of lung cancer was apparently all right; it was having fun she objected to.

He took a deep breath and looked around him. God, what was he doing at *Cianno's*? It was one of those terminally

33

trendy bistros with beige walls, a couple of strategically placed potted plants, and a menu designed for the wealthy anorexic. He'd have to tell his new patient, Sarah Heller, about this place; she'd love it. She could spend a fortune here and still go home hungry, watching her beautiful Chinese tiger come ever closer. But a forty-four-year-old man should not have to spend an evening surrounded by skinny trendies just to speak to his own wife. And where was she, anyway?

He looked at his watch. That's right, Judith. Be just a little bit late. Keep me waiting about fifteen minutes or so – that'll show me who's boss. Nice bit of passive aggression, that.

He looked around for an ashtray and couldn't find one. There was a little vase of flowers on the table; that would do. He lifted the vase and flicked some ash into the water. The waiter rushed over, wielding an ashtray, before he could even put the vase back down. The ashtray landed on the table with a metallic ping; the waiter vanished as suddenly as he had appeared. The ash in the flower vase trick had worked again; it always brought the waiters running.

Fitz amused himself by looking at the faces around him. They were chatting amiably enough, laughing and smiling enough, but it was all pretence. I can see through you, he thought, I can see through every one of you, to the heart of darkness within.

He focused on one: a woman, blonde, in her late twenties, leaning forward to listen to her companion for the evening, a man in a suit telling boring stories, most likely about his work.

How could he tell the stories were boring? By the look in the woman's eyes. So why was she leaning forward so intently, smiling so broadly, apparently so engrossed by every word? Because the man she was with was better than no-one at all. Because she was frightened of being alone.

Interesting you should pick on that one, Doctor Fitzgerald, he told himself, seeing as how your wife left *you* alone not so long ago.

34

And then he saw her walking towards him; she always had an uncanny knack for timing.

She looked good. But then she always looked good. Wearing printed leggings and a loose jacket, she had the body of a woman half her age. He stood up, smiling, and then he saw she wasn't alone.

'Hello, Fitz,' she said.

'Hello,' he said, looking at the man beside her.

'Graham. Fitz,' Judith said by way of introduction.

Graham leaned forward, enthusiastically shaking Fitz's hand. He was forty-something, with a receding hairline, big round glasses, and a thick brown moustache that completely hid his upper lip. His suit was the same shade of beige as the walls. 'I've heard a lot about you.'

Fitz turned to his wife, struggling not to show his annoyance. 'I've only booked for two.'

'We're not stopping,' Judith said, sitting down.

To Fitz's dismay, Graham sat down, too.

Fitz dropped back into his chair, waiting to see what would happen next.

Judith stared at him coldly. 'You want me to come home?'

Fitz looked at her, sitting there so stiff and formal – all business – and then at Graham, leaning forward and watching them both intently. And then he realised she'd brought this ferret-face along as some kind of arbiter. Just what the hell was she thinking of? 'Wait a minute,' he said.

'You want me to come home?' Judith said again, her voice flat, her expression steely.

Fitz gestured at the interloper sitting next to his wife. 'Who *is* this?'

Her face didn't change; still that steely expression. 'Graham is my therapist.'

Her therapist? Since when did Judith have a therapist? 'Judith, you don't need crap like that.'

She laughed: a short, bitter laugh. 'Twenty years married to you, I need more than therapy. I need a trip to Lourdes!'

Graham leaned across the table, his hands in a prayer position. 'I can understand your hostility,' he said soothingly.

This was more than Fitz could take: to be patronised by a twerp. He clenched his teeth, struggling not to explode. 'Oh, can you?'

Graham went on in his soothing murmur, 'Judith's told me things, intimate things. So you feel vulnerable . . .'

'Jesus wept!'

Graham nodded sympathetically. 'Of course you feel threatened. And you shouldn't evade those feelings . . .'

God, Fitz thought, I'll bet he runs bloody encounter groups: bloody psycho-drama role-playing, learn-to-express-yourself weekend retreats. 'I'm not discussing anything in front of this talking bloody text book,' Fitz told Judith angrily.

'Fine,' Judith said, standing up. 'Bye, Fitz.' She turned and walked away.

Graham hesitated a moment, then rose to follow her.

Fitz shook his head in despair. Why did it have to turn out like this? 'No, no. Wait! Cancel that last statement, Judith.'

She stopped and turned around, hesitating. Fitz couldn't help noticing that it was only after Graham nodded to her and gestured with one arm for her to sit back down, that she returned to the table. Then Graham pulled out the seat for her, mister bloody chivalry himself.

'You want me to come home?' Judith said again.

Of course he wanted her to come home. What did she think this whole thing was about? This whole bloody romantic dinner that was now completely ruined. It was all because he wanted her home. He wanted her.

'Yes,' he said, looking straight into Judith's eyes.

The next voice he heard was Graham's. 'Why?' he said.

Fitz could not believe it. The bastard – butting in like that, when he was trying to talk to his wife.

'I think Judith needs to hear it,' Graham added, nodding earnestly.

Fitz signalled to a waiter who was passing. 'Waiter,' he said loudly, 'a plate of humble pie for Herbert Lom there please.'

'We're not eating,' Judith told the waiter, dismissing him with a little shake of her head and one of her stock pay-no-attention-to-my-husband looks. She waited until the waiter was gone, then asked Fitz very quietly, 'Why do you want me to come home?'

He looked down at the table, acutely aware of Graham's intrusive presence, studying him as if he was a specimen in a bottle. 'Because I love you, that's why,' he mumbled, reaching for his drink. He saw Graham raise his ugly eyebrows, looking as if he'd caught him with his hand down a cookie jar. He held up the glass for his inspection. 'Diet Coke.'

Judith continued to stare at him coldly. God, where was the woman he'd married? The woman who'd smouldered with such passion, who'd stood side by side with him against the world, who would have laughed her head off at the posturings of a weedy, pretentious bastard like that so-called therapist now sitting so smugly beside her. Where the hell had that woman gone? 'I'll come back on three conditions,' she said. 'First: you go to Gamblers Anonymous.'

Fitz made no effort to hide his disgust. 'It's run by wankers for wankers.'

'*I'm* involved in the local branch,' Graham butted in, as if he thought that was a recommendation.

Fitz rolled his eyes. 'I rest my case.'

'It's just about the best in the country,' Graham added in his soothing drone.

'I bet you it isn't.'

'Second:' said Judith, 'we put the house in my name. My sole name.' She sounded like she was reading off an autocue. She'd rehearsed this; probably gone over it, word by word, with Graham. 'And third: we change the current account so that each cheque needs two signatures.' There was a long silence as they regarded each other across the table, Judith staring at him without blinking.

Fitz finally looked away, grinding his cigarette butt into the ashtray.

'Well?'

'Waiter,' Fitz called out. 'Could I have a very sharp knife, please? My wife would like to cut off my balls.'

'I used to enjoy that sort of thing, Fitz,' Judith began calmly. 'The way you'd toss a hand grenade into the conversation, sit back and watch it go off.' Her eyes narrowed, her voice became choked with anger. 'But now it's boring. The way you probe . . . is boring. The way you analyse . . . is boring. Your search for the bloody "pure motive" is boring! It's as boring as living with the bloody Pope!' She took a deep breath, struggling to compose herself. She turned to Graham. 'Would you get me a gin and tonic, please?'

'A large gin and tonic for the lady please,' Fitz called to a passing waiter; Judith was his wife, he'd be the one to order her drinks.

'Well?' said Judith.

Fitz leaned back, watching her face: her controlled, emotionless face. Just enough make-up to highlight her best features, glossy hair cut short for ease of care: that was Judith. Everything perfect, everything neat. 'My gambling,' he said. 'Is that boring?'

'I could think of a lot of words to describe it, Fitz. But no,' she shook her head, and for just an instant, she allowed herself a rueful smile. 'Boring wouldn't be one of them.'

'No,' Fitz said excitedly, encouraged by this brief flash of the old Judith, 'life needs a bit of risk. A bit of Bogart and Hepburn on *The African Queen*.'

'I'd prefer Judith and Fitz on the straight and narrow.' The old Judith had gone back into hiding, behind that controlled, emotionless mask.

This wasn't working; nothing was going to plan. The only hope was to get her away from this beige room full of nattering media types and jazz piano and waiters buzzing around like flies. 'Come on,' he said, rising. 'Give me ten minutes. I want to show you something.'

Judith remained seated. 'Just tell me whether or not we have a deal.'

One part of him knew that what she was asking seemed perfectly reasonable to *her* after what he'd done to finance his gambling: overdrawn the current account; forged her signature to put a second mortgage on the house.

Another, second part of him knew it would be so easy to say yes, Judith, I love you, I'll do whatever you want. Yes, we have a deal.

Everything would be so simple then. They'd get up and leave this bloody restaurant, they'd go home together, they'd spend the night in each other's arms. And wasn't that exactly what he wanted? Say yes, a voice inside his head urged him. Say yes.

But a third part of him knew he would never change. He might try, but something deep inside him would rail against the hypocrisy and the injustice of it all, would simmer and bubble and eventually explode. He loved Judith, he wanted to keep on loving her. If he let her make him her prisoner, he would resent her, and eventually the resentment would turn to hatred.

There was so much that was good between them, but in her anger over a little financial difficulty – something that would be sorted out in no time now he was working as a freelance consultant to the police, even if they did take their bloody time about paying his invoices, or even sooner if he could only pick a couple of winners for a change – she had forgotten just how good the good times had been, and still could be. All she needed was a little reminding. 'We've been married for twenty years, Judith.' He extended his hands, palms up. Imploring her. 'What's ten minutes?'

He waited while she turned to ferret-face for guidance. After a moment's hesitation, Graham nodded his approval, and they both stood up.

'Wellll,' Fitz said as they approached the house, nasally

drawing out his words in an imitation of Loyd Grossman on *Through the Keyhole*. 'I wooonder what kind of puurrrson lives in a place like this? Shall we go inside and see what seeeecrets their possessions might reveeeal?'

Judith rolled her eyes to show she was not amused.

Fitz opened the door and ushered them both inside, leading them up the stairs to his – and formerly Judith's – bedroom. 'That disgusting smell,' he informed Graham, temporarily lapsing into his normal voice, 'is my son's feet by the way. We've tried everything bar amputation, though that's still a possibility.'

They followed him into the bedroom, where he flung open the door to Judith's wardrobe. 'Wellll,' he said, becoming Loyd Grossman again. 'Whoeeever lives in this house obviously has extreeemely, extreeemely expensive taste in clothes!'

'Get to the point, Fitz,' Judith interrupted him angrily.

He reached into the wardrobe, grabbing hold of one of the dresses. 'I bought you this,' he said, reverting to his normal voice, 'when Cool Ground won the Gold Cup. This . . .' He grabbed hold of another dress, sliding the previous one down the rail, '. . . when Doctor Devious won the Derby.' He lifted a third dress out by the hanger. 'And this,' he said, holding it out for her inspection, 'when Party Politics won the National.'

'I've shared in your winnings, is that it?'

Smart woman, Judith. Quick on the uptake. 'Exactly.'

'And why do you think I left them all behind?' She turned and walked away, heading down the stairs and into the street with Graham trotting at her heels.

FIVE

Tina lit a cigarette and leaned back on the sofa, squeezing the bubbles on a sheet of plastic wrapping. Listening to them pop.

It was late afternoon, and Sean was in the shower; *pop*. She could hear him singing. *Pop*. He'd been in there a long time now. *Pop*. When was he getting out? They could go somewhere, do something.

She pressed another plastic bubble between her fingers; it wouldn't break. She dug at it with a fingernail. *Pop*; then something that sounded like an explosion.

She leapt up, heard another crash, saw a crowbar come through her door. Saw the wood splinter, saw the lock and the chain pull away from the wall. Sean was still in the shower, still singing. Couldn't he hear?

A man stepped through the shattered doorway. Thirtyish, movie-star handsome, wearing dark glasses and expensive clothes.

Cormack.

He strode into the room as if he owned it. Two others followed behind him – younger, more muscular, dressed in jeans and puffa jackets.

Tina stood frozen; she'd heard about Cormack's thugs, what they'd do to you if you made a single false move.

Cormack paused, removing his glasses. He looked at her, raising one eyebrow.

'What do you want?'

'You know what I want. You still owe me.'

'We've got nothing,' she said, keeping her voice calm and even. She hadn't worked since she'd met Sean; some men didn't mind that kind of thing, were glad of the money. But not Sean. Sean was different; Sean would hate the whole idea of it, it would rip him up inside. 'Get a giro on Wednesday. I'll pay you something then.'

'Telly,' he said harshly, keeping his eyes on Tina. One of the men picked up her television set and carried it outside; the other picked up her stereo.

Sean's voice carried through from the bathroom: '*Are you lonesome tonight? Do you miss me tonight? Are you sorry we drifted apart?*'

Cormack walked over to the bathroom door and twisted the knob.

She heard the shower curtain sliding on the rail. Heard Sean shouting, 'Hey! Wh-wh-what the . . .?' Heard the door slam, heard an evil laugh. Heard fists pounding against wood. 'Hey! Open the door!'

Then Cormack was back. He walked over to the collection of cups and trophies mounted on one wall. Began to toss them, one by one, into a sack.

Tina moved across the room to stop him. Those cups were all Sean had in the world; other than a few clothes, they were all he'd brought with him when he moved in the week before. 'Haven't I been paying you regular up 'til now? It's just the last couple of weeks've been hard, that's all. It's only been a couple of weeks!' He just kept filling the sack, ignoring her. 'You might as well give us a bit more time,' she said, reaching for the sack. She knew the cups were practically worthless, but they meant so much to Sean. 'There's nothing here worth taking!'

He pushed her away.

She could hear Sean pounding and shouting her name. 'Tina! Tina, what's going on?'

She ran into the kitchen, pulled out a drawer full of knives, reached for one, then hesitated, not sure she had the nerve to use it. A hand shot out from behind her, slamming the drawer closed. She swung around; Cormack pressed himself against her, pushing her back against the kitchen cabinet. 'I can make things easy for you or I can make them hard. The choice is down to you, love.'

She spat on his face.

He raised a hand as if to hit her; she stiffened, bracing herself against the blow. But it didn't come; he used the raised hand to wipe the spit from his face, then wiped the hand across her breasts. Slowly.

'TINA!' The pounding in the bathroom never ceased; the shouting went on and on. 'Tina, what's going on?'

The hand lingered briefly at her chest, then moved down. She looked away, revolted.

Cormack stepped back. 'So that's your choice.' He walked over to the kitchen door. 'Stay,' he ordered her, closing it behind him. *Stay.* He'd said it as if he was talking to a dog.

There was another crash; she heard Sean cry out in pain. What was happening? What were Cormack and his bloody goons doing to him? She pushed the kitchen door open, peering out into the hall. No sign of anyone; they were gone.

She ran to the bathroom door. The key was still in the lock; there was a large ragged hole in the wood, near the bottom. She turned the key and found Sean lying naked on the bathroom floor, his face contorted with pain, a small pool of blood forming beneath one badly cut leg. He'd tried to kick his way out, breaking through the wood with his bare foot.

She fell to her knees beside him. 'Oh, Sean.'

He pulled himself up to a sitting position. 'What's happening? What the fuck's going on?' he demanded angrily.

'It's all right, they're gone.'

'Who? Who? Who's gone, Tina? Who?'

'I'd better clean that leg up.'

He sat on the edge of the bathtub, silently seething, as she dabbed at his foot with cotton wool soaked in antiseptic. 'B-b-bastard's n-n-n . . .'

'The bastard's name is Cormack.'

'C-c-c . . .'

'Your cups? He took them.'

Sean closed his eyes.

'He's coming back when I get my giro. He always comes back.'

He curled his hands into fists. 'I'll k-k-k . . .'

'I'll ask my parents,' she said, soothing him. 'Get some money from them, pay that bastard off, get your cups back. It'll be all right, you'll see.'

She heard the dog barking as soon as they walked onto the balcony. It sounded big, and vicious. And it sounded close. She followed Sean to the top of the stairs, and then she stopped. 'It's on the stairs,' she said.

Sean shook his head. He grabbed hold of her hand, pulling her down the steps.

'It is,' she insisted, pulling back. 'I won't go down there, Sean.'

She tried to resist, but he kept tugging at her, not letting her go. They went down a few more steps and abruptly came face to face with something that looked like an Alsatian, teeth bared in a ferocious snarl. Tina froze, terrified. Then Sean bared his teeth, growling back at the dog. 'No, Sean,' Tina whispered.

He rushed forward, dragging her along with him. 'No, Sean!' The dog turned and fled down the stairs. Sean ran after it, barking. 'No, Sean!' she shouted again, but this time she was laughing.

They slowed down to a casual stroll as they left the estate, walking up and down the neighbouring streets, looking for transport. In a quiet road, temporarily free of traffic and pedestrians, Sean used a small length of lead pipe to smash the driver's-side window of a car. He reached in to unlock the door, brushed away the glass, and got in, reaching across to open the passenger side for Tina. He took a screwdriver out of his pocket, used it to pull out the ignition, then briefly fiddled with some wires. The engine came to life and they were off.

An unopened pack of Benson and Hedges sat on the dashboard. Tina ripped it open, took out two, and lit them, handing one to Sean. She opened the glove compartment and found a treasure trove: cough sweets, cheap plastic sunglasses, a wind-up alarm clock, a dozen or so cassettes. 'Bingo,' she said, sweeping the contents into her bag.

She slipped one of the cassettes into the tape deck: country and western. She clapped her hands, laughing and laughing as a film reel played inside her head: of beautiful young desperadoes on the run. The narrow street lined with council blocks became the open road; Moss Side became an endless prairie. The Dustbowl. The Badlands. She raised a fist in triumph as the car charged onto the motorway heading south of the city. 'Yee-ha!'

SIX

Fitz looked up to see Sarah Heller standing in his office doorway. She was wearing a dress today: red, mid-thigh length, with black opaque tights and boots. Red top half, black below; her narrow frame reminded him of a half-burnt joss stick.

'Come in, Sarah. Sit down.' He reached into his desk drawer for another pack of cigarettes. 'I went to a restaurant the other night: *Cianno's*. Ever hear of it?'

She nodded. 'I've been there.' She settled down into the padded chair across from his desk, back straight, legs tightly crossed.

'Thought so,' he said. 'I didn't eat anything while I was there, either.' He brushed a bit of ash away from his jacket, then leaned forward across his cluttered desk, resting his elbow on a stack of unanswered letters. 'So what's it all about, Sarah? Hmm?'

'What's what about?'

'Life, the universe and everything,' Fitz said, '. . . if we're speaking in general terms. Though I must admit I was thinking of something more specific. Like: I recently met this woman, Sarah Heller, and she's starving herself to death, I wonder what *that's* all about. Any ideas?'

'Why don't you tell me?' Her head inclined slightly forward. She waited expectantly, staring at him with deep-set hollow eyes. It was terribly easy to imagine that taut, hungry face crawling with maggots in a hole six feet below the ground.

'I'd say it's all to do with control,' Fitz said. 'As an infant, you have no control over situations around you. No control over what happens, over what is done to you. This is true of all of us. We gain control later, when we're adults, and that is enough for most people. Now you, Sarah, take it all one step further. You grow up, you work hard, you move right to the top. You don't just control your own life, you control the lives of others around you. You become the boss, the one who hires and fires, the one with the power. This should be more than enough control to satisfy you, more than enough to satisfy anyone. But it isn't enough, is it? You want more control, more power. So what's left to control? Your own body. You ignore the pangs in your stomach, because you're the one in control. You watch your flesh waste away with a kind of morbid fascination: I'm the one who's making that happen. I'm the one in control. I don't need food to keep going, I'll keep going by sheer force of will. And when I die, it'll all be down to me. No-one else can kill me, no-one else can destroy me the way I can destroy myself. That's control!' Fitz stubbed his cigarette out in one of several overflowing ashtrays on his desk. 'What do you think of that as a theory?'

'I'd hate to see the inside of your lungs.' Sarah shifted in her chair, uncrossing and recrossing her bamboo-thin legs. 'I'm a successful person in a highly competitive field. Of course I'm a control freak. Why don't you tell me something I don't already know?'

'Put your money on Lonesome Wanderer in the three-thirty tomorrow at Epsom. Sure thing, can't lose.' He picked up a polystyrene cup, took a sip of thick brown liquid, made a face. The coffee in this place was terrible, came from a canteen on the third floor where the food was even worse. Still, even bad coffee had its purpose: it was something to focus on, another minor irritant to keep him occupied. 'Who are you angry at, Sarah?'

She rolled her eyes, looking up at the ceiling with an exaggerated sigh.

Denial, Fitz thought. Definite denial. There was a raging

fury inside her; it came off her in waves. 'Something in your childhood, maybe?'

She raised a hand. 'Wait a minute. Stop right there. I told you before, I've read all the articles in all the Sunday supplements. I was not abused as a child, sexually or otherwise. My childhood was fine. I am not here to talk about my childhood. Have you got that?'

'Why are you here, Sarah?'

'I thought I had an appointment. Am I too early? Have I come on the wrong day?'

She wasn't a bad game-player. But he was a better one; he'd been at it longer, worked out his own set of rules. Applied them when and if it suited him. 'That's not what I meant, Sarah. You know what I meant.'

'OK,' she said. 'I know what you meant. But then, you know why I'm here.'

'No, Sarah, I don't know. Why don't you tell me?'

She gave him a look of complete exasperation. 'I'm here because Doctor Peterson suggested I see you. I come here a couple of times a week because I'm such an urgent case, remember? I'm the skinny one, usually comes on Tuesdays and Fridays.'

Fitz pursed his lips. 'That's it? Doctor Peterson suggests something, so you do it?'

'Yeah.'

'Let me get this very clear in my mind,' Fitz said, lighting another cigarette. 'You come here – you spend the money to come here privately – because Doctor Peterson suggested it? You do it simply because it was his suggestion?'

'Yes.'

'I'm sure he's suggested more than once that you start eating something like a normal diet, but you don't do that, do you?'

She waved one skeletal hand in a gesture of dismissal. 'OK, OK. Point taken.'

Fitz wasn't going to let her off that easily. 'What point?' he persisted.

'Huh?'

'What point have you taken, Sarah? What point do you think I'm making here?'

She pursed her lips in a show of concentration. 'The point you're making,' she began slowly and carefully, 'is that . . .' She paused to scratch her head. 'This is some kind of a trick question, isn't it? But I think I've got it. I don't do everything Doctor Peterson suggests, but I do come here. This shows I only follow the suggestions I want to follow, ergo: I must come here because I want to.'

'And why is that?' Fitz asked her. 'Why do you want to come here?'

'You want the truth?'

'I always want the truth Sarah. The truth is my Holy Grail.'

'Is it really? OK, the Holy Grail truth is: I agreed to see a psychologist because I know that I am all right. My work is not suffering; my agency is doing better than it ever has. People talk about the recession, and I say, what recession? I own a luxury flat overlooking a canal, I drive a BMW. I go where I want when I want. You were right about me being in control; I am in complete control. I don't eat because I don't want to. When I want to eat, then I will. Simple as that. I'm not stupid, and I'm not crazy either. I won't let it get out of hand; I've got it all under control. I know exactly what I'm doing.'

'So the reason you're here is you want me to confirm that for you? You want me to tell Doctor Peterson: don't worry, I've talked to her, and she's just playing a little game with herself. She'll quit when she's bored with it, and she'll get bored with it soon enough. Before it's too late. So there's really no need to keep hassling her; she'll be OK.'

'That's it exactly. You understand, don't you? I knew you'd understand.'

He rose from behind his desk, shaking his head. 'No way,' he said. 'No way in hell do I understand! You want me to confirm that you're all right? My God, Sarah, you're anything but all right! Whatever the game is you think you're playing, I absolutely refuse to go along with it! Do you understand me? I absolutely refuse.'

SEVEN

Tina pointed to a large, detached house at the end of a tree-lined suburban street. Seventy-six Brook Road, Hale. The house where she'd spent her childhood, the house she'd been so anxious to escape.

It was nearly dark, and Sean's face was obscured by shadows, but she didn't need to see him to be aware of his discomfort; she could sense it. Just the way she could usually sense what he was thinking, what he was trying to say, even when he couldn't manage more than a frustrated sputter. He didn't look at her as he pulled the car to a stop; he probably had a fair idea of what was coming. Her parents would look down their noses at him; question him. Give each other meaningful looks as he struggled to answer. And then he would get angry.

There was an estate agent's board mounted on the front gate; it said 'Sold'.

Sold? Since when?

Her first reaction was one of hurt, one of a long line of hurts, going back, way back. Her second reaction was one of anger, and anger felt better than hurt. She got out of the car, ditching the hurt. Holding on to the anger. Feeling it course through her veins, straightening her back and making her strong.

She walked up the drive to the front door. She was aware of Sean beside her, nervously running a hand through his hair. She almost laughed out loud at the thought of it: Sean smoothing down his hair, trying to look presentable for her parents. She told herself it would be all right; she'd do all the talking. Get the money and get out.

She rang the bell and waited. She knew they were home; there were lights on inside. She saw a shadow move behind the curtain in an upstairs window; she knew who that was. She gritted her teeth and looked away.

The front door finally opened. Just a crack at first, then slightly wider. A woman peered out at them: middle-aged, with a tight, pinched face, high-necked blouse, dark cardigan and sensible shoes. She just stood there, looking as if she'd encountered a nasty fungus growing on the cellar walls.

'Can we come in?'

'*You* can come in,' her mother said finally. 'But he can't.' She pulled the door back just far enough for Tina to enter, then slammed it in Sean's face.

Tina marched past her mother, into the sitting room, where she found her father standing, hands in pockets, beside a padded armchair. He wore a white shirt, a too-short tie, and a dark blue cardigan just like her mother's. 'Sit down,' he said, gesturing to the sofa.

The sofa was long and deep, purposely designed to make a person feel small. She sank down into the cushions, feeling herself shrink. Her father remained standing, asserting his authority by making her have to look up at him, by making her little again. He knew exactly what he was doing.

Well, she wouldn't have it – she wouldn't let him crush her like that. She leaned back, crossing her legs and gazing at her surroundings with a superior sneer. Then she noticed the wooden packing crates stacked up against one wall, and it finally sank in that her own parents had been going to move away without even telling her.

Her mother came into the room and sat in the chair beside her father. Neither said a word. This was one of their favourite little ploys: the silent, accusing stare. Well, she could do that, too. She lit a cigarette and stared back, waiting for them to speak.

A Labrador appeared in the doorway, panting and

drooling. Tina glanced at it, then quickly averted her eyes.

This silent treatment was maddening; being in this house again was maddening. The dog panting in the doorway was maddening. Get it over with, she told herself. 'Look, could you lend us some money?' She looked from one accusing face to the other. 'I'll pay you back.'

Her mother leaned forward in her chair, eyes narrow. 'Where did you get the car?'

Tina waved her cigarette towards the stack of packing cases. 'You're moving,' she said, cursing herself for failing to disguise the hurt in her voice.

'Where did you get the car?'

'Sean bought it,' Tina answered quickly, looking away. 'He's got a job; he's working.' The dog was drooling onto the carpet; it was disgusting. She turned her gaze back to her mother. Now it was Tina's turn to narrow her eyes. 'You never told me you were moving.'

'We tried,' her mother said. 'But we didn't know where you were.'

Tried? Tina thought, like hell you tried.

'Where's he working?' her father asked. He always did that. Always pried, always wanted to know everything.

'Some haulage firm.' She gestured towards the slobbering animal in the doorway – it was making her sick. 'Can you get rid of that?'

A door opened and closed upstairs. The dog darted into the hall and vanished up the steps.

Her father still wasn't satisfied. 'Which one?'

'I'm not sure where, but he's working,' Tina insisted. 'Right?' Her voice sounded too shrill, too high; they would know she was lying. She smiled, trying to bring her voice back to its normal pitch. 'But I'm not sure where.'

She raised her head to look at her father, standing there all self-righteous and disapproving, thinking he knew it all when he knew less than nothing, and it was all she could do to keep from screaming. 'Will you lend it me,' her throat constricted, her eyes burned. *No*, she told herself fiercely, *I will not let them make me cry again, not ever again.* 'Or not?'

Her mother broke in before he could answer. 'Sammy's upstairs,' she said, looking at Tina meaningfully.

Tina shrugged, exhaling a cloud of smoke. 'Yeah?'

Her mother's eyes flashed briefly. 'Well go and see her.'

She stubbed out her cigarette and rose slowly, heading reluctantly towards the stairs. She was about halfway up when Sammy appeared on the landing above her, looking like a younger version of their mother in her pristine blouse buttoned all the way up to the neck and her ankle-length skirt.

The dog sat on its haunches beside her, gazing up at her in adoration, a dripping tongue lolling from its open mouth. That's what *she* was supposed to do, fall down at Sammy's feet and worship. That's what they expected.

'Hello, Tina,' Sammy said.

The undisguised contempt in that voice sent a chill through her. Tina turned to face her parents, standing in the living room doorway below her. 'Will you lend it me or not?' she demanded angrily.

Her father shook his head. 'Not.'

Tina slammed her hand down on the railing, eyes watering. The muscles in her face and neck tightened as she made a conscious effort to turn the pain into fury. Never again, a voice screamed inside her head, never again.

'Get rid of him, come back with us,' her father went on. 'We'll talk about the loan then.'

Come back to them? Come back to fetch and carry, back to serve, back to be a good little doggy? She punched the wall. She wanted to smash the place, smash their stupid, smug faces in. She should have known better than to come here, she should have known they wouldn't give a damn what happened to her. They never asked how much she needed, never even asked what she needed it for; they didn't care what happened to her. They had never cared. They despised her.

She ran from the house, slamming the door behind her.

Sean was waiting in the car. 'W-w-w . . .?'

She'd told Sean some things about her childhood – but not everything. There was no reason for him to know it all, no reason for anyone to know. Just like there was no reason for him to know how she'd been earning the money to pay Cormack. If he knew, it might change the way he felt about her. It was all in the past now, anyway. It was better if he didn't know.

She kept her face impassive, not letting him see how upset she was. 'You want to know what they said?'

He nodded.

She got in beside him. 'They said no.'

'Sh . . . sh . . . shit!' His face contorted with anger. He gunned the engine, leaving a trail of rubber.

She leaned back in her seat, bracing herself, as Sean nearly turned a corner on two wheels. The car slowed down when they reached the high street. At first Tina assumed it was because Sean had managed to calm himself and was driving more sensibly, but then she saw the look on his face. He was seething.

'W-w . . . What w-w . . .'

'What will Cormack do?'

He nodded.

She changed the subject, keeping her voice light. 'They said they would've given it me but they're a bit short. They're moving house soon as well.' The car was slowing to a crawl; she could hear Sean mutter something under his breath. She didn't know what to do, so she just kept talking. 'And that's not cheap you know. Estate agents screw you. Lawyers screw you. Carpets, curtains . . .'

Sean managed to steer the car towards a kerb as it rolled to a stop. He pressed his foot down hard on the pedal; the engine made an empty, coughing sound.

'Petrol?'

He pounded his fists against the steering wheel, grunting in frustration, then one word came out crystal clear: 'Yeah.'

55

He turned and looked at her exactly the way she had looked at her parents. 'You're lying,' he said, speaking quickly and fluently. He could speak perfectly well when he was angry enough. 'They think I'm crap! They told you to get shot of me and then they'd give you some money!'

Tina tried to interrupt him, to tell him he was wrong, but there was no stopping him.

'You and all! You think I'm crap. You're ashamed of me!'

'I'm not!'

He got out of the car and kicked it.

'Listen, where are you going? Sean!'

He stormed off down the street, ignoring her.

She realised for the first time just how much she needed him. She had no family; her family didn't exist for her now. And friends? Not really. Women saw her as competition, and men only wanted one thing. But Sean was different than other men – it wasn't just sex. Sometimes she felt as if they were one person, like the Yin and Yang symbol on her wall – two separate halves of one whole, each incomplete without the other. He needed her as much as she needed him, maybe more; she was certain of it. She jumped out of the car. 'Sean! I love you!'

He kept walking. She couldn't lose him now – couldn't imagine life without him now. It would be like losing one half of herself. She followed after him, shouting, 'I love you! Sean!'

He still didn't stop; she shouted even louder, 'Ey, Billy-no-mates!'

He slowed his pace, twisting his head back to look at her.

She spread her arms out wide. 'I love you, OK?'

He stopped and waited for her to catch up, staring down at the pavement. Calm enough now to be embarrassed.

'I love you,' she said. 'OK?'

He raised his eyes. 'I l-l-l . . .'

She placed a finger on his lips to shush him. 'I know.' She put her hand in his, and they started to walk. It was a long way home.

EIGHT

Fitz had been trying to phone Judith ever since the night at the restaurant, but every time he tried to reach her at work she was 'in a meeting' and every time he phoned her father's house the old man told him she was 'out'. No-one spent that much time in meetings, and no-one spent that much time out.

The lights in his father-in-law's house were on, and Judith's car was parked across the street. They were in there, he knew they were in there. He could see shadows moving behind the living room curtains. He walked up the path to the doorway, calm but determined. He was going to see Judith. He was going to speak to her, that was all. He was going to say all the things he'd meant to say in the restaurant, but never got the chance.

He pressed a finger against the doorbell; he could hear it ringing. He could hear the dog barking. He looked towards the living room window and saw the shadows momentarily freeze.

One shadow grew larger; a corner of the curtain twitched, then the shadow receded. Fitz pressed the bell again, and once again the shadows froze.

He raised his finger one more time, and held it there. He knew they were in there. He kept on pressing the bell, just to let them know he knew.

They'd been walking nearly half an hour when Sean gestured towards some lights up ahead: a bus station. Tina shrugged, not sure what he was trying to tell her; they couldn't take a bus back to Manchester, they didn't have any money. Cormack had taken every last penny.

Sean started to walk very fast, pulling her along behind him.

She followed him past a tea stand where several men in drivers' uniforms were standing around, eating and chatting, then into the terminus where several single-decker orange buses sat with their engines running.

Sean headed straight for the one in the front of the queue.

'But we haven't got the fare,' Tina protested, pulling her hand away from his. She kept her voice low; the drivers were only a few yards away.

She watched in amazement as Sean climbed onto the first bus and got into the empty driver's seat. There were passengers on that bus: a couple of overweight, middle-aged women in cloth coats and head scarves, and an old man with a little dog. The women were deep in conversation and the old man had nodded off. She looked back towards the tea stand where the drivers were still chatting; they hadn't seen them. Then she looked up at Sean, urging her to hurry.

And suddenly it all seemed so hilarious, she could hardly stop laughing. She leapt onto the bus and took a seat at the back, behind the two women. The doors swung closed and the bus began to move.

She heard voices shouting behind her. She turned to see the uniformed drivers drop their tea and start running after them, as if they really thought they could catch a bus on foot. She gave them a little wave as she mouthed the word: 'Bye'.

The two women in front of her were too busy nattering to notice the bus they were sitting in had just been stolen. ' 'Ere, he's going a bit fast, isn't he?' one of them asked the other as the bus careered around a corner.

The old man jerked awake, looked around, blinking, then went back to sleep.

One of the women reached up and pulled the cord to signal a stop. ' 'Ey,' she said a moment later. 'He's gone right past it.'

'Hey love,' the other woman called out. 'You've missed

me stop!' She turned to her friend. 'Ding the bell, he hasn't heard.'

The first woman pulled the cord again. 'You've gone past the bingo! Stop the bus! You've missed the bingo!'

There was the sound of sirens. The bus plunged onto the motorway, followed by half-a-dozen police cars, their flashing blue lights giving everything a look of unreality, like the flickering of celluloid. Sean wove from lane to lane, blocking his pursuers, forcing them off the road and leaving them far behind. Tina laughed out loud.

The women turned to look at her, a mixture of astonishment and fear on their faces.

'It's just like *Bonnie and Clyde*,' she told them, eyes shining with excitement.

The dog was still barking, the shadows behind the curtains were still sneaking about cautiously, and Fitz was still ringing the doorbell.

'Excuse me, sir,' said a voice behind him.

He turned, and found a light shining directly into his eyes. As his sight gradually adjusted, he began to make out the outline of two policemen standing on the path that ran through his father-in-law's front garden. Behind them, a police car sat parked at the kerb, blue lights flashing, a stream of talk and static blasting from the radio. He couldn't believe he hadn't heard or seen them coming, but then he'd always found that ringing his father-in-law's doorbell induced an almost Zen-like level of concentration. 'Yes?' he said, finger still on doorbell.

'I'm going to have to ask you to stop doing that,' said the policeman shining the light in his eyes.

'Doing what?'

'That,' said the policeman, indicating the rather large finger pressed against the bell.

'Oh, *that*,' said Fitz, removing the offending finger.

So they'd called the police. He couldn't believe it; Judith would never call the police on her own husband. It had to be her father, that bitter old stick of a man. But she could have stopped him. She could have – should have – slammed the phone down on his bony old fingers. So why didn't she? This was definitely a matter that would require some discussion; this was just another of the many things he would have to talk to her about.

'Look,' he told the policeman, shrugging, being reasonable and calm and obviously harmless. 'All I want to do is to talk to my wife, OK?'

'That's a civil matter,' the policeman agreed.

'Exactly.' Fitz was pleased to see the policeman was a reasonable man.

'But we've had a complaint,' the officer went on. 'That's a police matter.'

Maybe he's not so reasonable after all – pressures of the job and all that, Fitz told himself. 'Must be hard to be a policeman,' he said, 'the terrible things you see.'

'If you don't leave these people in peace, I'm going to have to arrest you.'

No, Fitz decided, this man is anything but reasonable; he's a raving lunatic. Shouldn't be allowed out. 'You *are* joking,' he said.

The policeman shook his head.

'Just give me a minute,' Fitz said, holding up one finger. 'Just one tiny minute. I'd like to ask my wife about this, if you don't mind.'

He turned, still holding up the finger, and pressed it hard against the bell.

The bus left the motorway, barrelling down a wide road leading into town. It swerved off the road, tyres screeching, and hurtled down a ramp, the undercarriage throwing sparks as it bounced up and down over a row of speed bumps. There was a barrier up ahead, manned by a uniformed guard in a little glass booth. The women in headscarves gasped as the bus crashed headlong through the barrier, followed by an army of police.

They entered an underground car park lined with concrete pillars. Tina braced herself as Sean steered the bus in a desperate circle, trying to find a way out. There was another ramp at the far end; they raced towards it, burning rubber. Leaving the cops behind them one more time.

Tina held her breath, willing Sean on. Willing him to go faster than light. They were almost at the ramp; they were almost there.

A police car seemed to come out of nowhere. It was on the ramp, heading right towards them. It swung around sideways, then came to a dead stop directly in front of the bus, completely cutting them off. Sean slammed down the brakes, bringing the bus to a screeching halt.

They were surrounded within seconds. Tina sank down in her seat as a group of coppers leapt onto the bus. They dragged Sean away.

One copper stayed behind briefly, asking if everyone was OK, if anybody had been hurt. The older passengers just stared at him, speechless.

Then the copper noticed Tina; his eyes locked on hers. She swallowed, trying to control her sense of rising panic. He knew she was with Sean, he knew they were together and now he was going to arrest her, too. 'Are you all right, love?' he said, his gaze moving downwards along her body. She breathed a sigh of relief. Coppers were just men, after all.

She nodded to let him know that yes, she was all right. Finally the copper got off the bus and left them alone: the two women sitting with their mouths hanging open, the old man blinking and looking puzzled, the little dog wriggling and whining.

Tina looked out the window and saw Sean looking back at her. They shoved him up against the back of a van, twisting his arms as they cuffed him. He bared his teeth in a grimace of pain. Then they pushed him inside and drove him away.

NINE

Detective Sergeant James Beck smiled at the uniformed copper standing near the bare white wall of Anson Road Station's windowless Interview Room 1; this was going to be interesting. They told him this one hadn't said a word since he'd been arrested; not a single word. No ID. No address, no name. Interesting.

He lit a cigarette – casually, taking his time. He let his lungs fill with smoke while the young man seated across the table stared at him sullenly. More a boy than a man, Beck thought. He didn't look more than nineteen or twenty. And moronic with it; Beck doubted there was any intelligence there. What kind of idiot steals a bus full of passengers? He wasn't even a proper villain – just some kid out for a joyride. Maybe he wasn't so interesting after all.

'Interview commences twenty-two hundred hours. Present DS Beck, PC Withers, and one male suspect, yet unidentified, who has been cautioned.'

OK, Beck thought, let's start him off with something easy. He put down his cigarette and picked up a pencil, holding it poised above his notepad. 'Name?'

The boy twitched a bit, made a face, sort of grunted. Twitched a bit more, made another face. Maybe this was going to be interesting after all. 'Name?' he said again.

The boy's face went through some terrible convulsions. Finally three words came out: 'I'll w-w-write it.'

Beck tapped the tape recorder on the table beside him. 'I need to hear it.'

The boy's head jerked forward as he made a series of choking, guttural noises. He took a deep breath, and tried again. All he could manage was a grunt. He took another breath, and another; he was close to hyperventilating.

Beck's eyes widened in fascination.

The boy looked directly at him, slamming his fist down on the table. 'Kerrigan!' he shouted.

Beck let a long moment pass. He reached for his cigarette, took in another lungful of smoke, and exhaled it slowly. Right into the boy's face. 'What?'

The boy looked so exasperated, it was priceless. 'You heard,' he muttered.

Beck raised his eyebrows and shook his head, all innocence. 'I didn't.'

The boy's head jerked a couple of times before he managed another: 'You heard!'

Beck continued to protest his innocence, giving the boy his would-I-lie-to-you? face. 'I didn't.'

The boy deflated like a pricked balloon. Then he started those faces again. 'K-k-k . . .'

Beck couldn't control himself much longer – he was going to laugh. He dropped his pencil and turned to the uniformed cop behind him. 'Good job we've got all night.'

The boy leapt up from his chair, eyes blazing with anger. 'Kerrigan!'

Beck calmly told him to sit down.

'My name is Sean Kerrigan!'

Beck stood up and moved around the table. This wasn't amusing any more; this was getting out of hand. He pointed to the chair. 'Sit down.'

The boy paced up and down the white-walled, high-ceilinged room, gesturing wildly. 'Sean Kerrigan!'

'I told you to sit down!'

'And I want to see Tina. I want to see Tina, right?'

Beck changed tack, became conciliatory. 'You can phone. Now just sit down.'

The boy wouldn't stop pacing, wouldn't stop waving his arms. 'We're not on the phone! All I've done is stole a vehicle! I've got to *see* her! We're not on the phone!'

Beck had had enough of the boy's histrionics; it was time he realised who was in charge around here, who was the law. 'Tough! Now sit back down!'

The boy rushed at him, screaming, 'I want to see Tina! I want to see Tina!'

It took five officers to get him down to the cells. In the end, they had to lift him off the ground and carry him down the twisting corridor, spread-eagled, each desperately clinging to a separate thrashing limb while Beck led the way, walking backwards, holding on to the boy's twitching head. Occasionally giving in to the temptation to twist one of the boy's ears a little, or wrap a strand of hair around his fingers and give it a good hard tug. The boy was screaming anyway, might as well give him a reason to scream.

Sean squirmed and kicked and shouted threats, but they eventually managed to squeeze themselves through the narrow doorway of a cell, where they dumped him on the floor and held him down. They let go on the count of three and ran. Sean leapt to his feet, running after them. Beck was the last one out of the cell; he slammed the door behind him just in time.

Sean growled and kicked the door with all his might. 'I want to see Tina!' He took several steps back, then rushed forward, trying to force the cell door with his shoulder. He made another attempt at the door, then he started on the walls, running from side to side, kicking at the white tiles, wailing, 'I want to see Tinaaaaah!'

A thin plastic-covered mattress sat on a long shelf attached to the wall; Sean picked the mattress up and kicked it. He threw it over his head, bashing it against the wall, then against the floor. 'I want to see Tina!'

He ran back and forth across the cell, from wall to wall, kicking and punching and shouting for Tina. He picked up the mattress again, flinging it over his head, roaring like a lion, before going back to kicking the walls.

In the corridor outside the cell door, Beck scratched his head and sighed, watching the boy kicking the hard tile walls, over and over again. Should have taken the boy's shoes when he had the chance.

He watched and waited for another minute; Sean was still going at it. Completely berserk. And he showed no signs of tiring.

Beck slid the spyhole closed, and reluctantly made his way down the hall.

Fitz sat in his cell in the euphemistically entitled 'Custody Suite', smoking a cigarette and listening to all the banging and shouting. And this used to be such a nice neighbourhood, he thought.

He still couldn't believe that some bloody over-zealous PC had actually arrested him, and then, to add insult to injury, brought him back to Anson Road: his own bloody nick. He'd told him, 'I work here, for Christ's sake! I am a consultant to the CID, you can't dump me in a bloody cell!'

But that's what they'd done. Made him empty his pockets onto the table in the charge room. Took his watch. Even took away his belt.

Fitz rubbed his temples. That racket down the hall was giving him a headache. And so was the air in this place. The plastic mattress – exactly one-quarter-of-an-inch thick – smelled of sweaty feet; the floor stank of disinfectant, and the lidless toilet in the corner reeked of an assortment of fetid odours he'd rather not think about. The sergeant who'd locked him up said he was lucky to get this cell; it was the nicest one they had, with private en-suite facilities. Room service, too. Fitz was glad he hadn't eaten anything before he left home; he doubted he would have been able to keep it down.

Causing a Public Affray, the arresting officer had called it. Fitz called it bollocks. All he'd done was ring a doorbell – since when was that a crime?

'I can't believe it,' he'd protested all the way back to the station. 'I simply can't believe it!'

'That's good,' said the PC driving the panda car.

'What?' Fitz asked him.

'You sound just like that old man, what's his name? Victor Meldrew. I love that show; he's dead funny.'

Fitz turned to the uniformed officer sitting on the back seat beside him. 'What's your name? Do you mind telling me your name?'

'Smith.'

'Smith!' Fitz rolled his eyes. 'Do I look like the desk clerk in a bloody hotel?'

'That depends on the hotel, I suppose,' the PC shrugged.

'OK, PC *Smith*. Let me ask you something else. Do you think this is going to advance your career, PC Smith? Do you think you're going to get a promotion for this? You think this will make the streets safe for innocent people – arresting a man for ringing a bloody doorbell? Can you imagine it, when the judge sends me upriver to the big house, and I'm there on death row? All the mass murderers will gather round and ask me,' he put on an American accent to play the part of a standard B-movie mass murderer. ' "So what're you in for, boy?" and I'll tell 'em: "It was a fair cop. They got me for ringing a doorbell." '

Fitz rubbed his temples and sighed. The screaming and banging down the hall showed no signs of letting up.

The cell door opened and there was a uniformed officer, and next to him was Beck. Shirt crumpled, hair dishevelled, moustache twitching. Of course, Fitz thought, where there's trouble there must be Beck. The Dirty Harry of Anson Road, the local papers had called him after that incident with the pickpocket and the bus.

Beck tilted his head in the direction of the noise. 'He's throwing fits, Fitz.' Yet another classic example of Beck's feeble wit.

'I'm in custody, custody.'

'You scratch my back . . .'

Fitz rolled his eyes. Scratching Beck's back – what a

repellent idea. Still, anything to get out of this cell. He stood up.

'Ten minutes, Frank,' Beck told the uniformed officer.

The shouting was louder than ever: 'I want to see Tina!'

Beck opened the spyhole, and Fitz saw a young face twisted in torment. The boy was pacing relentlessly back and forth in the confined space of the cell, lashing out with kicks and punches directed at nothing in particular. Screaming in anguish. 'I want to see Tinaaaah!'

'His name's Sean Kerrigan,' Beck told him. 'Took a GM bus on a joyride.' Beck was smiling; he was enjoying this.

'Open the door.' Beck turned a key in the lock and Fitz stepped into the cell. 'Hello, Sean.'

Sean turned to look at him. 'Who are you?'

'My name's Fitz. I'm a psychologist.'

'I don't want a psychologist, I want a lawyer, right? So piss off,' Sean said quickly, still pacing. Then he turned his attention to Beck. 'Just do one! Right now! Just do one!'

'You're not exactly winning friends and influencing people, are you Sean?' said Beck.

Sean rushed forward; Fitz stepped in front of Beck, spreading his arms and blocking Sean's way.

'Get rid of that feller will you?' Sean screamed. 'Will you get him out of my sight, 'cause I'm not gonna be responsible for my actions!'

The boy's face was a mask of bitterness and hatred. Probably understandable where Beck was concerned; Fitz had seen Beck's method of dealing with prisoners. 'Out,' Fitz told Beck.

Sean was gesticulating wildly. 'I'm not gonna be responsible for my actions if that walking turd stays in here much longer!'

Beck hadn't moved; he was just standing there.

Fitz glared at him. 'Out!'

Beck shrugged and left the cell.

Sean began to pace again, words coming out in an

unstoppable torrent. 'All he's done is wind me up right from the start! That's all he's done, wind me up. Right? OK?'

Fitz nodded agreement, parroting the boy's words: 'Right. OK.' He stepped closer to the boy, mirroring him as he walked from side to side. 'Now calm down.'

'I want you to tell my bird where I am, right? She needs to know where I am!' He slapped his forehead. 'She'll be going off her cake! She must be going off her cake! Wondering what's happened to me. She needs to be told. We're not on the phone so a phone call's no good. Do you understand?'

Fitz kept nodding. Kept his voice quiet and soothing. 'Of course I understand. Calm down.'

Sean turned away in despair, raising both hands to his face. 'I feel like I'm speaking a foreign language! No-one understands what I'm saying!'

Fitz reached out with one hand, trying to touch Sean's arm. 'Listen to me, Sean. Calm down, calm down.'

Sean batted Fitz's hand away, started pacing again. 'I need to tell a woman called Tina. Right? Tina Brien. I need to tell a woman called Tina Brien where I am. It's essential. Do you understand? Essential. That means very, very necessary. Do you understand? Very, very necessary for me to contact Tina.'

Sean wasn't listening; it was time to make him listen. Fitz grabbed him by both arms, pinning them down to his sides. 'Sean, calm down. I'm here to help you.'

They stood eyeball to eyeball. The muscles in Sean's face were taut as wire; his voice became low and threatening. 'Let go of me. Let go of me right now or I won't be responsible for my actions.'

Sorry, Sean, Fitz thought, threats like that don't work with someone my size. 'You butt me,' he told him, 'and I'll butt you right back, harder. OK? Now calm down. Deep breathing. Deep breathing . . . easy.'

Sean took several deep breaths. 'Let go of me.'

Fitz released him. Sean moved away, pacing in restless

circles. But he was quiet now and his movements were more subdued.

'So where does this Tina live then?' Fitz asked him, taking a pack of cigarettes from his jacket pocket.

Sean was still breathing heavily. 'With me.' His voice had become thicker, less distinct.

'Where's that?' Fitz sat down on the long shelf that ran along one wall, holding out the cigarette packet, offering one.

Sean nodded and took a cigarette. Fitz gave him a light.

Sean's mouth opened and closed several times. He took another deep breath. 'F-f-f . . . f-f-f-flat . . . I'll write it,' Sean said, waving one hand to mime the action of writing. 'I'll write it.'

Fitz reached into one pocket for a pen, then searched the others for some paper. He found a used betting slip, which he handed over to Sean. 'A loser,' he explained.

Sean took the betting slip and the pen, and sat down on the far end of the ledge, balancing the slip on his knee.

'You don't stutter when you're angry,' Fitz said while Sean wrote his address.

Sean shook his head. 'No.'

'Because it's the first thing that comes into your head – before it even comes into your head. You don't see the words, so they don't frighten you.'

Sean glanced at him sideways, shrugging. 'That's right.'

'There's speech therapy.'

Sean laughed, then raised his eyebrows and opened his mouth unnaturally wide. He began to speak extremely slowly, dragging out every syllable, his voice sounding forced and artificial, but without the slightest trace of a stutter. 'I've triiied speeeech theeraapyy. I'm fiiine if I taaalk liiike thiis. But thiiis isn't meee speeeaking; thiiis is some dickhead.'

'So you'd rather get angry?'

'S-s-s-s . . .' Sean scowled and shook his head in disgust and frustration. "Occasionally.'

'Sometimes,' Fitz prompted him.

'Sometimes,' Sean repeated after him. 'Sometimes, yeah. Sometimes I get angry. Sometimes.'

'You don't mind me helping you?' Fitz said carefully. 'Some stutterers do, you know.'

Sean looked down at the floor and shook his head. 'No.' Then he looked back up at Fitz, his face hard. 'Get me out of here.'

'I'll see what I can do,' Fitz said, standing up. 'But I can't promise anything.'

TEN

'You must let his girl know where he is,' Fitz told Beck as
they walked up the corridor leading away from the cells.
'And I'd like him remanded on bail for psychiatric reports.'

Beck's expression told Fitz he had to be joking. 'Psychiatric reports? For taking and driving away?' He waved his
hand in a gesture of dismissal.

'He needs help,' Fitz insisted.

'Bollocks. I wound him up a bit, that's all.'

'I'm talking prevention here.'

Beck stopped in his tracks. 'Prevention?' he said, sneer-
ing. 'I want twenty serious crimes a day. I enjoy them; they
pass the time.' He rubbed his fingers together to indicate
money. 'Overtime as well. Bollocks to prevention.' He
turned and walked away.

Detective Sergeant Jane Penhaligon stood behind a counter
just a few feet away from them, listening to every word. 'You
take a look at him, will you?' Fitz asked her, approaching the
counter.

She didn't have to look at him; she'd heard the banging
and shouting. She wouldn't be surprised if most of Greater
Manchester had heard it. She didn't need Fitz to tell her the
boy wasn't right in the head. But that wasn't the point.
The point was she didn't intend to piss anyone off at the
moment, even a prat like Beck. She had a lot at stake right
now, and if she wanted to get ahead, she had to keep
reminding herself that there were politics to play. That's
how Bilborough got where he was, she was sure. Playing
politics, getting to know the right people. Not getting mixed
up with someone who didn't give a damn about the rules.

She pushed a sheet of paper towards him, then handed him a pen. She pointed at the place on the sheet where he had to sign. 'Beck's the officer in charge,' she told him.

'I know,' Fitz said, leaning on the desk to write his name. 'But he doesn't have to find out, does he?' He gave her his mischievous look, his let's stir up some trouble look. He'd given her that look before and she'd helped him before, bent the rules just a little, just for him. And the pleasure of showing the others up, proving them wrong when they'd been so certain they were right. She could bend the rules again, if she wanted to.

She didn't want to. It wasn't like the last time; it wasn't a case of clearing an innocent man of murder. All he was talking about this time was some messed-up joyrider. It was no big deal, nothing to jeopardise her career over. 'Forget it. I have no intention of upsetting a fellow officer. I'm up for promotion, Fitz. I'm keeping this,' she tapped her nose, 'clean.'

'Promotion?' Fitz said, raising both eyebrows. 'Ooh, I'm dumbstruck.'

She raised her eyebrows back at him. 'Well, well, well,' she said. 'You dumbstruck? That must be one for the record books.'

He was giving her another one of his mischievous looks: the one that usually preceded one of his come out for a drink lines. Strictly platonic, he'd insist, you'll have to keep your hands to yourself. Probably use the fact she'd mentioned her promotion as an excuse: *Come on, Panhandle, we have to celebrate.* No, she decided, she wasn't getting mixed up in all that. The reason he'd been arrested in the first place was for harassing his wife. He still wasn't finished with her, maybe never would be. He opened his mouth to speak, 'Pan . . .'

'You can see your daughter tomorrow, by the way,' she interrupted, sliding the signed sheet of paper back across the desk. She handed him the plastic bag that held his personal effects. 'Meanwhile, consider yourself cautioned.'

• • •

Sean stood in the dock at the magistrates' court, listening to some copper read out the charges against him. Three magistrates, two women and one man, sat behind a long desk, wrinkling their noses as if he smelled or something. They asked him how he wanted to plead. He took a deep breath. 'G . . . g-g-g . . .' Everyone was looking at him as if he was a bug in a jar. He took another breath and tried again. 'Guilty,' he said, forcing the word out with a rush of air. Then one of the magistrates – the one sitting in the middle, an old woman with white hair and little pearl earrings – asked him if there was anything he'd like to say.

What a stupid question. There was so much he wanted to say; there were all these words swirling around inside his head. If only he could make the words in his head come out through his mouth, he could tell them things they wouldn't believe. He could tell them what it's like to live in a world where everything revolves around words, where words are power, words determine who you are and what you will be, and what it's like to find yourself excluded from that world because the words in your own head have turned against you. They're in there, he would tell them, the words are in there but they won't come out.

Unless he sang them.

He could sing them. Singing, he became the person he wanted to be, the person he should have been. Someone confident and expressive, someone people listened to. Someone people applauded and admired. Someone other people accepted as someone just like them. But they wouldn't let him sing in court.

Or he could shout them.

When there was enough anger boiling up inside him, then the words would come out all right. Come out so fast his brain couldn't keep up with the relentless, non-stop flow of them. But he couldn't shout in court.

The words were in his head, but no matter how hard he tried, he could not form them.

'Mister Kerrigan,' the magistrate repeated, 'do you have anything to say?'

He shook his head.

He stood waiting while they talked among themselves. The hearing so far had taken less than a minute; the magistrates' conversation lasted less than thirty seconds. The old woman in the middle told him they were going to put him on probation for two years, but it would take some time to arrange. In the meantime, he was to report to his local police station every two days. 'Failure to do so,' the old woman said, 'will result in a custodial sentence. Bearing in mind the reckless nature of your actions.' And then she told him he could go.

He left the dock fuming. Two years probation, have to report to the police every two days, all because of Cormack. It was all Cormack's fault; he never would have gone to Hale if it hadn't been for Cormack. Never would have stolen that bus, never would have been arrested.

Tina was waiting for him in the wood-panelled hall outside the courtroom. 'Bastard,' he told her. 'Bastard Cormack.' She placed a hand on his cheek, soothing him. 'It's OK,' she said.

'Bastard,' Sean said, shaking her hand away. Still angry. A man in a suit glanced at him as he walked past. 'Have you got a problem?' Sean demanded. ' 'Ey? Have you got some sort of a problem?'

Tina grabbed hold of Sean's arm, pulling him back. 'It's OK, Sean. It's OK.'

He turned to face her, the anger in his eyes already fading.

She raised his hand to her lips, lightly kissing his fingers, kissing away the humiliation, the fury. 'It's going to be all right,' she told him. 'Trust me.'

Once again, Fitz found himself walking up the grim little path that led to his father-in-law's front door. The old man's vicious little dog was on the lawn, barking furiously, straining at a leash secured to a pole. Fitz sneered at it, growling. That drove the dog into a particularly satisfying frenzy. The stupid thing leapt into the air, nearly strangling itself.

Katie opened the door before he could even ring the bell; she'd been waiting for him. She ran towards him, leaping into his arms. 'Hiya.'

She was so small and fragile in her little green leggings and big floppy tee shirt, brown hair pulled back from a smiling, elfin face. That's what she is, Fitz thought, she's a little elf, a tiny little forest sprite. He lifted her off the ground, swinging her in a dizzying circle.

'Daddy!' she giggled. 'Put me down!'

He did as he was told, lowering her gently. 'Hiya! How are you?'

'OK.'

'Where would you like to go?'

'The park,' she said. There was never any umming and ahhing with Katie, no exasperating rounds of: 'I don't know, what do you want to do?'

'OK,' Fitz said. 'That's settled then.'

It was a gorgeous day, sunny and mild. He bought her a greasy hamburger and crisps and lots of sweets and fizzy drinks and a huge ice-cream cone, sprinkled with bits of chocolate – all the things that were bad for her. All the things that Judith would object to.

He cursed himself for falling into the trap, for wanting to spoil Katie rotten for the brief time he was allowed to be with her. For feeling the need to buy his own daughter's affection. But the way things were going between him and Judith, it would be so easy to lose Katie, too. So easy for her to drift out of his life, for them to grow further and further apart, until they became strangers to one another. He'd seen it happen many times – to friends, to patients – but it had never once crossed his mind that it might happen to him and Katie. Until now.

Katie wanted to ride around the lake on a pedalo, so Fitz took out his wallet and paid the money. This was Katie's day.

They spent the next half hour pedalling in lazy circles, under overhanging branches of trees, around little islands full of nesting birds, past all the other pedalos full of all the other fathers – either separated or divorced – buying their children's devotion one day at a time.

'What would you do,' Katie asked him playfully, 'if, all of a sudden, there was a great big earthquake?' This had always been their favourite game: 'What if?'

'Oh,' Fitz said, thinking. 'I'd quiver and shiver all over, like a big bowl of jelly. And you . . . you'd shake and rattle and roll, like a little bag of bones.'

'What would you do if there was a hurricane?' her little voice piped up again, almost immediately.

'I'd spread the arms of my jacket out wide, like a sail, and let the wind carry us off to exotic lands and pastures new.'

'You couldn't,' Katie corrected him. 'I've got another week before the school holidays start.'

Oh, Katie, he thought, only ten but I can already see the practical woman you will grow up to be – so very like your mother. 'Oh all right. I'd huff and I'd puff and I'd blow the hurricane right back where it came from.'

'What would you do if,' Katie said, pursing her lips in concentration while she tried to think of something suitably dramatic to top the earthquake and the hurricane. 'If . . . if a great big dinosaur came out of that lake to eat us?'

'I'd say: "Eat Katie first. She's young and tender like a lamb chop; I'm just a stringy old tee-bone steak."'

She shook her head, unconvinced. 'You wouldn't.'

'No,' Fitz said, pointing at a metal fence around one of the islands. 'I'd get one of those railings and I'd sharpen it up and I'd stab it through the heart.'

'You wouldn't have time to sharpen it,' Katie reminded him, ever practical, ever the miniature Judith.

'No, that's true,' Fitz conceded, thinking. 'Oh – I'd do what Tarzan does! You know when the alligators try and bite him and he sticks a bit of wood in so they can't snap them shut? I'd do that. No,' he said, waving his hands in

76

childish excitement. 'I know what I'd do! I'd bang it over the head with a mallet. I'd leap up and hit it over the head with a mallet and I'd keep leaping up and hitting it and hitting it until it got smaller and smaller,' he moved his hands together to indicate it shrinking, 'and smaller and smaller . . . And do you know what he'd be then?'

'What?'

'A tiny sore dinosaur.' He winked and nudged her gently with his elbow. 'Not bad, eh?'

It was late afternoon and Tina was in the bathroom, washing her hair. Sean rolled over onto his side, scrunching the pillow into a ball beneath his head, listening to the flow of water. There was a small chest of drawers at the foot of the mattress. He sat up, keeping one eye on the slit of light beneath the bathroom door, and pulled the top drawer open. Nothing in there but costume jewellery. The second drawer was full of lacy underwear, the bottom drawer held mostly tee shirts and jumpers, neatly stacked. He lifted the stack of tee shirts and found what he was looking for: Tina's photo album. She'd hidden it after that first night.

He opened the album, carefully examining each page; the outline of the scratched-out figure present in every photo. He noticed things this time that he hadn't seen before. It wasn't just a person that had been scratched out, in some of the pictures it looked as if certain objects had been deleted, too.

He suddenly realised he couldn't hear the water any more. He looked up and saw her standing naked in the living room doorway, a towel wrapped around her head. 'I . . . I . . .'

'It's all right,' she said, walking towards him.

'Wh-wh-wh . . .'

'Why,' she said. 'You want to know why?'

He nodded.

'I didn't want you to know, Sean,' she said. 'I didn't want you to know what I was, what she made me. I was afraid you wouldn't love me any more if you knew.'

He wanted to ask her what she was talking about. He wanted to tell her that nothing could ever make him stop loving her; she was everything to him. She was his whole life. But all he could manage to say was: 'Sh-sh-she?'

His father-in-law's bloody dog was barking at him again. It didn't matter that he was with Katie, and for the moment at least, Katie was part of the beast's household; somewhere inside that stupid animal's head lurked the notion that Fitz was always to be barked at.

He noticed Judith standing in an upstairs window; she stepped back at their approach, obviously not wanting to be seen.

Fitz blew a raspberry as Katie reached up to ring the doorbell. 'Dad,' Katie moaned in mock disapproval.

'What an interesting bell,' he said.

They were both laughing when Judith's father came to the door. He opened it, and the laughter stopped.

'Can I see Judith, please?' Fitz asked him.

'Come in, Katie,' the old man said, looking as if he'd swallowed a lemon.

Katie started to step forward; Fitz grabbed her by both shoulders, holding her back. 'No, I'd like to hand over my daughter to my wife, thank you.'

Katie squirmed in his grasp. 'Dad, please . . .'

Oh God, Fitz thought, I'm doing it. I'm putting Katie in the middle; I'm using her like a pawn. Thirty years from now, she'll be telling some thoughtfully nodding therapist like Graham how her fourth marriage is on the verge of breaking up, and she'll say her troubles all began the day her father wouldn't let her go into her grandad's house. He released his grip; she hurried inside, without looking back.

'She doesn't want to speak to you,' Judith's father told him firmly. 'Goodbye.'

A searing pain shot across Fitz's forehead. Inside the house, the dog was still barking.

'You train that dog to bark at me, don't you?' Fitz said as the door closed in his face. 'Quite specifically of course, don't you?' Locked out and abandoned, Fitz raised his voice to a shout. 'You train it, don't you? You ill-natured old Polack bastard!'

The pain in his head gradually subsided to a dull ache. He walked away down the path, imagining that he shook the dust of his father-in-law's house from his shoes.

Old man's dust, dry as brittle bones.

Judith sat with her elbows on the kitchen table, resting her chin on her hands.

Her father entered the kitchen, regarding her from the doorway. 'I assume you heard all that?'

'I should think they heard it in Bolton, Dad.'

'I don't know why you married him in the first place,' her father said. 'I never understood it; you could have had anyone. Anyone you wanted.'

She sighed. 'Trouble is, he was the one I wanted. And still do, I suppose.'

Her father snorted in disapproval. 'Weeks now, he's been phoning all hours of the day and the night, pounding on my door so hard I think he's going to break it down, tormenting my dog, and shouting abuse for the whole street to hear. And you're telling me you still want him. Well, why don't you ruddy-well go back to him then, and leave me in peace!'

She looked up at her father, glaring at her, his arms crossed in front of his chest. 'I can't go back. It's not that simple, Dad.' She stood up. 'Look, I'm sorry. I didn't mean to put you in the middle like that. Katie and I will go to a hotel for a few days, until I find a place.'

'You'll not take Katie to a ruddy hotel,' her father said, uncrossing his arms. 'I won't let it be said I drove my own grandchild from my house. Nor my daughter, even if she is a fool.'

'You're saying I'm a fool?'

'Yes,' he said. 'Twenty years married to a drunken gambler – that's what I call a fool.'

'Maybe it would be better if we left.'

He walked over to the sink, filling a kettle with water. 'Sit down, I'll make us a pot of tea,' he said, his back to her. He turned to face her. 'I said, sit down.'

She sat.

He put the kettle on the hob and went to sit across from her. He looked at her face for a long moment, his deep-set brown eyes seeming to look right through her. 'Now you're going to tell me you love him,' he said.

'I'm angry at him, Dad. I'm bloody furious. But that doesn't mean I can erase more than twenty years of my life,' she snapped her fingers, 'just like that. I can't. But I can't speak to him either. Every time I try to speak to him, he twists every word I say, turns it inside out and upside down until it means something different entirely. So what am I supposed to do? I can't talk to him.'

Her father raised his eyebrows, completely incredulous. 'Can't talk? You? You never stop. You talk so much, you have to pay someone to listen.' Another dig at her therapy. Her father didn't approve of therapy. In his day, he always said, there was no time for that kind of nonsense, if things went wrong, you pulled yourself up by your bootstraps and you got on with your life.

'I don't pay Graham to listen!'

'Oh, it's free of charge, is it? This therapy of yours?'

'Well, no.'

The kettle was whistling; the old man stood to switch off the hob. 'And what does a typical session with your therapist consist of? What exactly does he do in return for his fee?'

Judith shook her head, exasperated. 'OK, you're right. Mostly I talk and he listens. Dad, you know why you've never got on with Fitz? Because both of you are always right! You're always so infuriatingly right!'

● ● ●

Sean took several deep breaths, then spoke very slowly, drawing out every syllable. 'I ha-a-a-te her. I ha-a-ate an-y-one who would ever hurt yoooou.'

Tina sank into his arms, tears running down her face. 'What about Cormack? He wants to hurt us both, and he'll do it, Sean. He'll do it.'

All the humiliation and the fury flooded back with the mention of his name. 'If he ever touches you, I'll kill him.'

'He's tried to Sean. He's tried more than once.'

'I'll kill him!'

Tina raised her head to look into his eyes. 'He's got money, Sean. Lots of money. Carries it with him, likes to show it off.'

The patio doors were open and the stereo was on full blast, filling the night air with a mournful country-rock ballad. Fitz sat alone, in a plastic chair beside a plastic table topped with a festive yellow umbrella, systematically working his way through a large bottle of whisky in a futile attempt to stop the relentless churning of his mind. To stop him going over and over the last twenty years with Judith, and the last four weeks without her.

He had always wanted Judith. The first moment he saw her, he knew he had to have her. Of course he wasn't so naive as to believe in love at first sight – in those days, he didn't believe in love at all. Love came later, much later. After she became such a part of his life that living without her was simply unimaginable.

And now she was gone. The unimaginable had become reality, and reality had become ugly and empty.

Reality was a fat man rapidly approaching middle age, sitting outside in the dark, pouring himself drink after drink in a feeble attempt to blot that reality out, and by the very act of trying to blot it out, perpetuating it.

Round and round it goes, he thought, raising a full glass to his lips and emptying it in a single gulp.

He heard a voice shouting somewhere, 'Do you mind?'

He looked up and saw an irate man in striped pyjamas leaning out of next door's open window.

'It's nearly midnight, you know.'

Fitz knew there were at least a dozen witty things he could say to the man, sharp put-downs that would shut the bugger right up, but he couldn't be bothered. He didn't have the energy.

Just as next door's window slammed shut, another slid open. This time, the voice came from directly overhead, and the voice belonged to his teenage son, Mark. 'Dad, are you gonna come inside or what?'

'What,' he muttered, pouring himself another drink.

'Dad!'

He looked up again.

'Turn off that music and come inside, will you?'

It was dark out in the garden; he could hardly see what he was doing. He waved his arms up over his head until the intruder light came on.

'Dad, act your age, not your shoe size, eh?'

Next door's window slid open again. 'Would you show a bit of consideration? That's all. A bit of consideration!'

'Shut up,' Fitz muttered under his breath.

'You know what you are, Dad? You're a bad joke. A really bad joke! Jimmy Tarbuck wouldn't even use you!'

'Shut up!' Fitz leaned back in his chair, putting his feet up on the table.

The chair tipped over backwards, dumping him onto the grass.

ELEVEN

Tina stood before her dresser-top mirror, naked. In front of her stood a selection of jars and bottles. Behind her, Sean paced nervously from wall to wall, his head twisted towards her, watching everything she did.

She picked up one of the jars; it contained a scented skin cream. Wild Musk. She unscrewed the lid and slowly rubbed the jar's contents over her entire body, paying special attention to her breasts and her inner thighs.

She put down the jar and bent over to take several items from a drawer. Skimpy black lace pants hardly bigger than a G-string, black stockings, black suspender belt, black bra. She slipped them on, one by one, tugging at straps, adjusting pieces of elastic, smoothing tiny creases. Turning left and right to check her profile. Never taking her eyes off the mirror. Watching Sean watching her; watching him become more and more agitated by the minute. That was good; it meant he wouldn't let her down.

She reached over to the wardrobe, selected a red leather skirt – very short – and a denim waistcoat. She tried on the skirt; if she moved a certain way, her stocking tops peeked out from just below the hem. The skirt would do nicely.

She slipped on the waistcoat, buttoned it all the way up, then thought again and undid the top button.

Next came the shoes and the jewellery and the make-up and the hair, streaming down her back in long black ringlets. 'Well?' she said. 'How do I look?'

Sean's face twitched; he clenched and unclenched his fists several times before he finally spoke. 'Y-y-you l-look,' he paused, taking several deep breaths, '. . . beautiful.' He punched the wall, his face contorting with anguish as the word ricocheted around his head like a bullet: beautiful. Tina looked *beautiful*. Beautiful for Cormack. Beautiful for that bastard; it was more than he could stand. More than any man could stand.

'Think of the money, Sean,' Tina said.

Tina said that Cormack always carried money. Enough money for them to go away, somewhere Cormack and his henchmen would never find them.

'Think of what he did to you.'

Sean's lips curled back into a snarl as he remembered the way that bastard had burst in while he was in the shower, the way he pulled the curtain back. The way he stood there, all flash clothes and gold rings, scrutinising Sean's body as he swung round, startled and naked and dripping wet. The way he laughed as Sean fell back against the wall, stammering, his hands cupped protectively around his genitals. The way he flourished the bathroom key in Sean's face before he locked him in, trapping him. Making him feel helpless and humiliated.

'Think of what he wants to do to me.'

A sickening picture flashed before his eyes: Tina's legs spread wide, Cormack's bare arse heaving as he sweated and pumped on top of her.

A surge of blood rushed to Sean's head; his face felt red and hot as fire. 'Let's go,' he said.

It was a short walk to Cormack's shop: the place where he sold the various possessions he'd confiscated from those unfortunate enough to owe him money. They walked it slowly, taking time to build up their courage.

Sean's cups were on a shelf in the window. The lights in the window were out and the curtains behind the shelf were drawn, but the lights were on upstairs, in the flat where Cormack lived.

Tina knocked on the door and waited. A light went on inside the shop, and a shiver of fear ran down her spine. She felt sick and cold; she wanted to run.

The door opened, and there was Cormack, in an expensive sports jacket and flash trousers. He was dressed for a nightclub, not sitting around at home after midnight.

She pushed away her fear, put on her most winning smile. 'Hiya.'

Cormack looked her up and down, raised one eyebrow. 'Yeah?'

Tina tossed her head to one side, flicking a strand of hair back from her face. 'Can I have the cups back, please?' she asked him, her voice high and breathy. Cormack just looked at her. She pointed to the shelf in the window. 'The little silver cups?'

'No chance,' Cormack said, laughing.

Tina looked him right in the eye, lowering her voice to a husky, suggestive whisper. 'I'd be very grateful.'

Cormack stopped laughing. He took one of the cups from the shelf and held it in his hand, weighing it. Then he looked at Tina the way he'd looked at her that afternoon in her kitchen. Violating her with his eyes.

A woman's shrill voice called down the stairs. 'Who is it?'

'Business,' Cormack called back.

'At this hour?'

Tina steeled herself; she mustn't lose her nerve now, mustn't leave Cormack in any doubt about what she was offering. She arched her back slightly – a move she knew from past experience made her breasts appear more prominent – then circled her lips with her tongue.

'Yes, at this hour,' Cormack yelled over his shoulder. 'I'm going out.'

'Out where?'

'I told you it's business! I'll be right back.'

'This way,' she said, leading him into the alley where Sean was waiting. The second they were out of sight from the street, Cormack thrust his hand up her skirt.

She backed up against a wall, lit by the dim yellow glow of a single street lamp. Cormack worked his fingers past the lace-trimmed elastic of her tiny knickers and slipped one of them inside her.

'Oh yes, oh yes, that's good,' Tina whispered, firmly grasping the back of his head, holding it so he couldn't turn it to either side. He pressed his mouth against hers. Cormack's eyes were closed; Tina's darted up and down the alley, looking for Sean. Where was he?

Cormack's finger moved gently. Expertly. Tina gasped as he slid his tongue down her neck and into the hollow between her breasts. This was going too far, much too far. Where was Sean? Where was he?

She closed her eyes as Cormack grunted, pinning her to the wall, ramming his cock inside her. 'Oh baby, baby,' he whispered in her ear.

Sean cowered behind a semi-circle of metal dustbins, wondering how he could ever have got himself into this situation. He had never done anything like this before. Never. He'd stolen things, yes. He'd hit people, yes, and sometimes he'd lost control and hurt them worse than he'd intended. But never like this, never cold-blooded, never premeditated. He'd only agreed because he couldn't bear the thought of losing Tina, didn't want her to think he was a coward. He'd told her he'd do anything for her. Anything. But now he didn't think he could do it after all. He knew he couldn't do it.

He saw them in the yellow glare of a streetlamp, further up the alley. Cormack was kissing her, touching her. And Tina was kissing him back! He felt sick; he wanted to throw up. The only thing he had in the world was being stolen from him. And then he saw Cormack push her skirt up around her waist, saw him fucking her against the alley wall. He felt as if a lightning bolt had struck him in the head. His doubt and hesitation vanished, swept away by a flood of uncontrollable rage.

Tina opened her eyes to see Sean standing behind Cormack, holding a brick in both hands, his face twisted into a look of maniacal fury. She froze, her eyes wide with horror.

Sensing that something was wrong, Cormack opened his eyes. Sean raised the brick high above his head, then brought it down hard, smashing the back of Cormack's skull. Blood spurted everywhere as Cormack slid to the ground, his expression one of disbelief.

Cormack was dead – killed by the one blow. But Sean wouldn't stop hitting him; couldn't stop hitting him. Cormack had become the alcoholic father who abandoned him, the mother who beat him, the schoolchildren who laughed at him, the teachers who could never wait for him to give an answer. The social workers, the foster parents. Tina's mother, slamming the door in his face. That slimy copper with the moustache, winding him up. The magistrates, asking him if there was anything he wanted to say. Everyone who had ever hurt him, everyone who had ever humiliated him. Everyone who had ever reminded him that he was not like them, that he was different, when all he wanted to be – all he ever wanted to be – was a part of the world around him, be like everyone else. But they wouldn't let him in, the bastards would never let him in. And now he was showing them, now he was showing them all.

Tina averted her eyes, sickened, as Sean mercilessly pummelled the body, smashing Cormack's once-handsome face into jelly, spattering his flashy clothes with gore. Kicking him in the ribs until he heard them crack, crushing his balls with the heel of his boot.

She finally recovered enough to remember why they were there in the first place: the money. She bent down and searched Cormack's pockets. 'I've got it, Sean. I've got his wallet.'

He didn't hear her. He was on his knees beside the prone body, making incoherent, animal noises, pounding the corpse with his fists.

'Sean!' she cried, grabbing hold of one of his arms. He didn't even know she was there; the arm kept up its relentless rhythm, moving like a piston, up and down, up and down. 'Sean, please,' she pleaded, pulling with all her strength as she tried to drag him away from the body.

He shook her hand away and she lost her balance, falling over an overflowing bin liner filled with stinking rubbish.

Sean leapt over the body, giving it a final kick, and pulled her to her feet. In the dim yellow light of the alley, his face was strange and savage. He smelled of sweat and blood. Smelled so strongly she could feel it at the back of her throat.

He shoved her back against the wall, only feet away from the spot where Cormack lay murdered. She was his. *His*. He had to prove that she was still his, had to make her his again.

They kissed passionately, tongues entwining, bodies writhing. They struggled with their clothing, popping buttons, tearing threads. And then he plunged inside her, shuddering. Smearing her face and her body with Cormack's warm, wet blood. Tasting of salt and copper. Scraping her skin against the rough brick wall.

It started to rain. Little spits of rain that quickly gave way to large, heavy drops that landed with a splash. Warm rain, blood temperature.

Tina threw her head back, letting the blood-warm rain roll down her face. 'Oh God, Sean,' she gasped, her body erupting into spasms. 'Oh God! Oh God, I love you!' Her voice faded into a whimper. 'I love you.'

Sean stepped back, staring at her coldly as he buttoned up his jeans. He couldn't look at her without seeing Cormack, bathed in a garish yellow light, his tongue down her throat. And then he realised what he had done. What she had made him do. He turned and ran. 'Wait!' Tina shouted, following after him. 'Sean, wait!'

By the time they got back to Tina's estate, the rain had become a downpour. Hair and clothes dripping, they stopped in a covered passageway between two concrete pillars, each clinging to opposite pillars for support as they struggled to get their breath. Tina couldn't understand why Sean was so angry with her, why he stayed so far away.

'You!' Sean cried, pointing an accusing finger.

Tina clutched at her chest, feeling as if her lungs were about to burst. 'Me?' she rasped, barely able to get the word out.

'The things you let him do!'

She shook her head, gasping, confused. 'I didn't.'

He shook with rage, punching the pillar. 'You did! You bleedin' did! I was watching; I saw you!'

She gulped, trying hard to swallow. Her heart was pounding wildly, her throat was dry and raw; it hurt to breathe. 'I wanted you to stop him!' she shouted hoarsely, bracing herself against the pillar. Didn't he understand? Didn't he remember what they'd planned? She walked across to where Sean stood, shivering in his dripping clothes. 'I wanted you to stop him doing those things.' She gripped his face with her hands, moved forward to kiss him.

He pushed her away and charged up the stairs, never once looking back.

The bathroom door was open. Sean stood beneath the shower head in the bath, fully clothed. Tina watched his head roll back, eyes closed. Mouth open. Watched the water run off his body, tinged with red. Watched him collapse back against the wall, exhausted.

She walked towards him slowly, dropping her blood-stained clothing onto the wet bathroom floor.

TWELVE

Fitz opened his eyes to find himself lying in bed, still dressed, a blanket draped across his stomach. He had a vague recollection of someone dragging him in from the rain by his feet; must have been Mark. Or perhaps it was a dream.

It was light outside, but only just. The clock on the wall said five-thirty. And the phone on the bedside table was ringing – loud and insistent enough to burst a man's aching head wide open.

Across the hall, Mark was groaning. His precious sleep had been disturbed.

Fitz lifted the receiver. 'A bit early in the day, isn't it?'

'I'll be round to get you in fifteen minutes,' said a voice he instantly recognised as belonging to Detective Sergeant Jane Penhaligon.

'Panhandle, I know you want me desperately, but surely you can hold on to your virginity for just a few more hours? It will be worth the wait, I promise you,' he said, ending with a massive belch. Well bugger that for perfect timing, he thought, rolling his eyes.

'There's a murder, and it's a messy one. Be ready in fifteen minutes, Fitz.'

'Oh all right, you mad, passionate temptress you.'

He put down the phone, walked across the hall to Mark's room, and knocked. 'Wha'?' Mark croaked as Fitz opened the door.

'I'm going out in a minute,' Fitz said.

Mark rolled onto his side, pulling the blanket up over his head. 'Good.'

'I just wanted to ask you, was it you brought me upstairs last night?'

Mark threw back the blanket and raised his head, his long dark hair a mass of tangles, his mouth hanging open in astonishment. 'What? Me carry you up a flight of stairs?' He threw his head back onto the pillow, tugging at the blanket as he rolled onto his other side. 'Don't be daft.'

It was a damp, chilly morning and Jane Penhaligon had dressed for tramping up and down an alley full of puddles: waterproof hooded jacket, heavy grey trousers, and boots. All thrown on in a matter of seconds. She'd been sound asleep when the call came: 'Get down here in a hurry, and bring Fitz with you.'

She pulled up to the kerb and saw him wave at her from an upstairs window.

There'd been no time to put on make-up, no time for breakfast, not even a cup of tea. Hardly time to comb her tangled hair; she twisted it into a plait down her back while she waited for Fitz to come out of the house. She caught a glimpse of her reflection in the rear-view mirror and shook her head in dismay. She looked every bit as tired as she felt. Then she saw Fitz shambling towards her, eyes bloodshot, bulldog face as crumpled as his suit. He looked a lot worse than her; that was some small comfort. 'God, Fitz,' she said as he got in the car, 'you look terrible.'

'It may have something to do with the fact there's at least a dozen jackhammers banging away inside my head, and I think someone's been using my mouth as an ashtray. I tell you Panhandle, if I was a house I'd be condemned.'

'Good night, was it?'

'Bloody awful,' he said, belching again. He rolled his eyes in a combination of embarrassment and disgust. 'You'll pardon me if my gullet decides to explode.'

She shook her head. 'Like hell I will. Your gullet wants to explode, let it explode outside. Not in my car, thank you very much.'

'I was in bed when you phoned – you knew that of course, the thought of it excited you, don't deny it – but I'll be buggered if I can remember how I got there. And that's one thing I've always prided myself on: remembering how I got into a bed.'

'I thought men prided themselves on forgetting.'

'Ooh, you are the astute one, aren't you, Panhandle?'

'So I've been told,' she said drily.

They drove through a police cordon, down a narrow street lined with terraced houses. Despite the earliness of the hour, the street was full of curious onlookers. The local residents seemed to be out in full force, many of them in bathrobes, lifting small children up to give them a better view as they strained to see around the uniformed policemen guarding the entrance to an alley.

And then there was the media. Notebooks and Nikons, microphones and camcorders, everywhere Fitz could see. Ghouls, he thought, we're all ghouls, drawn to death like flies to shit. He opened the can of Diet Coke he'd insisted they stop off to buy, and took a large swallow.

Penhaligon flashed her badge as they got out of the car. 'Body's that way, Miss,' a uniform told her, pointing into the alley.

They ducked beneath a strip of yellow tape marked with black lettering: POLICE LINE DO NOT CROSS, turned a corner, and came across a group of people drinking coffee from polystyrene cups, chatting beside another line of tape, beyond which lay several overturned rubbish bins and one large sheet, spread over something on the ground. The sheet was white and red. The white was the sheet's original colour; the red was not.

The centre of attention seemed not to be the badly-stained sheet on the ground – or more important, what lay beneath it – but a blonde-haired woman with a notebook. Beck, Giggs, Bilborough: they gathered around her like puppies with wagging tails.

DCI Bilborough was still handling the initial introductions as Fitz and Penhaligon approached, so the woman had obviously just arrived. 'DS Beck,' Fitz heard Bilborough say, as Beck reached his hand out for a shake.

'Beck,' the woman repeated thoughtfully. 'Are you the same Beck that was in all the papers the other week? Something about a pickpocket and a bus.'

'If you had been there . . .' Beck began.

'And this is Detective Sergeant Giggs,' Bilborough added quickly, cutting Beck off in mid-sentence.

'How do you do?' Giggs asked the woman, smiling ear to ear, his round, boyish face lighting up like a department store window at Christmas. Nothing made Giggsy happier than to meet an attractive woman. He shook her hand for a long time, as if he never intended to let go.

'So you all work on this major enquiry together?' the woman asked, finally tugging her hand free.

'That's right,' Bilborough told her. 'All part of a team.'

People always seemed to expect a Detective Chief Inspector to be a sombre, grey-headed type – and to Bilborough's frequent dismay, he looked even younger than he was. In someone as ambitious and as anxious to be taken seriously as Bilborough, Fitz had observed that this often resulted in a tendency to overdo things. At the moment, he was overacting the part of the generous superior, always happy to give the major share of credit to his jolly little band of hard-working underlings.

'How long for?' the woman asked, reaching into her bag for a pen.

'As long as it takes,' Bilborough told her. 'Tenacity, that's what being a detective is all about. Like a dog with a bone. You sink your teeth into a case and don't let go until it's solved.'

Fitz hadn't dragged himself out of bed with a massive hangover just so he could stand around and listen, unnoticed, to Bilborough spouting a load of pompous rubbish. He took a large swig of his drink and belched loudly, this time on purpose.

Bilborough finally became aware of Fitz's presence. 'Nikki Price,' he said, introducing the woman. 'Researcher with the Lenny Lyon TV Show.'

Television. So that's why Bilborough and the others were falling all over themselves.

'DS Penhaligon,' Bilborough said as Panhandle leaned forward to shake the researcher's hand, mumbling something about how nice it was to meet her, despite a look on her face that said it wasn't nice at all. Panhandle wasn't keen on media types with big hair and perfect nails, oohing and aahing to the men about how exciting police work was, how dirty and gritty, then looking at *her* as if she was there to make the tea.

'And Doctor Edward Fitzgerald,' Bilborough said, waving a hand towards Fitz. 'We pay Fitz a retainer. He helps me out now and again.' He waited while Fitz and the woman exchanged greetings, then rubbed his hands together, as if to say, 'Let's get started.' He bent down to cross beneath the waist-high line of tape separating them from the body. 'Right,' he said, slipping on a pair of rubber gloves before he raised the blood-stained sheet. 'Kevin Cormack, loan shark.'

Nikki Price turned away, a hand across her mouth. Even Fitz found the sight hard to take, but then he could always blame his hangover for the way his stomach seemed to leap into his throat. He swallowed hard, forcing himself to look; to take in every detail. To visualise the ferocity, the savagery of the attack. To understand what had happened here.

Bilborough looked up at Penhaligon. 'Will you take the wife? Tea and sympathy and everything she knows about his business. You know the sketch.' Then he nodded to Beck. 'Jimmy, door to door, both sides of the alley. Statements from everyone.'

'Right.' Beck downed the last of his coffee and walked away, crushing the empty polystyrene cup in his hand.

Penhaligon stood where she was, hands in trouser pockets, expression glum.

'Are you all right?' Bilborough asked her.

'Yes, sir.'

'Then get on with it!'

'Yes, sir.' She turned and marched away.

Bilborough looked up to see Fitz rubbing his throbbing temples. 'You look worse than he does, Fitz.'

'Thanks.'

'It started raining about one,' Bilborough went on. 'He was found at five. That's four hours of rain we could've done without.'

'Yeah.'

'The scene-of-crime lads have already been, and you just missed Murphy. She's taken the photos back to the lab, they're being developed now,' Bilborough added.

'Hmm,' Fitz said, not really listening; Bilborough was just waffling on at him for the TV researcher's benefit. *Police procedure, you know. All terribly complicated, terribly precise, but I'm on top of the situation, got it all under control.*

Fitz wandered down the alley, looking and thinking, as Bilborough returned his full attention to Nikki Price, asking her if she was all right, and did she want another cup of tea?

A couple of yards from the body, several large metal bins stood arranged in a semi-circle beside the opposite wall. Plenty of room for someone to hide behind here, Fitz mused. He noticed that the alley's brick paving was still wet from the rain, and that a puddle had formed behind the bins, perfectly rectangular in shape. He called up the alley to Bilborough, 'What did he use?'

'A brick.'

Fitz nodded. 'Came from here,' he said, indicating the puddle with his foot.

Bilborough turned to Giggs. 'Get me the brick.'

Two minutes later, the brick – sealed in a plastic evidence bag – was lowered into the puddle by one of the forensics team. It was a perfect fit.

●   ●   ●

Jane Penhaligon stood with her arms crossed, leaning against a dusty metal shelving unit stacked to the ceiling with second-hand electronic equipment, wondering what to say to the woman who sat before her on a folding chair, hunched and trembling.

The woman lit a roll-up cigarette, inhaling with a ragged gasp. They'd told Penhaligon that Kevin Cormack was only thirty; his widow looked at least ten years older, with too much make-up and bleached hair the colour and texture of straw.

Penhaligon hated the fact that Bilborough always expected her to be the one to handle grieving relatives. Some couple's fifteen-year-old daughter has been raped and murdered; *you* tell them, Penhaligon. It'll be better coming from you. It's better coming from a woman. Someone's twelve-year-old son crashed a car head-on while he was joyriding, and now he's in a coma. Penhaligon, you be the one to tell his mother. I'd ask one of the blokes, but they'd go about it all wrong, you know that.

Now she was supposed to ask this total stranger, whose husband's body had been discovered less than an hour ago, what she knew about her husband's business. How was she supposed to do that? How was anyone supposed to do that?

She decided on the direct approach. 'Mrs Cormack, what can you tell me about your husband's business?'

'We had a shop together, bought and sold things.'

Penhaligon looked around at the eccentric mishmash of objects on display. Everything from satellite dishes to a beaded wedding dress. She found herself wondering how much of it had been stolen. She took her notebook out, started jotting down an inventory.

'What are you doing?' Mrs Cormack asked her.

'Just taking a few notes. Where do you get your stock?'

She shrugged. 'All over. Jumble sales, car boot sales, people coming in off the street. Why are you asking me this?'

'Just routine.'

'Oh.' She looked down at her lap, shoulders rising and falling as she struggled to keep herself from sobbing.

'I'm sorry, Mrs Cormack, I know this is difficult for you. But you told one of my colleagues that your husband said he was going out on business. So we need to determine what that business was.'

Mrs Cormack closed her eyes and nodded, a single tear glistening on her cheek.

Penhaligon moved away from the dusty shelves, bending down in front of the woman. *Tea and sympathy, Penhaligon. You know the sketch.* 'Would you like me to make you a cup of tea, Mrs Cormack?'

'No.' She opened her eyes and saw that her roll-up had gone out. She took a lighter from her dressing gown pocket.

Penhaligon straightened up, back to business. 'Did your husband receive or make any phone calls last night?'

'Don't think so.' She shook her head. 'Don't know.'

Penhaligon made a note to check with the phone company. 'Do you have any employees, Mrs Cormack?'

'Kevin had a couple of lads helped him out now and then.'

'I'll need their names and addresses.'

'There's an address book on the desk over there.'

'And I'll need to see your husband's accounts, bank statements, credit card statements, insurance policies, bills, correspondence . . .' Penhaligon shrugged, throwing up her hands. 'Everything.'

'I thought you were the police, not the bleedin' Inland Revenue.'

'It's routine,' Penhaligon assured her. 'In a . . .' she paused, catching herself before she said the word: murder. She didn't want to start the woman crying again. 'In an enquiry like this one, everything I'm asking you is strictly routine.'

'Should be in the desk,' Mrs Cormack told her. 'It should all be in the desk.'

Penhaligon walked over to the desk, and started pulling

files out of the drawers. 'I'm going to take these back to the station,' she told Mrs Cormack. 'You'll get them back as soon as we're through with them.'

'Uh-huh,' the woman said, relighting her cigarette one more time.

Penhaligon signalled to a PC standing on the pavement outside. He took the stack of files and letters out to her car, while she remained with the victim's widow. It was time to go into more detail about the events of the previous night. 'You say a man knocked on the shop door a little before one?' she asked, referring to her notebook.

Mrs Cormack nodded, spilling cigarette ash onto her dressing gown. 'About a quarter-to. Yeah. I was upstairs.'

'And your husband told you he had to conduct some business.'

'That's what he said. Yes.'

'So why couldn't he conduct that business here? Why a back alley?'

Cormack's widow stared straight ahead, thinking and smoking. 'Will it delay the claim?'

'You mean the insurance?'

'Yeah.'

Penhaligon wished she could tell her no, it won't make any difference. Then maybe the woman would open up, tell her something useful. 'I don't know,' she said, shrugging. 'Possibly.'

Mrs Cormack tensed. 'Oh.'

'Did you see this man?'

'No.'

'Did you hear him?'

She thought a while before she said, 'Yes.'

An idea was forming in Penhaligon's mind. She kept her voice as gentle as possible; this was a delicate situation. 'You heard a male voice. It was definitely a *male* voice?'

Cormack's widow looked up at her angrily. 'Will you get out of my shop, please?'

● ● ●

Fitz stood beside the circle of bins, thinking. The victim had come out to the alley willingly. Why? 'Was this Cormack fellow a drug user? A dealer, maybe?'

Bilborough shook his head. 'Not that I know of. We're checking that of course.'

Fitz scratched his head. One person came to the door, another was lying in wait. Cormack was quite happy to leave with the first person, but not so happy to tell his wife who was there or where they were going.

Two men lifted Cormack's body onto a stretcher and carried it away. While Bilborough and Giggs continued their cosy chat with Nikki Price, Fitz crossed the alley to stand where the body had lain.

As far as anyone could tell so far, the blow that had killed Cormack, the one that smashed his skull, came from behind. But Cormack would have entered the alley from the top end – that was the nearest to his shop – and the bins were further down, towards the bottom.

Cormack never walked past his attacker; the spot where he was killed was the furthest he'd got down the alley.

So why didn't he see the attacker coming towards him? Because he wasn't looking. He was facing the wall. But why didn't he hear him?

He must have been preoccupied.

Fitz was beginning to suspect what that preoccupation might have been, but he had to be sure. He reached into his pocket for a pair of wire-framed half-spectacles and slipped them on, bending forward to examine the wall more closely. He moved a couple of feet along it, stepping over the spillage from an overturned bin, and then he saw it: something that made him want to shout 'Eureka!' Something that told him his suspicion was right. His horse was out in front of the pack, breaking through the finish line, paying fifteen-to-one. *He was right*.

'There's two killers,' he announced. 'One male, one female.'

Bilborough, Giggs, and Nikki Price turned their heads

in unison.

Fitz gestured to the spot where the body was found. 'The female leads him up here for sex. The male is hiding,' he gestured towards the cluster of bins across the alley, 'behind there. He's strong. He thinks he can kill him with his bare hands. He has second thoughts, pulls the brick out, and . . .' He raised and lowered one hand, going through the motions of hitting someone with a brick.

'Absolute bollocks,' Bilborough said, showing off for the researcher.

Fitz looked at Bilborough, then at Nikki. He reached into his trouser pocket and pulled out a roll of banknotes. 'Forty-five quid,' he said, holding up the money for Bilborough's inspection.

'We're conducting a murder enquiry,' Bilborough reminded him, taking refuge in his dignity.

Fitz waved the wad of notes at him, challenging him. 'Your money where your mouth is.'

Bilborough hesitated a moment before thrusting his hand into an inside jacket pocket and removing his wallet. He counted out forty-five pounds, then pointed to the spot where Cormack had been found. 'That's where you're wrong, Fitz. Cormack's murdered *there*, right? You don't walk up an alley to have sex, then have it in the full glow of a street-lamp.' He handed his forty-five pounds over to Giggs for safekeeping. 'Hold that.'

Giggs grinned and winked at the blonde-haired researcher.

'It's broken,' Fitz said, handing his money over to the smirking Giggs as well.

Bilborough shook his head, looking pleased with himself. 'It isn't. I checked.'

Fitz visibly deflated at the news. But streetlamp or not, he was right; he knew he was right. 'Get Panhandle,' he said.

Penhaligon appeared at the top of the alley. She walked straight over to Bilborough. 'Sir, I have something to tell you. I've had an idea.'

'Later,' Bilborough told her. 'Fitz wants you.'

'But, sir –'

'Panhandle,' Fitz called out. 'Get down here, I need you!'

'I'll talk to you in a minute,' Bilborough promised her.

She walked up to where Fitz was waiting. 'What do you want, Fitz?'

Fitz placed Penhaligon into position facing the street-lamp, making sure she stood far enough from the wall behind her not to disturb any evidence. 'I'd like that wall checked for human hair,' he told Bilborough as DS Giggs, who Fitz had drafted to represent Cormack, moved into position facing Penhaligon.

'I knew it was a woman that came to the door,' Penhaligon insisted to Giggs. 'I knew it all along. I tried to tell him,' she said, indicating Bilborough, 'but he wouldn't listen.'

'Come on, Jane,' Giggs said. 'You're supposed to be a seductive temptress luring me to my death. Be seductive.'

She blew him a kiss. Giggs moaned and stuck his tongue out.

'You've been to drama school, haven't you?' Penhaligon said, giggling.

Fitz played the part of the attacker, moving out from behind the bins. 'He steps out. He comes down here.' Fitz stopped behind Giggs, raising both arms. 'Bang, bang, bang,' he said, gently tapping Giggs's head. 'Giggsy drops down.'

Penhaligon creased with laughter as Giggs crossed his eyes and slowly crumpled to the ground.

'He grabs his accomplice by the hand. They start running up the alley.' Fitz held out a hand to Penhaligon. She took it, and they started to walk away from the murder scene, followed by everyone else in the alley.

Fitz turned to Nikki Price. 'Do you remember the soldiers coming back from the Falklands?'

'Just about,' she said, puzzled.

'Remember all those women that lined the quays, waving

101

their knickers and their bras in the air? Patriotism?' He shook his head, answering his own question. 'No. *Lust.* Some of those men had killed and those women wanted them.' They stopped beside an overturned bin, a torn plastic bag lying beside it, smelling of fish and old cabbage. He turned back to Penhaligon. 'What is death, Panhandle?' he asked her, indulgent teacher to favourite student.

'The finest aphrodisiac in the world, Doctor Fitzgerald,' she answered, teacher's pet.

'Right,' Fitz said, congratulating her on her word-perfect delivery. 'Now there,' he pointed to the ground, 'is a button off a pair of Levi's. Somebody undid his trousers in a hurry.'

Bilborough glanced at Beck, an unspoken order on his face. Beck obediently bent down, using a handkerchief to pick up the button.

'And there,' Fitz said, pointing at the brickwork in the wall. 'There's long strands of hair.' Giggs and the others leaned forward to get a better look.

Fitz grabbed Penhaligon by both shoulders; the demonstration wasn't over yet. 'So what happens is: they run up the alley, they stumble and they fall.' He bent slightly to one side, pulling Penhaligon down with him.

'They help each other up.' He and Penhaligon straightened up again.

'They're frightened. But they're turned on, too. So . . .' He turned to face Penhaligon. 'Excuse me,' he said, putting his arms around her waist and pulling her towards him. 'He pins her here to the wall. He tears at his trousers. The button goes flying and they have sex.'

He tilted his head forward, staring Penhaligon right in the eyes. 'Great sex. The earth doesn't just move, it measures eight point nine on the Richter scale. Mass evacuation of Southern California time. Rip-roaring, riveting, shaking, shuddering sex.'

'You're sick,' Bilborough said, walking away.

Nikki Price and the others followed him up the alley,

leaving Fitz and Penhaligon alone.

'Eight point nine?' Penhaligon asked him, raising one eyebrow.

'Give or take a tremor, yeah.'

She took a moment to consider the implications. 'I'd sooner watch Arsenal,' she said.

Nikki Price was waiting at the top of the alley. The television researcher immediately latched onto Fitz. 'Excuse me, Doctor Fitzgerald. Can I talk to you for a minute?'

He glanced at Penhaligon, a question on his face.

'I'll wait for you in the car,' she said, walking away.

She found Giggs sitting on her car bonnet with his arms crossed, waiting. 'Took your time with the good doctor, didn't you?'

Penhaligon took a deep breath and bit her lip. 'What is that supposed to mean?'

He raised his hands in surrender. 'Nothing.' He reached into his pocket and took out a small origami unicorn. 'Made it especially for you,' he said, handing it to her.

'God, Giggsy,' she said. 'A unicorn? Let me guess, *Blade Runner* was on TV again last night, wasn't it?'

'Nah,' he said, 'Emma rented the video. Which reminds me, you're still coming round tonight, aren't you?'

She shook her head. 'I don't know about tonight. I'm so tired.' She pointed to the stack of paper on the back seat of her car. 'And I've got all this stuff to go through.'

'We,' Giggs corrected her. 'We've got all this stuff to go through. Bilborough wants the two of us to work together on this one. Unless you'd prefer to team up with Dirty Harry Junior.'

'Team up with Beck? Willingly? You've got to be joking.'

THIRTEEN

'The trouble with Fitz,' Judith said, leaning back in a chair in her therapist's office, 'is that nothing is ever simple with him.'

Everything around her was brown. The chair she sat in was covered in dark brown leather. The walls around her were panelled in dark brown wood. A brown box of tissues sat on a small brown table within easy reach of the chair. Graham hovered nearby, in brown trousers and cardigan. Brown suede lace-up shoes. Brown plastic frames around his glasses. Absent-mindedly stroking his bushy brown moustache.

'It's all so bloody complex,' she went on. 'No matter what you say, there's always some hidden meaning. No matter what you do, there's some motive behind it.'

Graham shrugged. 'He may be right, Judith.'

'That's not the point,' she insisted. 'Life with him is one long complicated game with multiple levels, where you can never be certain of the rules. I used to like the game, Graham. But now I'm sick to death of it and I don't want to play any more.'

Graham walked across to the window, his hands in his pockets. Dust particles danced briefly in a beam of sunlight, then vanished from sight as the sun went back into hiding behind the clouds. Somewhere down the hall, a telephone was ringing. 'Why does his gambling upset you, Judith?'

She shook her head, puzzled. 'What do you mean, why?'

Graham's glasses slid down his nose. He pushed them back up. 'I mean . . . why?'

'It's obvious isn't it? It's an obsession, an addiction. And he knows that, Graham. He knows, but he thinks so what? So what if I destroy myself and my family, it's all part of the game. All part of some bloody game!'

'Is that the only reason?'

Judith's mouth dropped open. 'Isn't that enough?'

'I didn't ask you if it was enough,' Graham corrected her. 'I asked you if it was the only reason.'

'I don't know, Graham,' she said, rubbing her forehead. 'Sometimes, I think of what we had, the house, the children, jobs we actually liked doing, and I think: why wasn't that enough? Surely that would have been enough for most people, wouldn't it? So why wasn't it enough for him? Why wasn't I enough for him?' She paused, throwing her head back with a sigh. 'Maybe that's it, Graham. Maybe I see the gambling as some exciting, exotic mistress that I can never compete with. That I have no hope of competing with. Maybe the problem is me. Maybe I am not enough.'

Graham sat on the window sill, staring down at his feet. 'I think you're more than enough for any man,' he said eventually. He stood up and walked over to his desk. 'I'm cancelling our next appointment, Judith. I know someone very good. Her office is just around the corner, in Deansgate, and I'm sure she'd be more than happy to take you on.'

'Take me on? What are you talking about?'

'What I'm trying to tell you, Judith, is that I can't see you as a client any more. I can't be your therapist.'

Judith stiffened, horrified. 'But why? I don't understand! Was it something I said? Something I did?'

Graham shook his head. 'It's a matter of ethics, Judith. I can't have a personal relationship with a client; it would not be ethical. And a personal relationship with you is something I would like very much.'

Judith started to speak, but he held up a hand to stop her.

'Platonic friendship,' he said, 'that's all I'm suggesting. I would like you to think of me as your friend.'

● ● ●

105

Fitz purposely chose the desk next to the coffee pot. The fact that it was in the furthest corner of the senior officers' incident room – as far away from the others as he could possibly get – was an added bonus. He poured himself another cup, wishing they'd get this homicide team meeting over with, so he could go home and maybe get an hour's kip before he had to be at the studio. But so far, it hadn't even started. Half of them weren't there yet, and the other half were just sitting around nattering while they waited. What a bloody waste of time. He felt his eyes drift closed.

He heard someone whistling. He opened his eyes to see Giggs pinning something to the noticeboard on the rear wall. A photocopied picture of Beck, blown up to poster size, with the handwritten caption: Go ahead punk, make my day.

Giggs turned around and saw Fitz looking at him. 'He'll go spare when he sees it,' Giggs said, eyes twinkling. Across the room, Panhandle was giggling like a schoolgirl.

'Very droll,' Fitz said.

More coppers started drifting into the room. Eventually, there were about fourteen or fifteen of them scattered around the room, about a fifty-fifty mix of CID and uniforms, hand-picked by Bilborough, who had been placed in charge of the investigation.

Beck and Bilborough entered the room together. Beck sat down at his usual desk; Bilborough remained standing. Neither of them noticed Giggs's poster, which prompted Giggs and Penhaligon to nudge each other repeatedly with their elbows.

Fitz's eyes were starting to close again.

'Are you two all right?' Bilborough asked Penhaligon.

'Yes, sir. Just fine, sir.'

Giggs tried to hide the fact he was laughing by pretending to sneeze.

'Do you mind if we get started?' Bilborough asked him. 'If you're ready, that is.'

'No, sir,' Giggs said. 'I mean yes, sir.' He threw up his hands. 'Whatever.'

'Right,' Bilborough said. 'Jimmy?'

'Checked out the wife,' Beck told him. 'No boyfriend. No money troubles.' He flicked through some notes. 'There's an insurance on him but it's shirt buttons. He had a few bits on the side but she knew nothing about it. She's in the clear.'

Bilborough looked at Penhaligon.

'Giggsy and I have been going through his papers, and we found a list of names and addresses.'

'And there's a lot of them,' said Giggs.

'We think these might be people who owed him money. So if it's OK with you,' Penhaligon went on, 'we thought we'd split the people on the list between us; I'll do half, he'll do half.'

'Yeah, all right,' Bilborough said.

'Any women on the list?' Giggs whispered to Penhaligon. 'I'll handle the women, gladly.'

'Shut up, Giggsy,' she whispered back. 'One of these days, I'm gonna tell Emma about you.'

'You wouldn't.'

'Are you two finished?' Bilborough asked them.

'Yes, sir,' Penhaligon answered, shooting a look at Giggs.

'Good.' Bilborough turned to address the room at large, 'I've been upstairs to talk overtime. He's not prepared to sanction it yet. Until it's sanctioned we use every resource available to us. Now, Fitz is one of those resources . . .'

Fitz's eyes popped open at the mention of his name. Across the room, he saw that Beck was sniggering.

'Jimmy,' Bilborough said angrily. 'Jimmy! He's not the fount of all wisdom, but we're paying him good money. So just shut it and listen.'

Beck was quiet.

'Right,' Bilborough went on, 'you've all got his profile in front of you. Study it. We're gonna release it to the media tomorrow morning. OK?'

Fitz cleared his throat. 'Tonight.'

'What?'

'I'm gonna be talking about it on the Lenny Lyon show tonight.'

Bilborough's mouth dropped open. 'You're going on Lenny Lyon?'

'Yeah.'

'But she wanted *me*.'

Glances were exchanged around the room; Beck was practically shaking with suppressed laughter.

Fitz shrugged. 'She must have changed her mind.'

Bilborough glanced at Beck before turning back to Fitz. 'Why?'

'I don't know,' Fitz said, exasperated.

Bilborough swung around to face Beck. 'Is something tickling you, Jimmy? Have you heard a funny joke?'

Beck shook his head, fighting to control himself. 'No.'

'Listen,' Bilborough said, standing over him. 'If you've heard a funny joke, let's all hear it.'

'I haven't, Boss.'

Bilborough turned back to Fitz. 'I've organised a press conference for tomorrow morning. 'Til then, you keep shtoom about it. You don't mention it to anybody, especially Lenny the Lyon. OK?'

'Right,' Fitz said, feeling too tired to argue.

Bilborough walked back to his office, slamming the door behind him. Beck pounded his fists on the desk top, howling with laughter. Then he turned around and saw the poster pinned to the noticeboard. 'Hey,' he said, leaping up, 'what the hell is that supposed to be?'

The room erupted into laughter.

'I don't think that's funny,' Beck said, tearing down the poster. Giggs laughed so hard he fell off his chair.

FOURTEEN

Jane Penhaligon walked through the open gate of a scrap metal yard. She saw a pair of legs sticking out from beneath a battered wreck of a car. 'Gary Langston?'

The legs slid out on wheels, followed by a broad torso and a shaven head. 'Who wants to know?'

'I do.' She held out her ID. 'Are you Gary Langston?'

He laughed. 'I reckon I fit the description.'

'Sorry?'

'Yeah, that's me, love.' He pulled himself to a standing position. He was at least six foot five, maybe eighteen stone, either an ex-soldier or someone who did his shopping in an army surplus store, wearing a dark green tee shirt, baggy camouflage trousers, thick black lace-up boots. His muscular arms were covered in tattoos. He crossed them in front of his chest. 'Come to arrest me, have you?'

She raised her head just enough to look him straight in the eye. 'Is there a reason I might be here to arrest you?'

He shook his head. 'No reason. That was a joke.'

'Maybe there's something you think you should be arrested for?'

'I told you I was joking, love. That's the trouble with you coppers, you've got no sense of humour.'

'Yeah. Sad, isn't it?' She nodded towards the wrecked car. 'You trying to fix that thing? Looks like a total write-off to me.'

'That's why I got it for nothing. Get it running again, I'll make a tidy profit. They call it free enterprise, love. But that's not why you're here, is it?'

'You know a man named Kevin Cormack?'

'I did, yeah. Used to do a bit of work for him now and then.'

Worked for him, she thought, that made sense. One of his collectors, most likely. The sight of someone like him at the door would be more than enough to put the frighteners on most people. She noticed his use of past tense. 'You know he's dead, then?'

'Word gets around.'

'Any idea who might want him dead?'

He laughed. 'And to think I said you had no sense of humour.'

Detective Sergeant George Giggs knocked on the door of a terraced house. A woman opened the door on a chain. 'Yeah?'

'Mrs Marjorie Chapman?'

The woman nodded.

Giggs flashed his ID. 'Police. Can I come inside, please?'

She slid the chain off the door and he stepped into the hall. The air in the hall smelled of damp and mildew. The paper was peeling off the walls. He put his hand up to a dark patch on the wall; it felt soaking wet to the touch. He looked down at the skirting boards, saw something that looked like fungus. 'You should do something about that,' he said.

'I'd like to, but it takes money,' Mrs Chapman said, coughing. 'Everything takes money.'

Giggs looked at the woman standing before him. Probably about the same age as him, but looked quite a bit older. Overweight, with frizzy, greying hair and deep lines around her eyes and mouth. Wearing pink leggings and a bulky grey sweatshirt, neither of which flattered her in the least. She opened the door to a small, bare lounge, almost completely empty of furniture. There was a settee against one wall, a bare bulb hanging from the ceiling, yellow curtains, a thin brown carpet. Nothing else. 'Have a seat,' she said, gesturing towards the settee.

'That's all right,' Giggs said, staying where he was. 'This

will only take a minute.' He reached into his jacket pocket for a notebook. 'I understand you know a man named Kevin Cormack.'

She looked at him suspiciously. 'What's all this about?'

'Kevin Cormack,' Giggs repeated. 'Do you know him?'

'Yeah, I know him,' she said cautiously.

'You know he was murdered?'

'He's dead? You're telling me he's dead?'

Giggs nodded.

She sank down onto the settee, her head in her hands. 'I don't believe it,' she said. 'I just don't believe it.'

Giggs blew out his cheeks. 'I'm sorry, Mrs Chapman. I didn't mean to break it to you like that; I assumed you already knew. Everyone I've spoken to so far has either seen it on the news or heard about it or . . .' He stared up at the ceiling, searching for something comforting to say. 'I'm terribly sorry.'

'You're sorry?' She started coughing again, a deep, hacking cough. She looked up at Giggs, squirming uncomfortably in the doorway, and reached into the waistband of her leggings for a crumpled tissue. 'You may be sorry,' she said, 'but I'm over the moon.' She waved the hand with the tissue, gesturing to the empty room. 'Look around you. He did this. He came in here with a bunch of thugs and cleared the place out. Took the telly, the stereo, the microwave. Everything. Then he said I still owed him! Said he'd be back. And now, if what you're telling me is true . . . It is true, isn't it?'

Giggs nodded.

'That means he's not coming back. Not ever.' She blew her nose and stuck the tissue back into her waistband. 'You know what this is? This is the happiest day of my life.'

Jane Penhaligon took a deep breath, steeling herself for what was to come. This was not going to be easy. *This is going to be delicate, Penhaligon, needs a woman's touch. You know if I send one of the blokes, he'll make a right balls up of it.*

111

'Oh bugger it,' she said, reaching up to ring the bell.

An elderly woman stuck her head out of an upstairs window. 'Clear off!' she screamed. 'Clear off! I'll call the police!'

Penhaligon stepped back so the old woman could see her. 'I am the police. Detective Sergeant Penhaligon, Anson Road Station. I was here this morning. I need to speak to Mrs Cormack; is she in?'

The woman's head disappeared back inside the window. Penhaligon heard the sound of heavy footsteps on the stairs, and then the door opened. The woman who answered it was small, with a thin, puckered mouth and a cap of tightly permed bluish-silver hair. 'What is it now? Why can't you lot leave my daughter in peace?'

That answered Penhaligon's unspoken question as to who the woman was. She put on her most soothing and reasonable voice, assuring the woman it was of vital importance that she speak to her daughter, and that it would only take a couple of minutes. The woman grudgingly stepped aside to let her in.

'You again,' Mrs Cormack said, narrowing her eyes. She was lying on a sofa in the living room, head propped up against a stack of pillows, a duvet draped across her legs, a glass of light brown liquid in one hand. She held the glass balanced on her stomach. She was still wearing the dressing gown she'd had on that morning. Her haggard face, free of make-up now, was red and swollen from crying. A bottle of Jack Daniels sat on the table beside her, half-empty. 'What the hell do you want now?'

'I'm sorry to bother you, Mrs Cormack. But I need samples of your lipstick.'

'Lipstick?' she repeated. 'Why do you . . .' She raised the glass to her mouth and emptied it in one gulp. 'How dare you come in here with your bloody innuendoes. Who the hell do you think you are, eh? You make me sick, you do. You make me bloody sick.'

● ● ●

At least Emma Giggs seemed glad to see her. She rang the Giggs's doorbell a little after eight o'clock. The door was opened by their fourteen-year-old daughter, Joanna. Joanna was the spitting image of her father, with wavy dark hair and a round, mischievous face, completely at odds with the way she was dressed: black leather jacket dripping with chains, short leopard-print dress and Doc Marten boots.

'Hi, Jane. Bye, Jane,' Joanna said, rushing past her.

She stepped inside the house and saw Emma's head sticking out of the kitchen doorway. 'Going to a friend's house,' Emma explained. 'Says they're working on a project for school.' She shrugged. 'And pigs might fly, right?'

'They might,' Penhaligon agreed, closing the front door behind her.

Emma disappeared back into the kitchen. 'Come talk to me while I make the salad.'

Penhaligon walked down the hall towards the kitchen, where Emma was leaning over a chopping board, slicing tomatoes. She was dressed as usual in a tee shirt and jeans. Her dark hair was almost as short as her husband's, with several tiny wisps combed forward to frame her plump face. Penhaligon had once jokingly asked Giggsy if he'd married his twin sister; the two of them looked so much alike.

'Can I help you with anything, Emma?'

'You certainly can. Sit down and tell me all about your love life,' Emma demanded, eyes twinkling. 'I want names, dates and places.' They talked alike, too.

She sat down at the kitchen table. 'There's not much to tell.'

'Has Peter moved in with you yet?'

Penhaligon shook her head.

Emma put down her knife and placed a head of iceberg lettuce under the cold tap in the sink. 'Why not? He seems like an awfully nice bloke, Jane.' She tilted her head, indicating a bottle on the table. 'Help yourself to some wine, by the way. Maybe it will loosen your tongue, know what I mean? Nudge, nudge, wink, wink.'

Penhaligon sighed and poured herself a glass. 'I told you, I've been busy. And . . .' She hesitated, biting her lip.

'And what?'

'And I've met someone else. Kind of.'

Emma put down the lettuce and sat down at the table. 'What do you mean, kind of?'

'I mean . . . nothing, really.' She took a sip of wine. 'How can I put it? He's obnoxious, loud, and overbearing. I don't find him physically attractive. And he's married. Separated, actually. His wife left because of his drinking and gambling.'

Emma pursed her lips. 'Sounds like a real catch, Jane.'

'But there's something about him, you know? He's completely infuriating, but he's kind of charming, too. And there's a lot going on up here.' She tapped the side of her head. 'That's his trouble, I think. He's got too much going on up there.' She saw that Emma was looking dubious. 'Don't worry, Emma. I have no intention of making a fool of myself. I'm not going to do anything stupid; for all I know, his wife could take him back tomorrow. Tonight.'

'There's always that possibility,' Emma said, pouring herself a glass of wine. 'Is he anyone I know?'

She shook her head. 'But Giggsy does.' She leaned forward, touching Emma's arm. 'Promise you won't say anything to him? You know what he's like; might as well put an ad in the paper.'

Emma rolled her eyes. 'Ha! Do I look that stupid? Don't you worry, I never tell George anything.'

Giggs appeared in the kitchen doorway, dressed in jeans and a jumper, his hair wet from the shower. 'So what is it you're not supposed to tell me?'

'None of your business,' Emma told him firmly. 'Jane and I have the right to our secrets.'

'It's not about her and Fitz, is it? That's no secret; the whole station's been talking about the two of them for weeks.'

Penhaligon's mouth dropped open. 'Talking about what?'

114

she demanded. 'There is nothing to talk about! Absolutely nothing!'

'That's not what I hear,' he said, teasing her. 'Especially after that little demonstration in the alley.' He turned to his wife. 'Emma, you would have been shocked.'

Penhaligon narrowed her eyes, tapping her fingers on the table top. 'Emma, is it OK with you if I murder your husband? I mean, would you mind?'

'Not at all,' she said. 'Be my guest.'

FIFTEEN

Sean held a black and purple bowling ball in front of him, muscles tense as he struggled to concentrate on the ten white pins at the end of a polished wooden lane. He stepped forward, swung his arm, and sent the ball hurtling. The ball changed shape and colour; becoming a brick as it connected with a resounding crash, splintering bone and splattering the alley with blood and brains.

He raised his hands to his head, gasping for breath. Around him, people were drinking and laughing and jotting down scores. Glancing up occasionally at the television screens mounted at the foot of every lane. They didn't see what he saw. Didn't hear what he heard: the last whoosh of air as it escaped a dead man's lungs.

Tina was sitting on the bench behind him, hair tumbling down her back, legs encased in black silk stockings. Looking at the scattered pins without a hint of concern. She didn't see what he saw, either. Didn't hear it.

Sean lowered his hands and saw that the lane was just a lane. The toppled pins being swept away were just pins. The ball rolling back towards him was just a ball.

No blood, no bones, no dead man's sigh.

Tina came up behind him and touched him on the arm. 'Sean,' she said, looking up at the television screen above their heads. It was a local programme: the Lenny Lyon show. And sitting across from Lenny Lyon was the fat psychologist from the police station. They were talking about Cormack's murder; Lenny Lyon was saying he understood the police were now looking for two people, a man and a woman, and Fitz was saying yes, that's right.

116

Sean looked at Tina, aghast. She'd told him she was certain no-one had seen them.

Fitz sat squashed between the arms of a red and black padded chair, shifting uncomfortably in front of a huge backdrop of Lenny Lyon's face in a variety of poses: Lenny with his eyebrows raised, looking surprised; Lenny smiling, Lenny laughing, Lenny looking stern.

Lenny himself sat in a black and white chair, facing Fitz across a glass and chrome table. Lenny Lyon seemed comfortable enough in his seat, but then Lenny, unlike Fitz, was an unusually slender man.

Lenny Lyon asked him to comment on the sexual aspects of the case.

Fitz lit a cigarette and poured himself a glass of water. 'I'd rather not.'

'But there are sexual aspects to this case,' Lenny Lyon insisted. 'I understand you've done an offender profile based on that premise.'

That bloody Nikki Price must have told him about Panhandle and the wall. 'There's a sexual aspect to you sitting there with your tongue hanging out, wanting to hear every gory detail of a particularly vicious murder, don't you think?'

Lenny Lyon denied that his tongue was hanging out, and went on to deny he wanted to hear every gory detail.

Fitz sighed and rubbed his forehead. 'So what did you ask me the question for?'

'Because I'm interested.'

Fitz shook his head. 'You're nosy. You're voyeuristic. You get turned on by suffering just like – forgive me – your brain-dead vampire audience.'

'So why are you here?' Lenny Lyon asked him.

'I'm here because I thought we were going to have an intelligent discussion, but apparently not. You manage to make Barrymore's show look professional!'

The studio audience laughed at the crack about Barrymore; Fitz turned to confront them. 'What is it with you people? You've been queueing all day to watch this crap in the vague hope that you might see your face on television, is that it? For God's sake! All right, I'll tell you what you want to know: the killers are lovers.'

Lenny Lyon leaned forward in his black and white chair, nodding.

'*She* is young and attractive.'

The floor director signalled to one of the cameras, and it zoomed in for a close-up.

'She would have to be or he wouldn't have gone up the alley with her at that time of night. She's probably been on the game, so she'll have a few convictions for soliciting.

'He's young, too. And very strong. He was convinced that he could take his victim with his bare hands. He only picked up the brick at the very last minute. He didn't mean to kill him – so it's an organised robbery and a disorganised murder. But something happened. Something snapped. He's got a volatile personality so he'll probably have a few convictions for violence of some sort.

'And they're together these two. They trust each other. They're a team. They live together. So they're probably in a bedsit, a council flat, a squat, something like that. And they probably . . .'

Fitz was interrupted by Lenny Lyon telling him they were out of time.

Sean walked away from the bowling lanes, towards the amusements section. He put a pound coin in one of the machines, but couldn't concentrate on the game.

Tina came up behind him. 'He said nothing.'

Sean stared unseeing at the flashing screen.

'Young, strong and impulsive?' Tina went on. 'That's every bloke in here. It means nothing!'

Sean's head jerked forward with the effort of trying to speak.

Tina touched his arm. 'You're frightened.'

118

'Frightened?' he repeated angrily. Once he'd heard a word, he could repeat it. 'Frightened? He said you were on the game!' The most beautiful woman he'd ever known, the only woman he'd ever loved, the only woman who hadn't looked down her nose at him thinking he was stupid or something because of the way he talked, the only woman who'd made him feel like the person he was inside his head, the only woman who'd ever said she loved him – was on the game.

'He lied!' Tina insisted. 'He lied. He was winding you up, trying to upset you so you'd give yourself away.'

YOU LOSE appeared across the screen in bright red letters. Sean kicked the machine in disgust and stormed back to the bowling lanes.

'You want to go to prison?' Tina asked, following him. 'Is that what you want? Is it?'

He picked up a ball and he heard it again, the final rush of air from a dead man's lungs.

'Go to prison,' Tina said, blocking his way. 'Never see each other again – is that what you want?'

He brushed past her, swung the ball forward, and let go. It knocked out seven pins from the centre, leaving three. Two on the far right side, one on the left.

'Then we stay calm, right, Sean?' Tina said as he swung the ball again. 'We stay calm.'

The ball hit the two pins on the right. The one on the left stayed standing, became a man, backing Tina up against a wall.

Not Cormack – just a man. A faceless man, a stranger, anyone who had the money. Sean ran down the alley towards him, flinging a brick at him with all his might. The man's head exploded into gore; his lungs collapsed with a sigh.

The pin became a pin again, the brick became a black and purple ball, and Sean found himself standing at the far end of the polished wood lane, inches from the mechanism currently dropping a new set of pins into place.

He swung around and saw that everyone in the place was looking at him.

SIXTEEN

Fitz rang his mother's doorbell first thing in the morning — no answer. He walked around the back and found her sitting on a chair in the garden, studying the racing section of the sports pages through a pair of spectacles held several inches away from her face. She was a tiny woman, hardly taller than little Katie. Sometimes he looked at her and wondered how that fragile frame had ever produced a giant like him.

'Did you see Lenny . . .' he began.

'You promised you'd see to my roses today,' his mother said without looking up. It was barely eight o'clock, but she'd probably been sitting there for an hour, waiting. Unlike his son, who'd groaned and stuck his head beneath the pillow when Fitz offered him a cup of tea before he left the house that morning, his mother had always been an early riser.

'I'll need the key to the garden shed.'

'It's here.' She pointed at the patio table beside her, never taking her eyes from the paper.

Fitz sighed and took the key. There was no point talking to her about anything while she was studying the horses. He opened the shed, took out a trowel and a pair of shears, and knelt down beside his mother's roses, wiping his forehead. He hadn't done anything yet, and he was sweating already. The morning air was uncomfortably warm; it was going to be a hot afternoon. He looked over at his mother, a woolly shawl wrapped around her shoulders, shivering at the slightest hint of a breeze. Sometimes she reminded him of a delicate porcelain doll, riddled with cracks. He had a sudden vision of himself growing old alone. No Judith, no

Mark, no Katie. Just him. Sitting in a garden chair, a blanket around his shoulders, studying the horses. Turning into porcelain.

'Solo King?' his mother asked, reading from the paper.

Fitz considered the horse a moment, mentally going through its strengths and weaknesses, grateful his mother had given him something else to think about. 'Likes a right-hander,' he said eventually. 'Good to firm.'

'It's running at Chester.'

He shook his head. 'Now that's a tight left-hander. Doesn't stand a chance.'

'That's the one I'll have then,' she said, circling it with a pen.

'Mum, it doesn't stand a bloody hope in hell. It's never done anything on a left-hander in its life.'

'You couldn't pick your nose, never mind a winner.'

Fitz sighed, returning to the roses, forcing himself to focus on what he was doing. He didn't want to think about Judith, about being alone, about time running out, about turning to porcelain and then to dust.

'Just My Bill,' his mother said a moment later.

'Just My Bill,' Fitz repeated, relieved to be thinking about horses again. 'It ran quite well last time out. Stable's coming on form. If it gets the conditions it stands a good chance.'

His mother nodded thoughtfully. 'Then that's the one I'll leave alone.'

Fitz dug his hand in among the roses. 'Shit!' He glanced towards his mother and amended what he'd said. 'Sugar!'

She finally looked up from her paper. 'What is it?'

He stood up, sucking at his hand, and walked over to where she was sitting. 'A wasp bite,' he said, holding out his hand to show her. 'A bloody huge thing.' Something to think about, something to focus on.

'It's a tiny wee thing,' she corrected him.

He followed her into the house, where she removed the sting with a pair of tweezers. 'There you are, you big soft thing. All taken care of.'

'Ta,' he said, looking down at his hand. 'Did you watch it then? The Lenny Lyon show?'

'No.' Her tone of voice implied it was a silly question. 'I went to the bingo.'

Once again, he found himself ringing his father-in-law's doorbell. For once he couldn't hear the bloody dog barking – the old man must have taken it for a walk – and for once Judith actually came to the door.

'What do you want, Fitz?' Judith asked him, opening the door on a chain.

'I want to talk to you, Judith, that's all.'

'It's nearly eight-thirty, Fitz! I'm trying to get ready for work.' She wore a figure-hugging black dress and long earrings, and more make-up than usual. She never used to go to the office looking like that. She was making an effort to impress someone, and it was obvious it wasn't him.

'Lenny Lyon, did you see it?'

Judith shook her head, fingering the door-chain. 'I was out.'

He felt the muscles in his jaw tighten. 'Where?'

'At the pictures.'

'Who with?'

'A friend.'

He hadn't come to interrogate her, but now he couldn't stop himself. It was like scratching a rash or picking a scab until it bled; he couldn't leave it alone. 'What kind of a friend?'

She wouldn't look him in the eye. 'Just a friend.'

He pushed the door inwards, stretching the chain as far as it would go. 'A male friend?' He still had to ask, even if he already knew the answer.

She nodded, looking at something across the street.

Once again he felt the need to ask, the need to confirm what he already knew. 'Graham?'

'Yes,' she said, closing the door.

● ● ●

122

Bilborough, on the other hand, had seen the Lenny Lyon show. The minute Fitz arrived at the station, he was summoned into the DCI's office. 'I gave you strict instructions not to talk about it . . .'

'They'll kill again,' Fitz interrupted.

'We don't know that.'

'*I* know that,' Fitz told him angrily, leaning across the desk. 'They screwed after they did it!'

Fitz looked at Bilborough, sitting there all indignant. This wasn't about catching the killers, this wasn't even about following bloody police procedure. This was about Bilborough wanting to be the one on telly, the one with the brilliant, original ideas, the one who was so on top of the job, so gob-smackingly impressive (and so young, too!) that the bosses upstairs would have to sit up and take notice. 'There are two people on the street right now who get a sexual thrill out of murder, and all you care about is your wounded pride! Well, I don't have time to hang around and stroke your ego,' Fitz told him. 'Your bloody publicity-seeking ego.'

Bilborough stared at him, stung. There was a knock at the door. 'Yes!'

Penhaligon entered and placed a folder on the desk. 'Forensic found human hair at the scene of the crime. It matches what we found further up the alley. Long, traces of dye, probably female.'

Fitz tapped the folder triumphantly and stood up, holding out his hand. 'Ninety quid.'

Bilborough stared down at the folder, fuming.

Fitz studied Bilborough's face for a moment, then walked out, disgusted.

Bilborough looked up at Penhaligon. 'Yeah?'

She spread her hands in a gesture of innocence. 'Nothing!'

'Fitz!' he shouted, leaping up. 'Fitz!'

Bilborough followed him into a corridor where a team of decorators were painting a wall the same colour it was already. 'Fitz!' He had to scream in order to be heard over the decorators' blasting radio. 'Hey, Fitz!'

Fitz stopped and turned around, saw Bilborough hurrying after him, clutching the folder with the forensic reports. 'Hey, Fitz, I need you. You know I need you.' He came to a stop next to the decorators' scaffolding. 'You exploit the fact that I need you . . .' He paused, gritting his teeth at the radio blaring only inches away from his head.

'Ninety quid,' Fitz shouted above the music.

Bilborough threw his hands up in the air. 'I don't have it; Giggsy's still holding it.'

'Yeah,' Fitz said, walking away.

'Hey, Fitz, where are you going?'

'I have an appointment,' he called back over his shoulder. 'I still have patients to see, you know. And you still owe me ninety quid!'

Bilborough grabbed hold of the radio, turning it off. 'This is a police station, not a bloody discotheque!'

It was stifling in the flat; Tina opened all the windows, but it did no good. She'd been so certain there'd be enough money for them to go away. The night Cormack had given her the loan, he must have had at least five or six thousand pounds in his wallet, she'd never seen such a thick stack of notes – but that night in the alley, he'd only been carrying two hundred and eighty-five pounds. They'd spent most of that already, on clothes and booze and cigarettes.

They weren't going anywhere now.

And Sean was being moody. One minute he was hyperactive, pacing around the flat, touching everything. Then the next minute, he'd sit on the floor, rocking back and forth, hugging himself.

He was doing that now: the rocking. It worried her when he did that. Worried her even more than the manic pacing.

There were times when she could read his thoughts, when she knew exactly what he was thinking. She wondered if he could read hers. Stop it, Sean, she thought, concentrating hard. Stop it.

He didn't look up. Just kept rocking.

She was more relieved than disappointed. She didn't want anyone to know her thoughts, didn't want anyone to know what lurked inside her head.

Especially Sean. How could he love her if he knew? He'd seen a glimpse of it the other night, and he'd hated her. He'd hated her as they ran home through the rain, he'd hated her as he watched the blood disappear down the bathroom drain.

Maybe he was hating her now.

She walked over to where he sat staring straight ahead at nothing, and knelt down beside him. He seemed unaware of her at first, but with hands and tongue she soon got his attention.

He didn't hate her after all.

Fitz sat at his desk, smoking cigarette after cigarette, sipping bitter, tepid coffee from a polystyrene cup. He glanced at his watch for the twentieth time in as many minutes, tapped his fingers on his growing pile of unanswered correspondence, and finally stood up.

He walked out into the hall. 'No sign of Sarah Heller?' he asked the second-floor receptionist.

She shook her head.

'Perhaps she phoned? Maybe left a message while I was out, and you forgot to mention it? You can tell me, I won't be angry.'

'No, Fitz. There've been no messages.'

He nodded and walked back into his office. He'd been so certain she'd come back, if only to prove him wrong. If only to flaunt the fact she was still up and around, and tell him he was wrong.

He gulped down the last of his tepid coffee, then crushed the cup in his hand. He tossed it towards the bin, and missed. He shrugged and walked back out again, leaving the broken remains of the cup where they'd landed.

● ● ●

They had a shower after, but it just made the air inside the flat more humid, leaving their skin as sticky as before. They got dressed and went outside, walking along the concrete walkway that connected the flats.

Even the stale, fume-laden air rising up from the car park was a relief. They leaned their elbows on the railing, watching a teenage boy working on an old banger, listening to the cacophony of sounds around them. The choking rattle of the old banger's engine, the inane chatter of daytime television, the pounding bass lines of rap and reggae. Somewhere a dog was barking. And then there was a new sound: the unmistakeable crackle of a police-band radio.

A small blue car pulled to a stop below them. A man in a suit got out, speaking into a handpiece, 'Escort three to control.'

They jumped back from the railing and ran. Tina leaned against the wall, gasping for breath, as Sean fumbled in his pockets for the key to the flat. 'Come on,' she urged him, looking back over the balcony. 'Come on!' He opened the door, and grabbed her arm, pulling her inside.

Detective Sergeant George Giggs walked up flight after flight of concrete stairs, stopping on each landing to check the flat numbers for that floor, shaking his head and blowing out his cheeks each time the dreadful realisation hit him: there were still more stairs to climb. He wished he'd let Penhaligon handle this one; he'd only been joking when he insisted she let him visit all the women on the list. But Jane had called his bluff, said you want to see all the women, OK here's another woman; you go.

The flat he wanted was on the top floor. It would be, he told himself. He'd heard that a lot of people paid good money to do something called step aerobics, and here he was doing it for free, but the thought did nothing to console him. People paid money to go into a sauna and sweat; another thing he was doing for free. He reached up to loosen his collar, and made his way along the concrete balcony.

• • •

126

They stood face to face behind the closed door, leaning against opposite walls as they struggled to control their breathing.

It's going to be all right, Tina told herself in a desperate attempt to quiet her pounding heart. *It's a big estate, he could be here to see anyone, anyone at all. There's no way he's looking for us.*

There was a knock at the door. Sean stiffened, his eyes wide with terror.

'Hide,' she whispered.

She smoothed down her hair and put her hand on the knob, waiting while Sean got into the airing cupboard behind the kitchen. There was another knock. Louder this time.

She took a deep breath and composed herself, forcing her face into an expression of nonchalance. She opened the door just as the copper was lifting the metal flap across the letter slot. 'Yeah?' she said.

'Christine Brien?'

'Yeah.'

'I'm a police officer,' the copper said, quickly flashing his ID. 'Can I come inside?' He looked hot and uncomfortable in his dark three-piece suit; he'd undone his top shirt button and loosened his tie. There were beads of perspiration visible on his forehead and above his upper lip. She imagined he must be dripping inside his clothes.

'What do you want?' she asked him.

'Did you know a man named Kevin Cormack?'

She frowned and pursed her lips, as if she was trying to place the name. 'No.'

'I was told you knew him,' the copper insisted. 'Can I come in?'

She shrugged and stepped back, allowing him to enter.

He walked past her into the hall.

'I owed him money,' she explained, leading him into the living room.

'I know,' he told her. 'If you pay it back, fine. If you don't, fine. It's no business of ours.'

She moved closer to him, smiling a mixture of gratitude and relief. 'Thanks.'

She became acutely aware that the room reeked of sweat and sex. And he'd noticed it, too. She could tell by the way his nostrils twitched, the way his cheeks flushed red as his eyes fell upon a crumpled sheet with several rather prominent stains, lying on the floor beside the mattress.

Giggs tore his gaze away from the sheet, struggling to keep his mind on the job. 'You know Kevin Cormack was murdered?'

'Yeah.' Christine Brien took another step towards him, smiling. She was young, in her early twenties or even late teens. Unbelievable body, even more unbelievable clothes. Black fishnet stockings, the tops just visible beneath a pair of shiny black hot pants. Low-cut blouse, the same blood red as her lips. High-heeled black boots. An adolescent sexual fantasy come to life. 'Coffee?'

If he didn't know better, he would swear she was giving him the come-on. 'No thanks.'

'Sit down,' she told him, moving even closer. Her body had a strong, musky aroma. Pure animal. A tigress. He'd never met a woman who exuded sex like she did.

He backed away from her and sank down onto a sofa. Remember why you're here, George, he told himself, reaching into his jacket pocket for a notebook. 'Kevin Cormack,' he said. 'Do you know if he had any enemies?'

She threw her head back and laughed, a deep throaty laugh that sent a shiver up his spine. God, she was sexy.

'Can you think of anyone who'd want to kill him?' he persisted.

She pulled a large, padded chair into position directly opposite the sofa. 'Anyone who ever met him,' she said, sitting down across from him. She brought her feet up on the edge of the seat, hugging her knees to her chest. 'He was a bastard,' she added, letting go of her knees, allowing her legs to drift apart.

Tina nearly laughed out loud. If only that copper could

see the look on his face. Mouth open, gaping at her like a fish trapped in a net. Forehead glistening with perspiration as he struggled to force his gaze back to her face. 'I've got to ask you this, Christine,' he said, his voice husky. 'You understand?'

She leaned forward. 'Yeah.'

He cleared his throat, became all business. 'Where were you around midnight the night before last?'

She said the first thing that came into her head. 'At my parents'.' Spending an evening with her parents. That sounded good, didn't sound like the sort of person he'd want to question about a murder.

'Until?'

She looked up at the ceiling, counting on her fingers. ' 'Til about two, I think.'

'And where do your parents live?'

'Seventy-six Brook Road, Hale.' She watched him write the address down in his notebook, cursing herself for being so stupid. He was going to check up on her. He would go around there, and he'd find out that she was lying.

'Hale, eh?' he said, whistling in appreciation. 'Nice area.' He gave her a look, as if to say, so how did a girl from Hale end up in a dump like this? His gaze drifted towards the mattress in the corner, the crumpled, sex-stained sheets. 'You live alone?'

She had to stop him from going to Hale, had to stop him asking questions. There was no choice in the matter, he hadn't left her a choice. It was his own fault for turning up, for asking so many questions. And now she would have to stop him, the only way she knew how; it was self-defence. She raised a finger to her lips, lowering her feet to the floor. She leaned forward, her manner flirtatiously conspiratorial. 'You won't tell the social?'

He shook his head.

'Boyfriend stays occasionally,' she whispered. 'You live alone?'

He hesitated a second before he answered. 'Yeah.'

129

Tina tilted her head to one side, eyes twinkling with amusement. 'You're not married?'

'Divorced.'

The way he was looking at her, she knew he'd say anything now, anything he thought she wanted to hear. She laughed, teasing him. 'You're a bad liar.'

He couldn't stop looking at her. 'I know.'

'Doesn't matter.' She spent a long moment staring into his flushed round face, then reached around to find her cigarettes. She held the pack forward, offering him one, but he shook his head. She shrugged and lit one, leaning back in her chair, conscious of the fact that he was watching her every movement. She knew she could have him now – it would be so easy – but that wouldn't do her any good. She'd seen him talking into his radio, they knew where he was. 'I've got a problem,' she said. 'You see, my boyfriend will be back any minute, and I don't want him to know I owed money to Cormack.'

'I could call back,' the copper suggested.

Perfect. She made a circle with her lips, blowing out a perfect ring of smoke. 'When?'

'Whenever's convenient.'

She spent a moment thinking. She wanted to do it right this time: no mess, no fingerprints, no body. It would take some time to prepare. 'Tomorrow night?'

'What time?' the copper asked her, anxiously. The randy bastard couldn't wait.

She took a long pull on her cigarette. It would have to be after dark, she decided. 'About ten,' she said.

'Ten. Right,' the copper said, standing up to leave. She walked with him to the door and opened it, smiling. He hesitated a moment, looking awkward, as if he was trying to decide whether or not he should kiss her. 'See you,' he said finally, stepping out onto the balcony.

She giggled and gave him a little wave before she closed the door behind him. She closed her eyes and leaned forward, resting her forehead against the door. Then she walked back to the kitchen and opened the door to the airing cupboard. Sean was huddled on the floor behind the hot water tank.

She sat down beside him and explained the situation, keeping her voice calm and matter-of-fact. 'I lied to him. He'll find out I lied to him; he's bound to check.' She took a deep breath to steel herself, then found to her amazement that what she was about to say came easily; the words just poured out of her mouth with no effort from her whatsoever, as if someone else was speaking for her. So easy. 'We've got to kill him,' she said, snuggling close to Sean, resting her head on his shoulder. 'We'll do it tomorrow.'

SEVENTEEN

Gamblers Anonymous met in an upstairs room at an adult education centre. A small sign on a folding table at the back proclaimed: What you see here and what you say here, STAYS HERE.

Fitz didn't find the sign the least bit reassuring.

He leaned against the wall, sipping tepid coffee. Smoking cigarette after cigarette. Looking at the lifeless, blank faces all around him. Visualising Graham in a darkened cinema, sitting beside his wife.

So what did they do before the film? And where did they go after? Did they have a drink, a meal? A good-night kiss?

Graham arrived promptly at seven, wearing a buttoned-up brown cardigan over his blue shirt and tie. Jesus wept, Fitz thought, how could any self-respecting woman let herself be seen in public with a drippy little weed like that?

Graham moved to the front of the room and announced that they were starting. He sat down behind a table, facing the others, insisting that Fitz, as a "new member", come and join him in the front.

Fitz dutifully walked to the front, and balancing his bulk on a precariously narrow plastic chair, sat facing a room of the walking dead.

'So why have you come to Gamblers Anonymous?' Graham asked in his usual soothing drone.

Fitz didn't have any patience with this little ritual. 'You *know* why I've come to Gamblers Anonymous.'

'Would you like to tell us something about yourself?' Graham persisted.

'I was born September 19th, 1949. You know who else

132

was born that day?' He paused, waiting for an answer. 'Twiggy,' he said.

The walking dead were laughing – maybe there was hope for them after all.

'Anything else?' said Graham.

He shrugged. What do you say to a room full of the walking dead? 'There were two archaeologists dug up a mummy, and they started to unwrap it and this terrible face was revealed – the most depressed, angst-ridden face – and they said, I wonder what happened to this poor man. Look at the state of him! I wonder what made him so miserable? And they realise one of his fists is clenched. So they prise it open and there it is: a betting slip. Two hundred pounds to win, Goliath.'

Everyone laughed at that but Graham. 'I'm sorry,' Fitz said, getting up. 'This isn't for me.'

He was almost out the door when Graham shouted after him, 'Eddie, you're a fool!'

Fitz stopped and looked back at Graham, seeing him again in that darkened cinema with Judith. Seeing that pretentious, hypocritical, holier-than-thou bastard's fumbling hands groping his wife.

He turned to the man nearest to him, leaning in close, tantalising him, murmuring seductively in his ear. 'What happens if your horse passes that one on the rail? Wins in a canter? Two hundred smackers. Cocaine, heroin, they cost you. They'll kill you in the end. But gambling and winning!'

He straightened up to address the room at large, eyes shining with an evangelical fervour. 'To get that buzz, to get that jump-and-punch-the-air-and-scream buzz . . . and two hundred smackers on top, nothing like it on this earth. I was right. I'm holding a piece of paper that proves that I was right. I weighed up the odds and I studied the form and I exercised my judgement. I did what I'm not allowed to do at work. In that factory. In that office. Down that bloody dole. *I used this*,' he pointed a finger to his head, 'and *I was right*.'

The walking dead watched him, spellbound. Hungry.

He took a pack of cards from his jacket pocket and shuffled them, walking over to the table at the back. 'Oh, I know about the lows. I like the lows. The lows make the highs even higher. Peaks and troughs, mountains and valleys, give me that any day before the long, flat, boring road walked by the likes of,' he paused to point at Graham, 'him!'

He dealt seven cards onto the table: three clubs, two diamonds, two hearts. 'We're at Newmarket,' he said. 'Seven furlongs. Even money, spades. Three to one, hearts and diamonds. Five to one, clubs. Two pound minimum, five pound max.'

He looked up, saw them hesitating. 'Come *on*,' he urged them. 'How long has it been? How long since you felt your heart pounding, your hands shaking, your bowels turning to ice? How long's it been since you were *alive*?'

'Two pounds on clubs,' someone shouted.

'Fiver, hearts,' another voice shouted, this time a woman's.

And then they were all at it, shouting bets and dropping their money on the table. 'This is one in the eye for the puritans, one in the eye for the likes of that smarmy bastard there,' Fitz shouted, pointing an accusing finger at Graham, sitting helpless behind his table. 'When you go home tonight they'll say: How did it go, dear? and you'll say: Not bad at all, love, I told them all about my dreadful addiction and won two hundred smackers!'

Graham looked on sadly as Fitz whipped the walking dead into a frenzy.

'The white flag's up . . . they're under starter's orders . . . and they're off!'

Sean threw his head back, laughing as the car skidded into a sharp turn. He took one hand off the wheel to hold the car telephone to his ear. '*I just called*,' he sang, '*to say I love you.*'

'*I just called*,' Tina joined in, the camcorder in her hands jiggling and bouncing as the car spun in a dizzying circle around an empty car park, '*to say how much I care.*'

The car was white and shiny and brand new; probably belonged to some rich poser. The camcorder had been on special offer in a shop at the Arndale Centre.

Sean stopped the car so they could watch themselves on the camcorder's little monitor. He stared at the tiny image of himself in fascination, then rewound the tape, singing along in harmony.

Fitz stood in a doorway across the street from the adult education centre, waiting. It was nearly an hour before Graham emerged, head down, carrying a briefcase. Fitz crossed over to meet him. 'Fancy a pint?'

Graham studied him a moment, his bland face betraying no hint of expression. 'I'd prefer an orange juice.'

'All right,' Fitz said. 'Fancy an orange juice then?'

'Thank you.'

They walked to the corner pub in silence. It was a crowded, raucous place, thick with smoke. Not Graham's sort of ambience at all, Fitz noted with satisfaction, purposely leading him round to the saloon bar.

Fitz leaned an elbow on the bar, watching Graham sip his juice. 'I must say, you're handling this well. As one pro to another, I'm impressed.'

'Thank you.'

The wanker was nodding graciously, looking well pleased with himself. Smoothing his moustache with a little preening, self-satisfied gesture. The man didn't have a clue.

'I've got a wife,' Fitz reminded him, taking special care to emphasise the word: wife. 'A family, a house, a job I've always wanted to do.' He lit a cigarette, keeping his expression even. 'I don't gamble because there's a void in my life.'

Graham nodded, looked thoughtful. 'I see.'

Fitz laughed. 'Now I'd have said something different

there. Something provocative. Bullshit, maybe. Anything.'

'But I'm not a psychologist.'

Fitz lifted his glass and took a long swig of beer. He wiped his mouth with the back of one hand, sighing in satisfaction. 'I have this gift you see, Graham. I can talk to someone for five minutes and zoom right in there.' He pointed to Graham's heart. 'I can see what's going on in there.'

Graham's lips curled into a mirthless smile. 'You want me to ask you what you see.'

'You want me to tell you what I see.'

Graham shrugged, affecting unconcern. 'All right. What do you see?'

'He asked, determined to be cool regardless of the answer.' Fitz paused for effect, taking another swig of beer, followed by a long drag on his cigarette. 'I see a man,' he said eventually, 'who'd like to get into my wife's knickers.'

Graham's head twitched involuntarily, his eyes wide with surprise. 'Wrong,' he said. Somewhere beneath the thick brush of his moustache, Fitz noticed little beads of perspiration forming. 'So why do you gamble? What's your motive there?'

'I can't help noticing you've changed the subject.'

'Why do you gamble?'

Fitz shrugged. 'I'm bored, that's all.'

'And your motive in talking to me like this?'

Fitz looked down at his drink.

'You want me to say: "He disrupted the meeting, Judith, but he spoke to me in private afterwards." '

'Something like that, yeah.'

'I won't do it, Fitz.' Graham picked up his briefcase and started to walk away.

'All right,' Fitz called after him, 'I can't promise to stop, but I'll try.'

Graham kept walking, staring straight ahead.

'Do you believe in safe sex?' Fitz shouted, loud enough for the entire pub to hear. All conversation ceased, all eyes turned to the balding man scurrying towards the exit with his head down, aware that a room full of strangers were staring at him. 'Screwing my wife could be very dangerous. It could seriously damage your health!'

Graham turned around just long enough to shoot Fitz a look of exaggerated pity before he walked out the door.

EIGHTEEN

Sean and Tina stood on a rooftop across the street from Anson Road Police Station, watching and waiting. 'There he is, Sean.' Tina pointed up the street. The copper who'd been round the flat was walking towards the station with a red-haired woman. They stopped on the front steps outside the police station, talking.

Sean used the camcorder's zoom lens to focus in on the man, recording every facial expression, every gesture. 'He's big,' Sean said, 'strong.'

'You're stronger.'

Sean shook his head. 'I don't . . .'

'You've got to do it, Sean,' Tina insisted. 'Do you want to go to prison?'

'No.'

'Then we have to get rid of him, Sean.' She touched his arm. 'Don't worry, it'll be all right. You'll see.'

The red-haired woman went inside. The big copper was joined by someone Sean recognised instantly: Beck. 'I could kill *him*,' Sean said, panning across to Beck's face. 'Why can't it be him with the 'tache?'

'It's not the numbers that are important, it's the letters,' Giggs told Beck as they walked into the incident room. 'The letters give the cup size.'

'But the numbers have some relevance,' Beck insisted.

Giggs shook his head. 'Not unless you're playing bingo.'

Penhaligon looked up from her desk. 'You two are disgusting, you know that?'

'Would I be?' said Giggs.

138

Beck sat down with his feet up on a desk.

Bilborough stuck his head round his office door. 'What have you got for me, lads?'

Giggs and Penhaligon exchanged a look of sheer exasperation. Giggs sat down on the edge of Penhaligon's desk, picking up one of her pens and twiddling it in his fingers. 'Not a lot.'

Penhaligon shuffled through the contents of a folder. 'The man's dead. People aren't gonna rush forward to say they owed him money.'

Bilborough came out into the squad room, tossing a football from hand to hand. 'So who *have* you seen?'

'His family, his boozing partners, a couple of very large blokes who say they did a bit of work for him now and then,' Penhaligon said. 'All above board, nothing illegal, mind,' she added drily. 'But people who actually owed him money?' She looked up at Giggs. 'Six?'

'Seven,' Giggs corrected her. 'I've seen one already this morning, seeing two more this afternoon.'

Bilborough sighed, looking disappointed. 'Forensic?'

Penhaligon referred to her folder, taking out a couple of stapled sheets. 'Not a lot after four hours of rain. Lipstick on his shirt . . .'

'The wife's?' Bilborough interrupted.

'Oh no. You sent me round to check, remember? That was a bit of an adventure; the widow got hysterical. Started breaking things; a couple of glasses, anyway. I got the samples in the end, though. Not one of them matched.' She referred back to the stapled sheets. 'Time of death, cause of death, blah blah blah.' She stopped, at last coming upon something she considered interesting. 'His flies were open.'

Giggs leaned across the desk to nudge her, giving her a dirty laugh.

'Nothing else?' Bilborough asked her.

She glanced back at the report and shook her head. 'No.'

Bilborough wasn't pleased; she could tell by the way he

was clutching his soccer ball, squeezing it so tightly that his knuckles were turning white.

'You know what the problem is?' Giggs said, breaking the silence. 'They hated him because they hated him, or they hated him because they owed him money. But everybody hated him. Everybody wanted him dead.'

'Does that piercing insight get us anywhere?' Bilborough asked him.

Giggs shook his head, embarrassed. 'No.'

Bilborough headed back to his office. 'Keep me posted.'

Beck stood up. 'We're er . . .' He raised a hand to his mouth as if he was holding a large glass; his way of inviting the boss along for a drink.

'I'll see you over there,' Bilborough said.

Penhaligon got up to go with the others.

'Got a minute?' Bilborough asked her.

'Of course.' She followed him into the office and stood waiting while he carefully balanced the soccer ball on top of some books on the windowsill.

He sat down, arranging some papers on his desk. Placing a particular document directly in front of him. 'You're getting on OK with Giggs?'

'Fine,' she said, eyes on the document. It was her application for promotion. 'He's a good copper.'

'There's nothing you need?'

She shrugged and tried to smile. 'A bit of luck.'

'Has Fitz been any use?'

'Some,' she said carefully.

'You see a lot of him?'

This was getting a bit personal; she felt like telling him it was none of his business, but this wasn't the time. Not with her application for promotion sitting there on his desk. 'It's platonic,' she said, keeping her voice light and even. Remembering her vow that she would keep her nose clean.

Bilborough nodded. 'Don't tell him anything he doesn't need to know.'

The nerve of the man. What was he implying? 'I never

do,' she said, forcing herself to keep her voice and expression neutral.

Bilborough nodded. 'The Chief Super's had a letter from a member of the public,' he said. 'Sent me a copy. I thought you might find it interesting.'

'Yes, sir?' she said cautiously.

He reached into one of his drawers for a file, took out a small sheet of pink notepaper, and started to read: 'Dear Chief Superintendent, I want to thank you for sending that wonderful detective, Miss Sergeant Pendleton, to my house the other day. At least I think that was her name.'

Penhaligon closed her eyes and sighed, vowing to go back to Vale Road and kill the woman.

'You'd know her if you saw her,' Bilborough went on, 'she's a very pretty redhead, awfully clever, and so helpful and pleasant as well. In my humble opinion, she is a regular Miss Marple! Yours, Miss Anna Knight. P.S: The PC who came with her was very nice as well.'

She opened her eyes and saw that Bilborough was laughing. 'We don't get many letters like that one,' he said. 'Well done.'

'Thank you, sir,' she said drily. 'Is that all, sir?'

'No.' Bilborough put down Miss Knight's letter and picked up her application. He spent a moment leafing through it, then raised his eyes to look at her. 'You've made an application for promotion. I've got to do a report.'

She caught her breath, trying to stay calm. 'Yes.'

Bilborough put the application back down. 'Fan letters from the public aside, don't you think you're jumping the gun a bit?'

Penhaligon froze. How could he say that? After all the work she'd put in, the sheer determined effort to be not just as good as the men, but better. How could he do this to her?

'It's not that long since your last promotion,' he went on. 'Maybe in another six months. A year, no problem . . .'

'OK,' she said. She noticed to her horror that she was giggling. What was it Fitz had called it? A gallows giggle –

the laugh you laughed when you really wanted to cry. She nodded and left the office.

She came face to face with Fitz in the corridor outside. 'Panhandle,' he called in greeting.

All her anger and frustration boiled over at the sound of that patronising nickname. 'Penhaligon!' she shouted. 'My name is Penhaligon, you arrogant lump of lard!' She pushed him aside, storming past him, shouting one last time, 'Penhaligon!'

'Something's upset you,' Fitz said, looking after her. He tapped his nose. 'I can always tell.'

He found her in the pub across the road, sitting by herself while the other coppers nattered by the bar. He ordered a Scotch and a Diet Coke, and carried them over.

'I'm sorry,' she said.

'It's all right,' he said, lifting his glass of Diet Coke.

'On the wagon?'

He nodded. 'But it's a very bumpy road. I keep falling off.'

'He's right you know,' she said eventually. 'I know the system. I've applied too soon.'

'But?'

Across the room, everyone was laughing at Giggs, blowing his nose on a pair of women's panties. Penhaligon picked up her glass and knocked her drink back in one. 'Are you having one?' she asked, reaching into her bag.

'No.'

'Oh for God's sake, have one.' She pulled out her purse and started to get up.

Fitz grabbed hold of her arm, restraining her. 'But . . .' he said, 'the system's for other people. If you're special, it shouldn't apply to you. Right?'

'Right,' she mumbled, looking down into her lap.

A phone behind the bar was ringing. The barman picked it up, said, 'Jimmy,' and held it out to Beck.

'Yeah,' Beck said. He listened a moment, then shouted

ecstatically, 'YES!' He slammed down the phone and addressed the bar at large. 'They've used his credit card!'

The shop manager pointed to a camcorder in a glass display case. 'This is the sort.'

'I'll need a description of everyone who bought one,' Beck said.

'You're joking,' the manager told him. 'We've sold about a hundred in the last few days. Special offer, got Jeremy Beadle up to launch it.'

Beck gestured to a television set in the middle of the camcorder display. It was hooked up to one of the cameras, panning back and forth across the shop. 'What about this?'

'That's no good, either,' the manager said, shaking his head. 'The tape rewinds every two hours.' He shrugged. 'Buy now while stocks last.'

Tina fussed with the camera, looking through the eyepiece and positioning the tripod just so. Then she started moving Sean around, telling him to step forward, no back a bit. A little to the left, a little more, no that's too much. Yes, there.

She ran around from behind the camera and stuck a piece of tape on the floor beside Sean's feet. 'There,' she said, 'that's your spot.'

Then it was Sean's turn to get behind the camera. He spent a lot of time looking through the viewfinder, enthusiastically grunting and waving his hands to indicate which way she should move her chair. Finally they decided that everything was as perfect as they could possibly make it.

Sean moved to the spot Tina had marked for him. '*I, I who have nothing*,' he sang, gesturing wildly. '*I, I who have no-one . . .*'

Tina sat down in an armchair facing the camera. "We're going to kill a policeman,' she began.

NINETEEN

Fitz walked into the house to find Mark sprawled across the living room sofa, eyes closed and mouth open, snoring. Mark's eyes fluttered open. He raised his head, yawning. 'Wha'?'

'So what have you done today, Mark?' Fitz asked his son. 'What great things have you accomplished?'

Mark yawned again, rubbing his eyes as he rose to a sitting position. He was wearing a tee shirt, ripped jeans and a couple of studded leather bracelets. His shoulder-length hair was tied into a ponytail from which several strands had come loose, falling haphazardly across his face. 'I must have fallen asleep,' he said. 'Gran phoned. Said to tell you Solo King paid eighteen-to-one at Chester. Then she said something about you picking your nose.' He shrugged. 'She said you'd understand.'

Fitz left the room and headed for the kitchen.

It was a mess; dishes piled high in the sink, a bottle of milk slowly turning to yoghurt on the draining board, laundry lying crumpled and forgotten in the tumble dryer. Fitz sighed and switched on the radio, already tuned to the afternoon's racing.

He put the milk back in the fridge. He did the dishes and wiped down the table. Then he decided he might as well tackle the ironing. He emptied the contents of the dryer into a large basket and set to work, ironing tee shirt after tee shirt; Mark rarely wore anything else.

He noticed a number of little holes in one of them. Moths? He held the shirt up to the light to get a better look. No, not moths. These were burn holes.

He picked up another and examined it. More holes. 'Bugger,' he said.

He stormed into the living room, brandishing one of the shirts. 'What's this?'

Mark hadn't moved from the sofa, but at least he was awake now, his head propped up on a cushion to stare at something on TV.

Fitz moved in front of the screen to block his view, holding out the tee shirt. 'What *is* this?'

'It's a tee shirt.'

Fitz reached down to switch the TV off. He thrust the shirt towards Mark for his inspection. 'And what are these? These little holes?'

Mark looked at the shirt, then at his father. 'Is this a trick question?'

'No.'

'Then I'd say they're little holes.'

'Look, I buy you these,' Fitz reminded him angrily. 'I pay for these. You're obviously smoking some sort of dope that's doing your head in; you're dropping it all over your kit . . .'

Mark rolled onto his side, dismissing the accusation. 'I've had the shirt for ages.'

'You're obviously so far out of your cake, you don't even realise you're doing it!'

'I don't know what you're talking about.'

'Well, look, muggins here pays for these, OK?'

Mark rolled his eyes at the ceiling. 'Yeah, yeah.'

'So long as you're under my roof, you obey my rules.'

'Yeah, yeah, yeah.'

'Don't yeah, yeah, yeah me! This isn't the chorus of a bloody Beatles song! You just get rid of it,' Fitz ordered him. 'You don't smoke dope unless you prove to me that you can handle it.'

'Oh yeah,' Mark said, laughing bitterly. 'Says the man who's pissed out of his head every night, the man who's pickling his brains in booze.'

Fitz walked out of the room and resumed his ironing.

Mark appeared in the kitchen doorway. 'You want a cup of tea?'

Fitz looked up from the ironing board. A cup of tea: Mark's idea of an apology. 'Yeah, I would,' he said, apology accepted.

Sean studied the video of the two policemen talking and laughing on the steps of the station. Why couldn't it be the other one? The little slimy one, with the moustache? He could kill him with his bare hands; he could wrap his hands around his throat and squeeze. Squeeze and squeeze until the bastard's eyes popped right out of his head. Squeeze until his head exploded. But no, it had to be the big one.

He'd hated Cormack. Hated him more than he'd ever hated anyone. Even more than that little turd with the moustache.

Killing Cormack had been easy, surprisingly easy. But killing that big copper, that was going to be more difficult. Not because of the man's size, not because he was afraid of him, but because he didn't hate him. He had no reason to hate him.

Suddenly Tina was beside him. She touched him on the arm. 'He'll check my alibi, Sean. Find out I wasn't at my mum's. That's it, then. We're finished.'

'I kn-n-n . . .'

'You know.'

'I know. I know that. I know!'

'You'd kill the other one. The one who wound you up. You'd kill him.'

'Yeah.'

'This one's just the same. If he'd been in that cell he'd have wound you up just the same. They're all the same; they're all bastards, Sean. Every one of them.'

'I know.'

'You know what he wants to do to me, Sean. You know what he's coming here to do.'

146

He picked up a small piece of lead piping, felt the weight of it in his hands. 'I know.'

There were certain things about Judith that could always be relied on. One of them was when and where she did her weekly shopping.

He found her halfway down aisle seven: muffins, cakes and part-baked bread. She looked up in dismay as he took over pushing the trolley. 'What do you want, Fitz?'

'I have to talk to you. It's important.'

'It's always important, Fitz, and I'm bloody tired of it. I'm tired of talking, do you understand?'

'It's about Mark, Judith.'

Her face changed, became concerned. 'What about him?'

He was still with her at the check-out counter, and still with her as she unloaded the trolley in the car park. Still going on about Mark.

He was overreacting as usual. It was only a bit of pot; they'd both done it themselves when they were younger. 'There are worse things,' she told him, exasperated.

'No,' he insisted. 'A lot of dope.'

Judith threw up her hands. 'Then talk to him!'

'I've tried. But we just end up screaming at each other.' He gave her a helpless look. 'You know what it's like.'

'Oh, I know what it's like, all right,' she muttered, putting the last of the groceries into the boot of the car.

'What do you mean?' Fitz asked her, looking worried.

She pointed at the empty trolley. 'Would you get rid of that for me, please?'

'You'll drive off.'

Sometimes he could be so bloody silly. 'I won't,' she said. He didn't move.

'I promise!'

He slammed down the boot and took her keys. Then he wheeled away the trolley.

She slapped a hand to her forehead. Life with him was

like a game of chess she could never win; every move she made, he took another piece away from the board. Check and mate. 'Can I have my keys back, please?'

He tossed them back to her, point made. 'What do you mean, you know what it's like?'

She got into the car. Trolley disposed of, he stood looming over her, holding the door open as she strapped herself into the seat harness. 'You're a psychologist,' she said. 'You analyse people's problems, you solve their relationships, and you're totally incapable of talking to your own son!' She turned the key in the ignition. 'You don't talk, you spar. I'm not a mother, I'm a bloody referee! That's what I mean.'

'I'll book a table for us all tonight,' he began. 'We can . . .'

She shook her head, interrupting him. 'I'm going out.'

'With Graham?'

'Yes.' She tried to close the door, but he was still holding it. 'Let go.' He still held on. 'Fitz, let go of the door!'

'I'm not gonna make any promises I can't keep . . .'

They began to speak simultaneously, each shouting to be heard over the other: '*I'm not listening to you, Fitz* – Look, I'll cut down on the booze – *I'm not listening!* – I'll try and cut down on the gambling – *If I listen to you, you'll twist me round your little finger and I'm not going to let that happen* – I won't make empty promises; I'm not that kind of hypocrite – *I won't listen; I'm not going to let that happen!* – That's what you liked about me, for Christ's sake – *I'm not listening* – But I'll try! All I can say is I'll try – *Let go of the door, Fitz!* – I'll try; all I can promise is I'll try . . .'

'Let go of the door, Fitz,' Judith shrieked. 'I'm not listening to you!'

He took his hand away from the door. 'I love you.'

She slammed the door closed. Why was he tormenting her like this? Why couldn't he just leave her alone?

'I love you!' A giant of a man bent over almost double, nose pressed against the glass. 'I love you!'

She pressed her foot down and drove away, a single tear rolling down her cheek.

'I love you!'

Sean held a roll of black plastic bin liners in one hand. In the other, he held a large roll of Sellotape.

Tina tore one of the bags from the roll, then carefully cut along each side with a pair of scissors, turning the bag into one long strip of plastic. Sean handed her some tape, and she stuck the plastic to the living room wall.

They were both wearing gloves.

She took another bag from the roll and they repeated the process, Tina meticulously positioning the new plastic strip so that it slightly overlapped the previous one. The next strip of black plastic slightly overlapped the second, and the one after that overlapped the third.

She worked her way around the room, making sure every inch of wall was covered in plastic; if Cormack was anything to go by, there would be a lot of blood.

Then she started on the floor and ceiling.

'*Murder on the Orient Express*,' Giggs said, driving Penhaligon back to Anson Road Station.

'Huh?'

'You remember in *Murder on the Orient Express*, it turns out the murderer is everybody? That's what I figure on this Cormack case. Everybody we've spoken to hated him, everybody wanted him dead. Maybe they all killed him; made a party of it. That would explain a lot of things, wouldn't it?'

She laughed. 'You told Bilborough your theory yet?'

'Uh . . . no.'

'Well, I want to be there when you do. It's always good for a laugh, isn't it? To watch the way Bilborough's eyes glaze over every time you open your mouth, and this latest brainwave of yours should really get him.'

'Thanks, Jane,' Giggs interrupted her. 'I knew I could

rely on your support.'

She pointed towards a bus stop, near the next intersection. 'Hey, Giggsy, look. There's Fitz.'

Giggs pulled his car up to the kerb. Fitz didn't notice the car; he was staring up at a billboard advertising a new brand of jeans. Two nuns in habits stood a couple of feet away from him, waiting for a bus.

Giggs honked his horn as Penhaligon lowered her window. 'Hey, big guy!' she yelled, giggling. 'Want a lift?'

Fitz swung round, pointing at the advertising poster behind him: a gigantic close-up of a man's crotch, the flies on his tight-fitting jeans half-undone. 'Think about testicles,' Fitz said loudly.

She leaned out of the car window to get a better look. 'I do nothing else.'

'Cormack's testicles were crushed, right?'

'Right,' Penhaligon agreed uncomfortably, aware the nuns were listening to every word.

'Why?'

She shrugged. 'You tell me.'

'Sexual rage,' Fitz told her. 'Sexual rage. Look, I'll explain it over dinner.'

Penhaligon tilted her head, indicating Giggs. 'We're going for a drink.'

'We're not,' Giggs corrected her. 'I've got something on. A bit of business.'

Penhaligon turned to him, surprised. 'Oh yeah? What kind of business?'

'A mind-your-own sort of business,' Giggs said, looking away.

'With Emma?'

He still wouldn't look at her. 'No.'

'Well?' Fitz asked her, leaning into the window.

'OK,' she said. 'Get in.'

He climbed into the back seat.

'He's a nice boy, really,' she assured the nuns.

TWENTY

It was one of those restaurants where no-one dared to raise their voice above a whisper. That was an exaggeration, Judith realised, but everyone around her did seem to be speaking in a kind of hushed murmur. The waiter, the people at the other tables, and especially Graham. 'You must know how I feel about you, Judith,' he was saying. 'Surely you've guessed by now.'

'Graham, I'm sorry. But I'm just not ready for that kind of involvement.'

'I understand,' he said, nodding sympathetically. 'And I want you to know that I wouldn't dream of pressurising you.' He raised both eyebrows the way he always did when he'd had a piercing insight. 'That's a lie. My not pressurising you will pressurise you, because you won't be able to ignore the fact that I'm not pressurising you.'

Judith couldn't help laughing; that kind of convoluted logic was so typical of him.

Graham laughed, too. 'Relationships can be so bloody difficult, can't they?'

She nodded. 'I know what you're saying.' She noticed something moving in the corner of her eye. She turned her head slightly to get a better look, and felt a sudden urge to scream her head off. The waiter was leading two people across the room, and one of them was Fitz. Oh God, no, she thought, he's followed me here.

He was with a woman she'd never seen before: tall, with long reddish-brown hair, wearing a little yellow and black print dress. Judith doubted the woman was over thirty. Obviously nothing but a tart. Some bimbo her husband had picked up to taunt her with. Just another pawn in whatever sick game he was playing.

'It's all up to you,' Graham went on, unaware that Fitz was walking directly towards them, 'how far our relationship goes, where it goes, how long it lasts . . .'

Judith saw to her horror that Fitz and his bimbo friend had been seated at the table next to theirs.

Graham finally realised something was wrong. 'Are you all right?' he asked her.

'My husband's here.'

Graham turned to look.

Fitz nodded to them as if they were total strangers. 'Evening.'

'What's the big idea?' Judith asked him.

'I beg your pardon?'

Judith motioned to the waiter. 'Excuse me.'

'Madam?'

'Would you put them somewhere else, please?'

The waiter turned to Fitz and his companion, puzzled and a little embarrassed. 'The lady would like you to move.'

Fitz put on his glasses, looking perplexed. 'Do I know her?'

'He knows me all right. I'm his wife.'

Fitz raised a hand to his mouth in surprise, as if he had only just recognised her. He leaned towards the waiter, speaking confidentially, 'Actually, I'm a psychologist. It's very sad. She's a patient of mine.'

'I am not a patient! I'm his wife.'

Fitz leaned across the aisle towards her. 'Oh yes,' he said. 'Sorry, I didn't recognise you without the straitjacket.'

Judith turned her attention back to the waiter. 'Would you please put them somewhere else?'

The waiter stood where he was, looking puzzled.

Fitz leaned towards him, one man-of-the-world to another. 'I ask you, do you think I would take my mistress out for a meal and then bung her down right next to my wife? Large Scotch and dry please.' He tapped the woman on the arm.

'And for you, darling?'

'No thank you,' the woman said. Then she had another thought. 'A large jug of water, please,' she told the waiter. 'With ice.'

'Yes, madam,' said the waiter, hurrying away from the table.

'Would you please . . .' Judith called after him. But it was no use; he was gone. 'Who told you I was here?' she demanded of Fitz.

'No-one.'

'You just happened to walk in off the street.'

Fitz became Bogart in *Casablanca*, 'Of all the gin joints in all the world . . .'

'Isn't this a bit adolescent?' Graham broke in. The waiter came back with Fitz's drink and the jug of water. Graham raised a hand to signal him. 'Could we have the bill, please?'

'Is everything all right, sir?' the waiter asked him.

'No it isn't,' Judith answered for him.

The waiter put the jug of ice water down in front of the woman sitting with Fitz. She thanked him, picked up the jug, and stood up, holding the jug in both hands. She then calmly proceeded to empty the jug's contents over Fitz's head. The woman instantly rose in Judith's estimation; maybe she wasn't such a mindless bimbo after all.

The waiter didn't know where to look; he finally settled on a blank space several inches above Graham's head. Fitz's only reaction was to take one of the ice cubes that had fallen into his lap and drop it into his drink.

'Old Anglo-Saxon foreplay,' he told Graham before turning to tell the woman, 'Go straight to my bed. If I'm not there in half an hour, start without me.'

Fitz's woman friend walked out without saying a word, rising even higher in Judith's estimation. She felt like applauding.

Hair dripping onto the table, clothing soaked with ice-cold water, Fitz calmly began flicking through the pages of the menu. The waiter shrugged and took out his order book.

'Keeps on happening, doesn't it, Doctor Fitzgerald?' Judith said as she and Graham stood up to leave.

Sean stood in the middle of an empty room lined with black plastic. 'You'll have to take your clothes off,' Tina told him, unbuttoning his shirt. She reached down to undo his trousers; he brushed her hand away. 'You'll get blood on them,' she said. 'Evidence.'

He shook his head, angrily.

'He's coming to screw me Sean,' Tina reminded him, again reaching for his trousers.

Again he knocked her hand away; he would not face the man naked. 'I'll keep them on! I'll burn them afterwards, right? I'll burn them.'

The air in the casino was thick with smoke and tension; crowded with people in search of something to think about, something to focus on, something to make them feel alive. Fitz stood in the doorway, looking at a sea of faces creased in concentration, and imagined he was looking into the splintered fragments of a mirror, seeing his own desperation reflected back at him, over and over again.

Time to stop thinking about broken mirrors and desperation, time to stop thinking about becoming a cracked porcelain doll like his mother, wrapped in blankets in a lonely garden. Time instead to think about getting that buzz, that jump-and-punch-the-air-and-scream buzz. He sat down in front of the roulette wheel and opened his wallet.

He took out a wad of notes: the money he'd never got round to spending on his dinner date with Jane Penhaligon. He counted the money and threw it on the table, keeping twenty pounds back for later. The croupier passed him a stack of chips.

He shoved them across the table, placing them all on one number. He won. He waited for the buzz, the *I was right* buzz. It didn't come.

He placed all his chips on another number. He won again. And then again.

The stack of chips in front of him was enormous, almost a thousand pounds' worth. *Gambling and winning, nothing like it on earth.* And all he could think about was Detective Sergeant Jane Penhaligon, her hair hanging loose over her shoulders, laughing on the way to the restaurant. Oh Panhandle, he thought, I'm sorry. I'm genuinely sorry. He placed a final bet, and lost everything.

He got up from the table and walked over to the tuxedo-clad bouncer, standing just inside the door. 'Bar me, George.'

'Can't do it, Fitz.'

Fitz sighed and nodded. He reached around behind him and tipped over one of the tables, scattering cards and chips across the floor.

'You're barred,' the bouncer told him.

'Good boy,' Fitz said, slipping the twenty pounds he'd held back into the man's jacket pocket.

Penhaligon's flat was in a new development a short distance from a canal. He walked along the towpath, smoking and thinking. It was raining again, turning the plot of unlit waste ground that stood between him and the flats into mud. He tossed his cigarette into the water and made his way across, shoes squelching in the dark.

He heard the sound of drums as he entered the hallway, beating out a relentless rhythm. Bang, bang, clash, bang, bang, clash. Penhaligon, working out her anger. Taking it out on the drum set she kept in her living room. Taking it out on the neighbours, too: it was nearly ten o'clock.

He took a deep breath, and knocked. Bang, bang, clash. She didn't hear him. He knocked again, louder. The drumming stopped. He heard the sound of approaching footsteps, the metallic scrape of a chain sliding into place. The door opened slightly, her face glaring at him from behind the chain.

'Sorry,' Fitz said.

'So you should be,' she said sharply, slamming the door in his face.

He knocked again. The door opened again, still on the chain. 'Any chance of a coffee?' he asked.

She shook her head. 'A very slim one. Too small to measure.'

'Please?'

She unhooked the chain and let him inside. She'd washed off her make-up and changed into a baggy sweatshirt and leggings, the sort of thing Katie might wear. It made her look about fifteen.

She led him down the hall into her antiseptically clean living room, and left him there. He stood in the middle of the room, listening to her clatter about in the kitchen while he contemplated his surroundings. White walls, bare except for a single, framed print hanging above the floral-printed sofa. A couple of bamboo chairs with seat cushions to match the sofa, a bamboo coffee table topped with a spotless sheet of glass and a selection of magazines, neatly stacked. The Persian rug beneath his feet was immaculate, not even a hint of fluff. In her own way, Penhaligon was as much of a control freak as Sarah Heller.

It went back to her childhood of course, Fitz knew. The only girl in a house full of brothers. Strict mother, only strict with her. Kept her indoors while the boys ran wild outside. A lonely little girl, watching them with her nose pressed up against the window. Seeing them having fun, having adventures. Longing to join in the games from which she was always excluded. Longing for the freedom which the boys enjoyed but was denied to her. Being a good little girl, doing whatever she was told, totally under her mother's control. Seething inside. Chafing under her mother's domination, dreaming of the day she would lay claim to her own life. The day when she could do anything she wanted to do. The day when she would become an adult, be the one in control.

And then she grew up to find that nothing in life was

under her control after all. She had bills to pay, bosses to answer to. The only place she had any level of control was in her own home; if she couldn't control the world outside, at least she could control the dirt in her flat. Overcome the grime and the dust, make every surface shine. Control.

And then there were the drums. More control. Giving her power over the neighbours. The power to disrupt their sleep, the power to make their lives a misery.

Control, he thought again, trying to pinpoint the exact moment when he'd lost it. When everything around him began to fall apart.

He picked up a magazine from its neat little stack and started flipping through the pages, trying to focus his mind on something. He tried to read the first paragraph of an article, but the words didn't make any sense, became nothing more than black squiggles against a white background. He stared and stared at the page in front of him, but could find no meaning there.

Penhaligon finally broke the silence. 'You used me!' she shouted from the kitchen.

'I didn't mean to. I knew she was going out. I didn't think she'd use that restaurant. Sentimental reasons, Panhandle.' He paused. 'I thought you'd be amused.'

'What?'

'You know what the Chinese say?'

Penhaligon came back into the living room, wrinkling her nose. 'What's that funny smell?'

Fitz looked down at his shoes; he'd trodden in something more than mud. 'Oh God,' he said. He'd come here to apologise, and he'd tracked dog shit all over her Persian rug. 'I'll clean it up, Panhandle. I promise.'

'Bloody right you will!'

Tina stood in the darkened hallway, just inside the front door, waiting. Wearing a short black dress and long black gloves. The door at the other end of the hall – the one leading into the living room – was firmly shut.

At ten o'clock exactly, there was a knock. She opened the door, smiling. 'Hiya.'

The copper stood out on the balcony holding a bottle of wine. Wearing the same dark suit he'd worn the day before. 'All right?' he said, stepping into the hallway. He reeked of aftershave.

Tina closed the door behind him. 'Did you come by car?'

He nodded.

'You didn't leave it down there?' she asked, all wide-eyed concern.

'Up a side street.'

'Which one?'

'Sylvester Street.'

'You can't be too careful,' she told him, looking relieved.

'I know.' He offered her the wine.

She thanked him, rising on tiptoe to kiss him lightly on the lips. He pulled her towards him, forcing her mouth open with his tongue. His lips were large and rubbery; his tongue tasted of peppermint breath spray.

She led him down the hall, walking backwards.

'What's the rush?' she said, laughing between sloppy peppermint kisses. 'We've got all night, no need to rush. We've got all night.' He slid a hand up under her dress, pressing his lower body against hers, moaning. She laughed again, pulling away from his grasp. Taking him by the hand. They were almost at the living room door. 'I've got a surprise for you.' She handed him back his wine bottle, then reached up, playfully covering his eyes with her free hand. 'Now keep them shut,' she said, giggling.

He obediently did as he was told, laughing as she opened the door and led him into the room where Sean was waiting. 'Now wait right here,' she whispered.

Giggs stood perfectly still for a moment, eyes closed, smiling expectantly. Nothing happened.

He could hear someone breathing heavily. Panting, almost. But it seemed far away. Too far away. Something was wrong. He opened his eyes and found himself in an empty room, so

158

dark he could hardly see. Then he realised that it wasn't that the room was dark, it was that every surface: walls, floor and ceiling, was covered in something black.

He turned his head towards the sound of breathing, saw Tina standing in a corner. Backed up against the wall, head thrown back, mouth slightly open. Touching herself.

Tina watched the dawning of fear in the man's eyes. Gasped as Sean rushed forward, bringing the lead pipe down onto the back of the copper's skull with all his strength.

'Kill him, Sean,' she urged him. 'Kill him! Make sure he's dead.'

Fitz got down on his hands and knees, scrubbing brush in hand, bucket of soapy water by his side. Penhaligon supervised him from the sofa, pointing out the bits he'd missed. 'So what do they say?' she asked him eventually.

'Hmm?'

'The Chinese. You were going to tell me what they say, remember?'

Fitz bowed slightly, launching into an exaggerated Chinese accent, somewhere between Fu Manchu and Charlie Chan. 'You can appreciate the beauty of the tiger – even as it leaps to devour you.'

'Bullshit.'

'No, detachment,' he said, dipping the brush into the water. 'No matter what situation you're in, if you're detached enough – objective enough – you'll find it fascinating.'

'I did not find it fascinating,' she protested. 'I found it embarrassing! It made me angry.'

'That's because you weren't detached enough.' He looked up from his scrubbing. 'Because you fancy me too much.'

She laughed. 'That Chinese tiger's got more chance than you, Fitz. What were you trying to achieve?'

'You want the truth?'

'It would make a refreshing change.'

He got up from the floor and sat on a chair, facing her. 'It's the sort of thing I'd do years ago. Impulse, risk, intuition. It's the kind of thing she liked about me then. Of course you're besotted with me, Panhandle, so this may come as a bit of a shock, but . . . I do not have the ideal physique in the world.'

She shrugged. 'Love is blind.'

'But I could use this,' he pointed to his head. 'I had the gift of the gab. And I took risks.'

'You're forty-four now, Fitz.'

Et tu, Panhandle, he thought. Forty-four, no longer the young know-it-all with everything still ahead of him. Forty-four, too old to act on impulse. Forty-four, time to stop pushing, time to stop fighting. Time to let go. Time to leave this woman alone and go home in the rain. 'So I am,' he said quietly. 'Lend me a fiver for a taxi?'

'Yeah.' She reached for her bag, took out a note. 'Shall I call one for you?'

He stood up. 'No, I'll get one in the street.'

'Are you sure?'

'Yeah,' he said, heading for the door.

She followed him into the hall. 'You're welcome to stay,' she said suddenly.

He swung round, saw her looking down at her feet, embarrassed.

'I wasn't going to ask until I was sure,' she mumbled, still looking down. 'I didn't want to complicate things any further.'

She'd caught him completely off-guard. He hesitated, confused. 'Sure about us?'

'No,' she said, shaking her head. She giggled like a schoolgirl. 'I mean yes. But then I've always been sure, at least me personally. I meant until I was sure that you and Judith had burnt your bridges.'

Now he was even more confused; he hadn't said or done anything to give her that impression. 'But we haven't.'

She reached over to open the door, lowering her eyes back to the floor.

'What makes you think we have?'

160

'Go get your taxi, Fitz.'

He couldn't leave it alone; he had to find out what she was talking about, what could possibly have given her the idea he was finished with Judith. 'No, please tell me what makes you think we've burnt our bridges?'

'Will you just go and get your bloody taxi?' She pushed him out into the hall.

He stood in the corridor outside her flat, looking back at her. Pleading with his eyes.

'You just can't see it, can you?' she asked him.

'See what?'

She shook her head, exasperated. 'Fitz, you've driven her into bed with him.'

The door closed in his face.

Tina put on a pair of rubber gloves before she touched the dead man's wallet. She knelt down beside the body, carefully removed all the money, then replaced the wallet in his inside jacket pocket. She reached inside his trouser pocket, found his car keys, and handed them to Sean. She placed a video cassette on the dead man's chest, buttoning up his jacket to hold the cassette in place.

Sean helped her peel the wet plastic from the floor and walls, wrapping it round and round the body until it looked like a black plastic mummy. Sealing it with Sellotape.

Tina walked outside to check the balcony and stairs. It was well past midnight, windy and pouring with rain. No sign of anyone anywhere. She walked back to the flat and told Sean it was time to go.

He threw a coat over his blood-soaked clothing and moved the copper's car round to the bottom of the stairwell. Tina stood guard by the car while he went back upstairs to get the body. He dragged it down the stairs, holding it by the feet. Bumping its plastic-wrapped head on every step.

They bundled the dead copper into the boot and drove away, observed by no-one.

● ● ●

Penhaligon picked up the phone beside her bed. She had a pretty good idea who it was. 'Penhaligon,' she said, trying to keep her voice detached and businesslike.

'I don't believe it,' said Fitz.

'What?'

'I don't believe it.' He was slurring his words; he was drunk.

'What? What do you not believe?'

'Judith and that slimy little shit!'

'Go to sleep, Fitz.'

'Why did you say it?' he whined. 'There was no need for you to say anything.'

'Go to sleep, you self-centred, bloody . . . You can't see what's under your bloody nose. You've got the bloody cheek to talk about instinct . . . and intuition . . . and crap like that. And you can't even see what's happening right under your bloody nose!'

'Panhand . . .'

She slammed down the phone and switched off the light, fuming in the darkness.

They parked the car alongside a railway track, unloaded the boot and dragged the body through wet grass and mud, to the top of a hill overlooking a canal. They gave the body a shove and watched it roll out of sight.

Penhaligon's phone was ringing again. That bloody Fitz! She lifted the receiver and dropped it, cutting it off. A minute later, it rang again.

Sean sat shivering in a tub of pink water, nursing his right wrist.

'You've sprained it,' Tina told him. 'You shouldn't have hit him so hard.' She helped him out of the bath, gently dried him with a towel, and had him sit on the toilet while she wrapped his swollen wrist with a long strip of bandage.

'There,' she cooed, 'is that better?'

He nodded, still shivering slightly.

She stroked his goose-pimpled flesh, her warm, dry touch simultaneously soothing and arousing. Her lips curled into a smile.

She gently lifted his bandaged arm to her mouth; kissed it. She leaned forward, kissing him on the cheek, then the forehead. Then the lips. 'Shall we go to bed?'

He closed his eyes and nodded, no longer shivering.

TWENTY-ONE

Jane Penhaligon had finally managed to get to sleep, and now the bloody phone was going again. She picked up the receiver, determined to give Fitz a piece of her mind. 'Yeah?' she shouted.

It wasn't Fitz, it was the station. A voice was telling her something she didn't want to hear.

'Where?' she said.

This wasn't really happening, this was a dream. A bad dream.

The voice on the phone told her the name of a road.

'Fifteen minutes,' she said, still certain she was dreaming.

She reached into her wardrobe for some clothes and got dressed. She picked up her bag and her car keys, and went outside.

There was a chill in the early morning air; she shivered, knowing that she was awake, she'd been awake the whole time, and that no matter how desperately she wanted this to be a dream, it was real and there was nothing she could do but carry on and get there as fast as she could. She got into her car and started the engine.

You handle it, Penhaligon.

She put her foot down, speeding through the empty streets.

You tell them; it's so much better coming from a woman.

She swerved to avoid a milk float.

Tea and sympathy, Penhaligon, you know the sketch.

She turned down a dirt track leading to a field by the side of a canal.

Gently, Penhaligon. Break the news gently.

164

Up ahead, beyond the police cordon, there were cars and vans and a mobile incident unit. She flashed her ID and drove through.

Tea and sympathy.

There'd been no tea and sympathy for her, no breaking it gently. Just a terse phone call at dawn: Giggsy's dead, get down there quick. She got out of her car and walked across the grass, still damp from the morning dew.

Bilborough and Beck were already there, deep in conversation. 'Don't get mad, get even,' Bilborough was telling Beck. 'How do we get even? We catch the bastard. How do we catch the bastard? We stay calm, rational. We don't run around like headless chickens, that just wastes time and energy. We don't go after revenge, that'll just balls things up. Are you listening?'

'I'm listening,' Beck said.

'Are you hearing what I'm saying?' Bilborough asked him.

'I'm hearing what you're saying.'

They didn't even acknowledge her presence. And Fitz was there, too. Sitting on the bonnet of a panda car.

He jumped up as she walked past him. 'Look, your boss brought me here.'

She ignored him, ducking under another line of tape and heading down the hill to the canalside path where Giggsy's body had been discovered by a jogger. Fitz followed her, then waited while she marched up to the spot where several men in white coveralls bent over some *thing* lying on the ground.

This wasn't Giggsy – this wasn't her friend. This was an empty, battered shell. The face that stared up at her, unseeing, wasn't Giggsy's face – it was an unrecognisable mess. And that shattered, broken body, wrapped up like a mummy in something that looked like a bin liner – that couldn't be Giggsy.

She turned away, covering her mouth as they zipped up the body bag.

'What about the tape?' asked one of the men in coveralls, indicating the video cassette that fell from the dead man's jacket pocket.

'Leave it with the body for forensic,' a uniformed policeman answered.

'Are you OK?' Fitz asked Penhaligon.

'Yes,' she hissed, brushing past him. Her overriding emotion at that moment was anger. Anger at whoever had done this; that was a sensible kind of anger, one she expected of herself. But there was another, irrational anger that surprised her. She was angry at Giggsy for dying.

She walked back up the hill to confront Bilborough; she was angry at him, too. 'Does Emma know?'

'Is that his wife?'

She nodded, unable to conceal her annoyance; the way he always went on about them being a team, he should know Giggsy's wife's name. He shouldn't have to ask.

'The Chief Super's gonna tell her. He wants you there.'

Of course, she thought, it's always me. Always me.

'You worked with the guy,' Bilborough said.

'I'm not complaining,' she said, angry at herself now. 'They've got a son in Scarborough, a trainee chef. Can I tell her we'll fetch him by car?'

'Yes.'

Fitz followed Bilborough and Beck into the sterile white environment of the pathology lab. Brightly-lit shelves held an assortment of chemicals and equipment. Men and women in white coats sat at long counters around the room, bent over microscopes, examining slides. Occasionally speaking in hushed tones, barely above a whisper.

A white-coated woman led them to the small metal trolley where Giggs's personal effects lay. She handed them each a pair of surgical gloves, then left them.

They stood side by side, silently examining the items found on Giggs's body, looking for anything that might give them a clue as to where he'd gone, who he'd been with, what he'd been doing.

Fitz picked up Giggs's wallet. He took out a crumpled photo of Giggs and a woman he assumed was his wife, with Penhaligon and another man. They all had their arms round each other's shoulders. They were laughing and wearing party hats; Giggs was making one of his silly faces. A banner hung stretched across a doorway behind them, reading: Happy New Year.

'There's Panhandle,' Fitz said, showing the photo to Bilborough. 'Who's the bloke?'

'Don't know.' Bilborough passed the picture over to Beck; Beck shrugged.

Fitz turned the wallet upside down and shook it. 'No cash.' He turned to Bilborough. 'Go on, say it.'

'Say what?'

'He was holding our bet.'

'That's the last thing on my mind,' Bilborough told him.

'Sure,' Fitz said, his tone of voice implying he didn't believe that for a second. He picked up an unopened packet of three condoms. Ribbed for greater pleasure, according to the writing on the back. 'Did he have children?'

'Don't know.' Bilborough looked at Beck. 'Jimmy?'

Beck shrugged. 'Three, I think. I'm not sure.'

'Penhaligon'll know,' Fitz said.

Emma Giggs opened the front door before the Chief Super could even knock. 'It's about George, isn't it?' she said. 'He didn't come home last night. Something's happened to him, hasn't it?'

The Chief Superintendent introduced himself and suggested it would be better if they went inside.

Emma looked pleadingly at Penhaligon, standing beside the silver-haired, stern-featured figure looming on her front doorstep. 'What is it, Jane? Is George all right? Is he in hospital? Tell me.'

'Emma, please let's go inside.'

Emma stood in the doorway, shaking.

'Emma, please.'

She stood back, allowing them into the house. The Chief Super suggested she sit down. She turned again to Penhaligon. 'Jane? He's all right, isn't he? Everything's going to be all right, isn't it?'

Penhaligon took her by the arm and led her to the sofa.

'I'm very sorry, Mrs Giggs . . .' the Chief Super began.

'NO!' Emma screamed before he could finish the sentence. She threw her hands up to her face, knowing what he had come to say. 'Please God! Please Jesus! Please, please no!'

Penhaligon threw her arms around her, holding her as she sobbed. 'Oh Emma, oh Emma, I'm so sorry,' she murmured, stroking her hair. Rocking her back and forth like a baby. 'So sorry.'

The Chief Super stood by helplessly, staring out the window.

Penhaligon walked into Bilborough's office without knocking. 'You wanted to see me?'

He indicated the seat across his desk. 'Sit down.'

Bilborough wasn't alone; Fitz was with him, sitting at the far end of the room. 'How did she take it?' Bilborough asked her.

'She turned cartwheels.'

Bilborough crossed his arms, waiting patiently.

'I'm sorry,' she said.

'You know her well?'

'Yeah.'

'A friend?' Bilborough persisted.

She nodded. 'I like to think so.'

'Did they have kids?' Fitz broke in.

She looked at Bilborough. 'You know he's got kids.'

'He's not sure of their ages,' Fitz explained.

'Peter's sixteen. He's in Scarborough. Tony's fifteen, Joanna's fourteen.'

'Is she on the pill?' Fitz asked.

168

She snorted, deliberately misunderstanding him. 'At fourteen years of age?'

'Her mother,' Fitz said. 'Giggs's wife.'

'Emma,' Penhaligon corrected him angrily. 'She's called Emma.'

'Is *Emma* on the pill?'

'What's going on?' she asked Bilborough.

He held up a clear plastic bag containing a packet of three condoms. 'We found these in Giggsy's wallet.'

She forced herself to keep her voice nonchalant. 'So?'

'Is that what they used?' Fitz asked her.

Giggsy's dead, she thought, don't let them kill Emma's memory of him, too. 'Yeah,' she said. 'Sure.'

Fitz raised his eyebrows. 'For fifteen years?'

'Well, not the same packet!'

Bilborough and Fitz exchanged a knowing glance. 'You're lying,' Fitz said.

'Can I go now, please?' she asked Bilborough.

'No.'

Fitz stood up and walked towards her. 'It could have been you,' he said, standing behind her, towering over the back of her chair. 'It was Giggsy because Giggsy happened to be the one to call. He knocks on the door. She asks him in. A bit of chat and probably a lot of thigh. She invites him back – at night. Giggsy can't believe his luck. He's in the chemist buying a pack of three while the other bastard's flexing his muscles.' He moved round in front of her, bending down to look her in the eyes, his face less than a foot away from hers. 'Now, given what you know about Giggs, is that a realistic scenario, DS Penhaligon?'

She looked away, biting her lip.

'I know why you won't answer,' Fitz told her. 'You don't want Emma to find out he was playing around. Well, that's fine – she won't.'

She looked at Bilborough. 'Is that a promise?'

'Yeah.'

She sighed. 'It's a realistic scenario, yeah. Giggsy and

169

Emma didn't need condoms; he had a vasectomy years ago. He must have been worried about getting a dose from the bitch.'

Sean opened his eyes; Tina wasn't beside him. He sat up in bed, looking around frantically. He couldn't be alone. After all that had happened, all that he had done, he could never be alone again. Alone, his mind would fill with strange sounds and horrifying visions.

The whoosh of Cormack's last sigh. The gurgling sound the copper made as he fell to the ground, the rattle in his chest as he finally died.

Bricks and plastic, spattered with blood and brains. Dead eyes staring with huge black pupils.

'Tina!'

'Yeah?' She came out of the bathroom, dressed in her kimono, brushing her hair. He sank back onto the pillow, relieved.

She took her photo album from the bottom drawer where she kept it hidden, and sat beside him on the mattress, slowly flicking through the pages. 'I've been thinking, Sean,' she said.

He watched her face, waiting for her to continue.

She looked down at the album in her hands. 'All the things I could have done. The person I might have been, if only she'd never existed. She stole my life, Sean. The life that should have been mine – she stole.'

He closed his eyes, terrified of what was coming next.

'If she didn't exist now, then maybe I could still become that person. The one I should have been.' She touched his arm, leaned forward to kiss him. 'What do you think, Sean? What do you think?'

He didn't dare say no. If he said no, she might leave him alone with the words he could not form, with the visions of dead men that swirled inside his head. He needed her; he couldn't go on without her.

He nodded.

170

'Oh, I love you,' she said, kissing him again. Touching him. Running her tongue along the length of his body.

'Better get dressed,' she said, when he came out of the shower. 'You have to report to the police.'

He shook his head no. This was the one thing he couldn't do. He couldn't walk into Anson Road nick just like that. Not after what he'd done.

'You have to do it, Sean.'

He shook his head again, more insistently this time. If he walked into the police station, he might never walk out again.

'They're not going to arrest you, Sean. They're not even looking for you. They know nothing. They haven't got a clue. If you go in and report like you're supposed to, everything will be all right. But if you don't report, they'll come round here and arrest you. If you don't report, the magistrate'll change his mind. You won't get probation, you'll get sent down. Is that what you want?'

But they'd ask him questions, he'd have to give his name and address. If she was there, she could do the talking for him. 'C-c-c-c . . .'

'No, I can't come with you,' she said.

TWENTY-TWO

Detective Sergeant James Beck stood by the incident room door, cracking his knuckles. Waiting.

That was all he ever did these days: stand around waiting, doing nothing, while Bilborough and that fat psychologist sat on their arses, theorising. To hell with theory, he wanted action. He wanted to get out on the street, start getting some results: something tangible, that he could see. Something solid. Like his hand on someone's collar. Like a body down in the cells, a suspect to be questioned.

This wasn't just another killing, this wasn't just some sleazeball loan shark nobody gave a damn about, this was Giggsy. This was a cop.

Beck made a fist and punched his other hand. A cop. Some gobshite bastard had murdered – no, not murdered – *butchered* a copper. Butchered *one of us*, and what are they doing about it? Sitting around in Bilborough's office; he could see them through the glass. First they'd been talking to Penhaligon and now she was gone and they were talking to each other. He didn't have to hear them to know they were talking about another bloody theory. Talking about the bloody scientific approach.

Well, bollocks to science, he told himself. Bollocks to all that. You want to catch a villain, you don't sit around all day and talk about it. You get out in the street and you start feeling collars, and you keep on feeling collars, until you get the result you're after. That's the bottom line: getting the result.

He saw to his relief that they were finally standing up, finally leaving the office. Bilborough came out the door first.

'Ready to go, Jimmy?'

'I've been ready for ages, Boss,' Beck said, struggling to keep his voice even.

Fitz came lumbering out into the incident room and walked over to one of the phones. 'I'll be with you in just a minute,' he said, picking up the receiver. 'I have to make a phone call.'

'Boss,' Beck said.

'He said he'll only be a minute, Jimmy.'

Beck crossed his arms, seething, while Fitz dialled a number and stood waiting. 'Hello, Sarah,' he said, eventually. 'It's Fitz. I've been trying to get hold of you for a couple of days now. It's important that we talk. If I'm not at the office, please feel free to phone me at home. You've got the number.' He put down the receiver. 'Bloody answerphones,' he said to no-one in particular.

They walked downstairs and outside to the car park. Climbed into Bilborough's car. Fitz sat in the front passenger seat, talking non-stop to the DCI, expounding on his latest theories, while Beck fumed in the back.

They got out of the car at Manchester Central Hospital. Took the lift down to the lower basement, to the mortuary.

They walked down the long white corridor in silence. Beck sighed, relieved that the pointless pontificating was finally over, at least for the moment. They came to a stop in front of a large, clear window.

A woman stood on the other side of the glass, wearing surgical gloves and a plastic apron, bent over a table on which a body lay loosely covered by a sheet. She looked up at their approach, eyes sparkling behind a pair of huge round spectacles.

'Gentlemen,' her voice came over a speaker into the corridor, 'I've got a carbonised willy!' She gestured to the table beside her, waving a gloved hand. 'Young man, eight pints of lager. Stands on the edge of the platform, pees onto the track. It hits the live rail. The current passes through the arc of urine . . .' she traced a semi-circle in the air, '. . . kills

173

him stone dead.' She lifted the sheet from the corpse's lower torso. 'Voilà!' she said.

Beck stared at the woman in disbelief. He hadn't come here for more pointless chatter. And he certainly wasn't here for some kind of carnival side show.

He was relieved to see that Bilborough and Fitz did the same as him, just stare at the woman as if she had to be out of her tree.

The woman lowered the sheet, obviously disappointed with the men's reaction, and moved across to another table. She pulled back the sheet, exposing Giggs's naked torso. 'Now with your victim,' she went on brightly, 'at first sight it's a typical sustained frenzied attack. The first blows landed on the victim's arms.' She lifted one of Giggs's arms to show it to them. 'Hence the bruises.'

Beck walked over to a microphone mounted on the corridor wall and picked it up, shaking.

'The victim dropped his arms . . .' the woman went on blithely.

'Giggs,' Beck interrupted her, speaking into the microphone.

'Sorry?'

'He's not "the victim". He's Giggs. He's a policeman called Giggs. Right? Now I don't want to make a song and dance about it, but this is no bloody civilian you understand, this is a police officer called Giggs. Have you got that?'

'Point made,' Bilborough said.

'Not "the victim",' Beck went on, ignoring him. 'We'll have less of "the victim". This man was no victim, this man was law, do you understand that? This man was police . . .'

'Point made, Jimmy,' Bilborough repeated.

Beck was quiet.

'Very well,' the woman said. 'But the attack was not so frenzied. Several blows in succession landed on the same spot on the . . . on Giggs's skull. No doubt about it, the intention was to kill.'

Beck squeezed the microphone in his hand, breathing

deeply. He jammed it back into its holder and stormed off down the hall. Someone had done this to a police officer, and all they'd come up with so far was a couple of sheets of useless paper: Fitz's bloody offender profile.

Fitz and his theories were getting them nowhere. Fitz and his theories were letting a cop-killer run loose.

Well, Beck had his own theory. He had his own offender profile.

Fitz and the others were walking back to the car when someone called out Fitz's name.

Fitz turned and saw John Peterson walking towards him across the car park. 'Have you been up to see Sarah?' Doctor Peterson asked him.

'What? Nobody told me she was here.'

'She came in yesterday. Fourth floor, ward B,' Peterson said. 'I'm sorry, I thought you knew.'

Fitz turned to Bilborough. 'Look, I'll meet you back at the station later, all right? There's someone here I have to see.'

Beck took the stairs two at a time, burst through the incident room doors, and headed straight for Giggsy's old desk. He went through the murdered copper's notes, tossing the scribbled sheets of paper in every direction, until he found what he was looking for: Giggsy's list of Cormack's deadbeats.

He'd had enough of theorising, enough of sitting around doing nothing. He went downstairs, brandishing the list, and pointed at several uniformed officers: 'You, you, you and you. Come with me.'

Sarah Heller lay dozing on a bed halfway down a crowded ward, with a tube in each arm, each connected to a different bottle of clear liquid. A machine by the side of the bed monitored her heart and her breathing. 'I suppose it would be a pointless gesture to bring you a bag of grapes,' a voice said.

She looked up and saw a gigantic figure in a crumpled suit looming over her. 'I'd say it was practically useless,' she agreed.

Fitz sank down into a chair by the side of the bed. 'Do you still think you're all right, Sarah?'

'Why don't you just go away and leave me alone?' A television mounted on the wall was showing a daytime quiz show. The woman in the next bed started coughing violently, spitting something green into a bowl. 'But before you go,' she said, 'close the curtains for me, will you?'

Fitz stood up and pulled the curtains around her bed. 'It's not me you're angry at, Sarah,' he said. 'Who is it?'

'What difference does it make?'

'The difference it makes is that maybe you'll stop directing all that anger at yourself, Sarah. Maybe that's the only difference it'll make. But it's a significant one. It's one that might keep you alive.'

She laughed weakly. 'You do go on a bit, don't you?'

'You don't want to die, Sarah,' Fitz insisted.

'Why not? If this is life, stuck in a hospital bed, wired up to some bloody machine, with tubes stuck up my arms, then maybe I don't see an awful lot to commend it.'

'OK, you're in a hospital bed; that's your situation. Who put you in that hospital bed, in that situation? You did that! Only you! And who is going to get you out of that bed? I wish I could say that it was me, but the truth is that the only person who can do it is you. You want control, Sarah? OK, you've got control. What happens to you next is completely up to you. You're the one in control.'

'OK, you win,' she said.

'What?'

'Bring me a big steak with roast potatoes and Yorkshire pudding, and I'll have apple crumble with cream for afters.'

'You're taking the piss, aren't you Sarah?'

She closed her eyes. 'I'm humouring you. I'll say anything you want to hear, if it will stop you banging on about my childhood.'

'What about your childhood? I didn't even mention your childhood.'

'Oh didn't you? Well, you have before. More than once. Like you keep going on about control. Control!' She laughed. 'Look who's talking about control, will you? A fat slob who can't go two minutes without a cigarette; there's a man who knows about control!'

'Tell me about your childhood,' Fitz said.

'Is this turning into a session now?' she asked him. 'Will you be sending me a bill?'

'Just talk to me, Sarah. I'm here and I'm listening to you. Just tell me what you want to say.'

'What do I want to say?' She shrugged. 'I suppose I could say something like: what if you're right? I'm not saying you are right; I'm just saying what if you were. What if things happened to me when I was a child, things I don't want to think about. Things that I thought I'd brought on myself; things that I thought were my own fault. So what if I started thinking about them again? What would happen then? Would I suddenly leap out of bed and scoff a Big Mac?' She shook her head. 'I don't think so.'

'No,' Fitz said. 'But what might just happen, is you might stop taking things out on yourself. You might begin a healing process.'

'You think so, do you?' She pressed a button on the side of the bed, raising the top half of her body into an upright position. 'I'll tell you what. I'm not saying you're right. I'm not admitting anything, you understand? But . . . I'll think about what you said, OK? I can't say fairer than that, can I? I'll think about it.'

The first name on the list was Tony Rivers, and the address was a council house not far from Cormack's shop.

'OK, everybody ready?' Beck asked the uniforms gathered behind him. He pounded on the door and waited.

A woman opened the door a crack. She was dressed in a bathrobe. 'Yeah?'

Beck pushed the door in, shoving her to one side as he swept past her, followed by the others. 'Hey, what're you doing?' the woman screamed. 'What the hell do you think you're doing?'

Her husband was sitting on a chair in the living room, watching daytime television. An obvious no-hoper in a string vest. 'What's going on?'

Beck pulled the man to his feet and slammed him against the wall, handcuffing him. 'Let go of me,' the man said. 'What's going on?'

'Tony Rivers, I'm a police officer. I understand Detective Sergeant Giggs spoke to you on the day he died and I'd like you to accompany me to the police station, please.'

'Leave him alone!' the wife shouted, rushing towards Beck. 'Leave him!'

Two police officers wrestled her down onto the sofa, threatening to take her in with her husband.

'Get stuffed!' she screamed, trying to kick them.

Beck pushed Rivers ahead of him down the hall and into the street, where a crowd of neighbours had gathered to watch.

'One down,' Beck told the uniforms as they shoved Rivers into a car.

Bilborough charged into the incident room, pointing a finger at Beck. 'You do anything like that ever again and you'll be out on your bloody ear!' He turned to address the room at large. 'And that goes for everybody else.'

Beck leapt up, pointing an accusing finger right back at Bilborough. 'You don't want anybody to do anything!' he shouted, his voice verging on hysteria. 'We're supposed to sit around on our arses, doing absolutely nothing, while Giggsy's lying on a slab down at the morgue! Well, we're getting a bit pissed off with sitting around,' Beck told him. 'We're getting a bit pissed off with the bloody scientific approach.'

'If we're gonna crack this, we'll crack it as a team. A

team! Every member knowing what every other member is doing.'

'Crack this?' Beck repeated. 'You want to crack this, I'll tell you how to crack this!'

'A team! Every member knowing – '

'We go round to everyone Giggsy saw, we drag them out of bed at five in the morning – '

'– what every other member is doing!'

' – we pull them in here – '

'No bloody mavericks!'

' – and we keep them in here until we find out who it was!'

'I don't want bloody mavericks! We've got one already,' Bilborough said, pointing at Fitz. 'If we want a maverick, we've got a bloody maverick. We're paying him good money to be a maverick, everybody else is part of a team!'

'Dawn raids!' Beck shouted across the room. 'Dawn raids on everyone Giggsy saw!'

'Will you get out please, Fitz?' Bilborough said, never taking his eyes off Beck. 'Give us a couple of minutes.' He waited until Fitz had closed the door behind him. 'He's made a complaint,' he said, his voice cracking with emotion. 'We've got to spend precious time dealing with a bloody complaint! Giggsy would be cursing you, Jimmy, bloody cursing you.'

TWENTY-THREE

Fitz needed air. He needed out of this whole bloody station, with its internal politics and its rivalries and its constant friction between egos determined to rub each other up the wrong way. He walked down the hall, away from Bilborough and Beck in yet another screaming match, away from Penhaligon and her anger that was waiting for its chance to burst out as grief, away from all of them and all their problems.

He was at the bottom of the stairs, heading for the front door, when he saw someone he recognised: a young man in a leather coat, his head jerking violently back and forth as he struggled to give the desk sergeant his name, 'K-k-k . . .'

'Kerrigan,' Fitz said, walking up behind him.

'Kerrigan,' said Sean.

'Sprained?' said Fitz, noticing the bandage around Sean's wrist.

Sean nodded and looked towards the door, apparently anxious to get away.

'Your wanking hand, too,' Fitz said sympathetically.

Sean grunted, nervously shifting his weight from one foot to the other.

'How's Tina?'

'F-f-f-f . . .'

'Fine,' Fitz prompted, moving so that he stood face to face with Sean.

'Fine,' Sean repeated, still refusing to look Fitz in the eye. He scribbled his name on a sheet of paper offered him by the desk sergeant and hurried out the door without another word.

Fitz went back upstairs.

'What is it?' Tina asked as Sean got into the car. 'What's wrong?'

The engine wouldn't start; Sean pounded the dashboard with his fist. 'He knows.'

'Who?'

'Fitz,' he said, frantically trying to start the car. 'That bastard from the telly. He knows!'

'How?'

How could he explain the way the man had looked at him? As if he was looking right through him. As if he was reading the thoughts in Sean's head, as if he could sense the fear in his pounding heart. 'He just knows!'

Bilborough and Beck were still at it, but quieter now, off in a corner. Fitz headed for Giggs's old desk, and flicked through a scattered collection of handwritten notes. 'Is this Giggsy's stuff?' he asked Penhaligon.

She glanced up from her desk and nodded. Still not speaking to him, he noticed. Still blocking her grief with anger.

A uniformed policewoman came into the room and handed her the video cassette that had been found with Giggs's body. 'Tape's back from forensic,' she called across the room to Bilborough.

'OK, put it on,' Bilborough told her.

Penhaligon took the cassette from its plastic evidence bag and crossed the room, slotting the tape into the video which sat on a shelf above Beck's usual desk, along with a portable television set and a collection of box files. She reached up to press PLAY, and noticed a reddish-brown mark on her white shirt cuff. She walked away from the television, rubbing at her sleeve, telling herself that whatever was on her shirt couldn't have come from handling the tape, couldn't possibly be blood; not Giggsy's blood.

Fitz scanned the list of people DS Giggs had visited, looking for Sean's name. It wasn't there.

Bilborough was still talking to Beck, telling him they had to do everything by the book. 'If they want a lawyer, they get a lawyer,' he said. 'We owe it to Giggsy to do it right, we owe it to him to make it watertight.'

Sean pulled the cover off the cistern in the bathroom and took out the piece of lead pipe he'd used to kill the copper. He ran into the other room, tossing the pipe into the bag Tina was hastily packing.

Fitz found the name Christine Brien near the bottom of Giggsy's list.

I want to talk to a woman named Tina Brien, right? It's very, very necessary.

Christine Brien. Sean's Tina. He was about to say something to Bilborough when the sound of a woman's voice filled the incident room: 'We're going to kill a policeman.'

Penhaligon swung round to look at the television. 'Boss,' she said.

Bilborough looked up at the screen and his mouth dropped open.

Fitz walked over to stand beside Penhaligon, watching the bizarre scene unfold.

A man stood in the middle of a dismal little room, almost bare of furniture. There was a large poster mounted on the wall behind him: the Taoist symbol of Yin and Yang.

The man wore ripped jeans and a hooded jacket with the sleeves cut off, exposing a pair of muscular arms. He was singing, gesturing wildly, his movements choppy and ungainly as he began to dance, waltzing clumsily back and forth across the screen. Arms outstretched to hold an imaginary partner, face hidden behind a rigid plastic mask: the *Spitting Image* version of Prince Phillip. '*I, I who have nothing, I, I who have no-one, adore you and want you so, I'm just a no-one with nothing to give you but oh, I love you*'.

'People think that's worse than killing an ordinary person,' the woman went on. She was sitting in an armchair in the foreground, wearing a low-cut black dress and a grey John Major mask. 'Why?' she asked, as the man continued singing behind her. 'It's self-defence. If we don't kill him, we'll be put away for life. So it's self-defence.'

Fitz concentrated his attention on the man singing in the background, on his wiry frame and awkward movements.

'He can give you the world, but he'll never love you the way I love you . . .'

'You see a life sentence is worse for us than for ordinary people,' the woman said. 'We love each other. We love each other more than any two people have ever loved each other. If we're separated from each other, we'll die. So it's self-defence.'

'Sean Kerrigan,' Fitz said.

Bilborough turned to Fitz, looking gobsmacked. Beck raised his hands to his head, looking sick.

The masked woman on the screen spread her hands in a gesture of equanimity. 'It's self-defence.'

Fitz let the uniforms with their yapping dogs run on ahead while he took the five flights of stairs at a more leisurely pace. By the time he reached the flat, the door had been forced open and Bilborough was already ordering everyone out. 'Forensic's on the way; I don't want anyone in this room unless it's essential.'

Fitz sighed. Sean and Tina were obviously not at home. He stepped into the hallway, examining the door. It had been broken into before; someone had patched it up with some boards nailed onto the back.

He found Bilborough pacing the living room. He pointed to the large Yin-Yang poster on the wall; they both recognised it from the video. 'This is the place,' Bilborough said. He pointed to another poster: Hendrix. 'I thought you said James Dean.'

Fitz pointed to yet another poster: one for the film, *Badlands*, with Sissy Spacek and Martin Sheen. 'I wasn't too far wrong.'

Bilborough rubbed his hands together. 'Now we'll just sit down and wait for them to come home.'

Fitz looked around the room, empty except for the posters and a couple of pieces of cheap furniture. There was a clothes rail shoved up against one wall. No clothes, only a few wire hangers. 'I don't think they're coming home.'

'That's your most endearing quality, Fitz. Your optimism.'

Bilborough checked the kitchen – nothing in the fridge – and the bathroom – no toothbrushes, no shaving gear, cistern lid lying in the middle of the floor – before he finally agreed there was no point in hanging around.

But all was not lost, he told Fitz on the way back down the stairs, they had ID on Kerrigan, plus a photograph. 'Though nothing on the girl,' he admitted.

'We had Kerrigan,' Fitz told him. 'Beck let him go.'

Bilborough looked at him in disbelief. 'What?'

'Beck had him in custody. I recommended we hold him for psychiatric, and Beck turned him loose. Ask Panhandle; she was there.'

The fat man was in the car park, right across the street. Looking right at them. Sean reached for the wires hanging down from the dashboard; Tina put a hand on his arm to stop him. 'Not yet,' she said.

'But they'll see . . .'

'They'll see you if you start the bloody engine,' she snapped. 'Just stay calm, right? Look, they're all getting into cars; they're driving away.' She laughed. 'Look at them, running around like a bunch of headless chickens. They're only coppers, Sean. They can't help it if they're stupid.'

TWENTY-FOUR

Bilborough stormed into the incident room, eyes blazing. 'Beck, Penhaligon. In my office, now!'

Penhaligon looked up to see Fitz walk in behind Bilborough, surrounded as usual by a haze of smoke, giving them all one of his smug, know-it-all looks.

'I said now!' Bilborough shouted.

'Yes, sir.' She stood up, exchanging a puzzled glance with Beck, and followed him into the office.

Bilborough sat behind his desk; she and Beck stood, facing him. Fitz positioned himself behind them, leaning on one of the filing cabinets.

'Sean Kerrigan,' Bilborough said, holding up a mug shot of a young man with pushed-in features and a pudding-bowl haircut. 'The fucking son-of-a-bitch who murdered Giggsy. You had him in custody, and you let him go!'

'For taking and driving away, sir,' Beck protested. 'That's all.'

'Fitz recommended a psychiatric.'

'I don't recall that, sir,' Beck told him, adding slyly, 'Did he put it in writing?'

Fitz snorted, stubbing out a cigarette butt on the metal cabinet and tossing it into a bin.

'You were there,' Bilborough said to Penhaligon.

She took a deep breath, clasping her hands behind her back. 'I don't recall, sir.'

Bilborough picked up a piece of paper, referring to some notes, 'Fitz spoke of prevention. DS Beck said bollocks to prevention, he wanted the overtime.'

Go on, Panhandle, she imagined Fitz urging her. *Tell him*

*I was right. Tell him Giggsy would still be alive today if only
you'd listened to me. Jeopardise your career; grass on one
of your fellow officers. Do it for me, so I can tell them all 'I
told you so'.*

'I don't recall, sir,' she repeated.

'Hell hath no fury,' Fitz said, reaching into his pocket for
another cigarette.

*You let me humiliate you in a crowded restaurant, you let
me track dog shit all over your best Persian rug, you let me
phone you in the middle of the night to tell you how much I
still love my wife, so why can't you let me say 'I told you
so'?*

'If that conversation did take place,' Penhaligon said,
realising to her horror that her voice was trembling and she
was completely unable to control it, 'Doctor Fitzgerald
would have every right to say I told you so. He's obviously
dying to say I told you so. So let's assume it did take
place . . .'

'That's enough,' Bilborough told her.

'Let's hear him say it!' she shrieked. 'We're the ones
who've lost a friend but to hell with that because Doctor
Fitzgerald wants to say I told you so!'

'Finished?'

'I can recall no such conversation, sir.'

Fitz left the room, slamming the door behind him.

'Will that be all, sir?' Penhaligon asked her boss.

'No.' Bilborough looked at Beck. 'Get out.'

Beck nodded and left.

Bilborough studied Penhaligon's face for a moment. 'If
Fitz is right, you must be feeling bloody terrible.'

Penhaligon stared straight ahead, saying nothing.

'There's counselling,' Bilborough said.

'Will you offer Beck counselling?'

'Beck doesn't need it.'

'But I do?'

'Not because . . .' Bilborough paused; Penhaligon knew
he had been about to say: because you're a woman. He

stood up and walked around the desk to stand beside her. 'You've lost a close colleague,' he reminded her gently. 'Counselling can help. It's standard procedure these days.'

She shook her head. 'It'll go on my record.'

'It won't,' Bilborough assured her.

'They'll say the job's got to her. It hasn't. It's not the job. I can do my job as well as anyone. As well as Beck.'

'I know that.'

'It's not the job,' she insisted, angrily wiping a tear away from her cheek. 'I've lost a friend. I cried when I lost my father. There were coppers there, at the funeral; I cried in front of them all. Did they say the job was getting to me then? Of course they didn't. They said I cried because I lost my father. Same now. I've lost Giggsy. I've lost a friend.' The tears were streaming down her face now; she buried her face in her hands, unable to stop them. 'I'm crying because I've lost a friend. It's nothing to do with the job. I can do my job. I can do my job as well as anyone in this nick. Shit.' She blew her nose, sobbing, 'This is not the job. It's not the job.'

Bilborough looked on helplessly, arms crossed in front of his chest. He stepped forward, hesitantly reaching out a hand as if to touch her shoulder, then stepped back, recrossing his arms. 'My wife's pregnant,' he said.

Penhaligon didn't know whether to laugh or cry. The whole station knew his wife was pregnant; they'd known for weeks. Bilborough was obviously floundering, he didn't have a clue what to say, what to do. So he was telling her about his wife. She looked up from her handkerchief, sniffling. At least he was making an effort; at least he was trying, no matter how feebly, to make her feel better. A week ago, even a few hours ago, the last thing she would ever have expected was to receive any kind of comfort from Bilborough.

She looked at his face, studying it as if she'd never seen it before. It suddenly occurred to her that maybe he felt as vulnerable as her. Maybe he had just as much to prove, and was every bit as scared of screwing up. 'Is she really?'

Bilborough nodded. 'Nearly three months.'

'What do you want?' she sniffled.

'Anything. But if it's a girl, I'd like her to grow up to be . . .'

Penhaligon braced herself. If he said what she thought he was going to say, that would be it; she'd be in floods.

' . . . the total bloody opposite of you.'

Penhaligon raised the handkerchief to her face again, laughing and crying at the same time.

Tina outlined her lips in dark red pencil, then filled them in with a shade of gloss called Red Alert. She puckered them, admiring the effect in the rear view mirror.

All those coppers walking in and out of the station, right across the street from them, and not one of them even glanced in their direction. If someone's looking for you, Tina told herself, best place to hide is right under their nose.

Sean nudged her; she looked towards the station entrance and saw the fat psychologist walking down the steps, rubbing his forehead as if he had a headache. He never looked in their direction, just wandered away, rubbing his head. Looking old and miserable.

This was going to be easy, the easiest one yet.

Sean started the car.

TWENTY-FIVE

They followed him to a pub about ten minutes walk from the station. It was a huge place, set back off the road, with brightly-lit signs advertising live cabaret and karaoke.

Tina sat in the pub car park, studying her reflection in the rear-view mirror. She reached into her bag, feeling around for her mascara. She couldn't find it; she couldn't find anything any more. Everything she owned had been jumbled into a few bags; there hadn't been time to pack anything properly. She sighed at the thought of all her clothes squashed into a tiny holdall, thanks to that fat bastard of a psychologist. And she had no idea where they were going to sleep tonight. Somewhere on the road, she supposed. She liked the sound of that: on the road. She said it out loud: 'On the road.'

Sean gave her a puzzled look, and she kissed him on the forehead. 'God, I love you,' she said.

She climbed up over the seat, opening another bag, searching inside it for her mascara. Sean had packed this one, and it was mostly stuff from the kitchen: biscuits, tea bags, instant coffee, some knives wrapped in a towel. Under the knives, she found her photo album. 'I told you to burn this,' she said.

'N-n-n . . .'

'No time,' she said.

Sean nodded.

'We'll burn it later,' she said. 'We'll destroy every trace of her, as if she'd never existed, right? Once we're done with him, we'll go for her. OK?'

Sean nodded again, wrapping the lead pipe in his hands

with a long strip of black tape. He was so much calmer this time. It was getting easier for him, she could tell. She'd told him it would get easier and easier. She'd told him all you had to remember was that other people didn't count, they didn't have feelings – not like they did. Other people were just pretending, like actors in a movie.

She reached inside another bag, and breathed a huge sigh of relief; she'd found her mascara. She shook it and unscrewed the cap. 'I was thinking maybe we could go to London. There's a lot of people in London. We could vanish there; no-one would ever find us. Would you like that, Sean? The two of us, vanishing together forever?'

The pub's interior consisted of a single vast room, all red flocked wallpaper and rows of lights made to resemble Victorian streetlamps. The walls were lined with booths surrounded by ornate wrought-iron railings. On a stage at the far end of the room, a grey-haired man wearing a large pair of spectacles sang a spirited rendition of *When the Saints Come Marching In*. Several people were gathered at that end of the room, listening and clapping along. Not one of them looked under fifty.

Fitz walked up to the bar, ordered a Scotch, and gulped it down, thinking. For twenty years there had been only one woman in his life. Of course there had been flirtations – and plenty of opportunities.

Women who were vulnerable and needy: *Help me, hold me, help me.*

Women who enjoyed a challenge: *You think you know what makes me tick, do you? Well, let's see how much you really know.*

Some of them had been beautiful, but not one of them had ever interested him. Until now.

Detective Sergeant Jane Penhaligon was a problem in desperate need of a solution. In many ways, she was a lot like Judith. Attractive, smart, no tolerance for bullshit.

At least Judith never used to have any tolerance for

bullshit – until she met Graham. The man was as transparent as piss; why the hell couldn't Judith see through him?

Penhaligon had her blind spots, too, of course. One of them was a sometimes misplaced loyalty to her colleagues, whether or not they deserved it. Colleagues like Beck, for example.

Another was that – like Judith – she expected him to lie to her. Judith expected him to lie about his gambling; Penhaligon expected him to lie about the fact he still desperately wanted his wife.

He had no intention of lying to either of them.

He ordered another drink, walked over to a machine with lots of flashing lights, and started feeding it all the change in his pockets. After a couple of goes, he was winning. 'Collect,' a voice behind him urged. 'Don't gamble it; collect. For God's sake, take the bloody money!'

Fitz pressed the button marked: GAMBLE.

'No,' said the voice behind him. 'No, you shouldn't have done that.'

The lights flashed on and off. Fitz pressed several buttons, and lost everything.

'Two-to-one down, you go again,' the voice insisted. 'I know this machine, you should have taken the money when you had the chance.'

Fitz swung around to face a little bald-headed man.

'Right,' Fitz said, moving away from the machine. 'You play it.'

The man walked away, shaking his head. 'Never touch 'em.'

A woman entered the pub and planted herself in the centre of the room, staring at him. She had long black hair teased up high, heavy black eye make-up, dark red lips, long red nails. She wore a skintight long black dress with a black choker and dangling silver earrings. She slinked towards him, looking like a cross between a B-movie bad girl and a vampire.

Fitz moved over to the bar, watching her out of the corner of his eye.

Tina saw that she'd captured the fat man's attention; he was pretending not to look at her, but he was looking at her all the same.

She walked up beside him, sticking her face in front of his, eyes widening in an expression of amazement. 'You were on the telly, weren't you?' she asked him, looking ever so impressed. Gobsmacked, even.

He shrugged, looked embarrassed. 'Yeah.'

'I'm Michelle,' she purred. 'Can I buy you a drink?'

The fat man was looking her up and down; he couldn't take his eyes off her. 'Sure.'

'Bottle of dry cider,' she told the barman, then turned to Fitz and asked him what he was drinking.

'Double Scotch and dry please.'

She smiled and nodded at the barman, paying for the drinks with a twenty-pound note.

'So what do you do for a living, Michelle?' Fitz asked her.

'I'm a student,' she answered brightly. She took a pack of cigarettes from her bag and offered him one.

'A student,' Fitz repeated, taking the cigarette. 'What are you studying?'

'Criminal psychology.'

'Really,' he said, nodding. 'Going for a degree, are you?'

'Yeah.' She reached into her bag for a lighter. 'I'm in my third year.'

'Why criminal psychology?'

She lit her cigarette, then reached forward to light Fitz's. 'Violence interests me,' she said, blowing a ring of smoke.

Fitz raised both eyebrows. 'Does it really?'

'Oh yes,' she said, smiling.

'You from around here?' he asked her.

She took a sip from her drink. God, he was a nosy bastard. 'Yeah.'

'Leafy suburbia?'

192

'Yeah. Hale,' she said automatically, without thinking. She wished she'd said someplace else, anyplace else, but then she told herself it didn't matter; nothing anyone told him was ever going to matter again.

'Hale?' Fitz whistled appreciatively. 'They pick their noses with a hanky in Hale.'

She laughed and nodded. 'Yeah, they do.'

'So why go to university here? Why didn't you go away?'

She shrugged. 'I didn't want to.'

'You can't stand your parents.' He said it as if it was the most obvious thing on earth.

She laughed nervously. 'I didn't say that.'

'You didn't have to.'

'No, well.' God, what a know-it-all; he was worse than her father. She shrugged, keeping the smile on her face. 'My boyfriend lives here.'

'What does he do?'

'He's on the dole.' *Stupid*. She could have kicked herself for saying that; she should have said he was a student, too.

'Mummy and daddy wouldn't like that, would they?'

'How did you draw up that profile?' she asked him, changing the subject.

'How long have you known him, your boyfriend?' Fitz asked her, changing the subject back.

'Eighteen months,' she said; it was the first thing that came into her head. She wished he'd stop asking all these questions, catching her off guard like that. Most men didn't ask questions, most men didn't want to know anything about her. If they wanted to talk at all, it was always about themselves. It would be much better if he'd do all the talking, then she could just agree with whatever he said. It would certainly be easier. 'What makes you so sure you're right?' she asked him, steering the conversation back to his offender profile.

'Well, I'm not, really,' he said, leaning forward to support some of his weight against the bar; he really was big. Even bigger than he'd looked on television. Not just fat, but tall. 'Who killed JFK?' he asked her suddenly.

'Lee Harvey Oswald,' she answered instantly, relieved he was finally asking something easy.

'John Lennon?'

'Mark Chapman.'

'You see the point I'm trying to make?'

She shook her head, giggling a little. 'No.'

'It takes years to bring up a child. That child has a bit of talent, goes away to Hamburg, works all the hours God sends honing his talent, comes home to write beautiful songs, becomes world famous. Then one day some headcase comes along and blows him away. And then what happens? The headcase becomes famous, and people like you, still a little wet behind the ears, queue up to buy books about him.'

She forced herself to keep smiling.

'Two headcases killing for fun. And the sooner they're put away and forgotten the better.'

She felt her mouth draw into a narrow line. She tried to force her lips to turn back up again, but they wouldn't co-operate.

'That's my thesis; that's my profile. Of that I'm certain. The rest . . . ' he shrugged. 'Everything else is just guesswork.'

She moved in a little closer, close enough for the smell of her perfume to waft into his nostrils. 'My boyfriend, he's in London right now,' she said. 'Chance of a job.'

He looked thoughtful, as if he was taking in everything she said and weighing it up. 'So you're on your own?' he said finally.

She nodded, lips pursed into an early Bardot pout. 'I don't mind, though. I've got plenty of work to do.'

'Your thesis?'

'Yeah.' She took a drag on her cigarette, then leaned forward as if she'd just had the most marvellous idea. 'I hope you don't mind me asking, but would you read it?'

194

'Yeah.' He said it right away, without a hint of hesitation.

She moved another step closer, half-closing her eyes and lowering her voice suggestively. 'I mean tonight.'

'Ah,' he said. 'That could be a bit awkward.'

'It's only six-thousand words. I've got a car outside. I could drive us there.'

He looked at her for a long moment. 'I'm tempted.'

She had him! She leaned forward, moving even closer. 'I'd be very grateful.' Her voice was a husky, seductive whisper; her eyes left him in no doubt as to what she had in mind.

'I'll make a phone call,' he said.

'Right.'

'Wait right there. I'll only be a minute,' he assured her.

Fitz hung up the phone and walked back to the dark-haired woman at the bar.

'OK,' she said, 'let's go.'

'In a minute,' he told her. 'Let me buy you a drink first, OK?'

'Yeah, sure,' she said, smiling.

He ordered another round and carried the drinks over to a booth. He sat facing the door; she sat across from him, absent-mindedly twirling a long strand of hair around her finger.

'Cheers,' he said, clinking his glass against hers.

'Cheers.'

The little bald-headed man was tormenting someone else who'd had the nerve to press GAMBLE. At the other end of the cavernous room, an elderly woman had taken to the karaoke stage to sing 'We'll Meet Again'. The crowd down that end loved her; they were cheering and clapping and stamping their feet. 'You like Peter Falk?' Fitz asked the dark-haired woman sitting across from him.

'You mean Columbo?' she said. 'Yeah.'

'He did his best work for John Cassavetes. Did you see *Husbands*?'

She shook her head. 'No.'

'*Badlands*?'

'He wasn't in *Badlands*.'

Fitz looked confused. 'Wasn't he?'

'No.'

'You're sure?' he persisted.

'Positive.'

Suddenly Fitz became Columbo, doing a perfect impression of Peter Falk. 'Well, you see, I'm confused here. You say you're in your third year of college, right? You're doing your third-year thesis. Is that right?'

'That's good,' she said, laughing.

'And you've known Sean for eighteen months. That's what you told me?'

She stopped laughing. 'Who's Sean?'

'Your boyfriend,' he said, still Columbo.

'I didn't say his name was Sean.'

He shook his head, Columbo-style. 'Oh did you not?'

'No.'

'But you did say you didn't go away to college because you didn't want to leave your boyfriend.' He slapped a hand to his forehead, still playing Columbo. 'Now I'm really confused here, you see because, well, you hadn't even met him yet.'

He looked towards the open door where Jane Penhaligon was standing, accompanied by several uniforms. He watched her eyes scan the room, saw her see him. She said something to the coppers on either side of her. They spread out slightly, approaching the booth from behind, unnoticed by the pitiful self-styled vamp sitting with her back to them. Fitz became himself again. 'Other things, too, Tina.'

'Michelle.'

'You bought me a large Scotch and dry without a cough. On a student grant? You don't look like a student, you've got failure and resentment oozing out of every pore. And you don't dress like a student, either.' He gestured towards the red-haired woman standing behind her. 'This is Detective Sergeant Jane Penhaligon.'

Tina calmly reached for her glass and took another sip of cider.

'Tina Brien,' Penhaligon began, addressing the back of Tina's head. 'I'm arresting you for the murders of Kevin Cormack and . . .' she paused, struggling to control her voice, ' . . . DS George Giggs. You do not have to say anything, but anything you do say will be taken down and may be used in evidence. Do you understand?'

Tina took a drag from her cigarette and stared straight ahead, saying nothing.

Fitz picked up Tina's purse and removed several notes. 'You took this money from Giggsy's wallet. Ninety quid of it's mine, OK?'

She narrowed her eyes, shooting him a look of hatred, but remained quiet.

'Would you come with me please, Tina?' Penhaligon asked her.

She took a final sip from her glass and stood up. One of the uniforms handcuffed her and pushed her towards the door.

Fitz stood up and followed the others outside. The car park was crawling with police; there were panda cars and uniformed officers everywhere. A parked car suddenly came to life, swerving in a dizzying circle before it rammed its way past the two police cars blocking the entrance to the car park. It roared off into the distance, tyres screeching. 'Looks like he decided not to wait,' Fitz said to the uniform standing beside him.

A couple of uniforms shoved Tina into the back of a car. 'You wait 'til we get you alone, with no witnesses,' one of them told her. 'We're gonna do to you what you did to Giggsy, you murdering bitch.'

Jane Penhaligon walked up to the car. 'She's riding with me.'

'But Sarge . . .' one of the uniforms began.

'Put her in my car. I said she's riding with me.'

● ● ●

197

Penhaligon drove round to the rear of Anson Road Station, a WPC riding in the back with Tina. Bilborough was waiting for them. He came out to the car and opened the door. 'So this is her,' he said. 'So this is the bitch that murdered Giggsy.' He took her by the arm and led her inside.

There were more coppers waiting inside the door. Lining the twisting corridors leading down to the cells. Muttering taunts and threats: 'There she is, the cow ... Murdering bitch, wait 'til I get my hands on her ... Give the bitch a bit of what she gave Giggsy, the murdering slag.' Bilborough walked silently alongside her, accompanied by Penhaligon and the WPC who'd ridden with her in the car.

A thick metal door stood open before them. Beyond it lay a small, bare cell with walls of cold white tile, a hard, narrow ledge for a bed and a thin plastic-covered pad for a mattress. A lidless metal toilet stood in one corner. A blackboard mounted on the wall outside the cell had the words: 'Brien – Homicide', written across it in chalk.

Bilborough removed her handcuffs and pushed her inside. A uniformed copper tossed her a threadbare, nasty-smelling blanket.

Bilborough stood in the cell doorway, an expression of pure loathing on his face. 'Anticipation's nine tenths of the pleasure,' he told her. 'So I'm gonna look after you. No-one's gonna lay a finger on you. I'm gonna do everything strictly by the book. You see, I'm anticipating the last day of your trial, sitting there with Giggsy's wife, hearing the judge give you life with a recommendation for thirty years. I'm anticipating that with a certain amount of relish, you murdering bitch.'

TWENTY-SIX

Something was burning. Sean inhaled an acrid fume that scorched his nostrils and lungs, leaving a bitter taste in the back of this throat. 'Shit!' he said, 'Shit!' A plume of smoke rose from beneath the bonnet. 'Shit!'

He veered off the road and leapt out, reaching for the bags on the back seat. He only managed to get hold of two of them before he saw the first orange flickers. 'Shit,' he said again, running. 'Shit.'

He was on a side road around the back of an industrial estate. He had no idea where to go, he just kept running, visions of Tina in his head.

Tina in the pub that first night. He'd seen her from the stage, a tall, slender figure wreathed in black. Not exactly punk, not exactly goth, more like an Egyptian queen, he'd thought at the time. Strange, and a little frightening. And beautiful. Certainly not the type of person who'd want to know someone like him.

And then she'd come up to him at the bar and for the first time in his life, he'd met someone who treated him like a normal person. Someone who didn't laugh at him, or get impatient, or back away as if they thought there was something wrong with him.

And didn't overcompensate, either. Didn't handle him with kid gloves and a fake, exaggerated kindness, like some bloody social worker.

Just accepted him. No-one had ever done that before.

He couldn't believe it when she asked him back to her flat for a coffee. A woman like her. Couldn't believe it when she started kissing him, touching him, pulling him towards her, easing him inside her.

'I could stay with you here like this forever,' Tina had told him that night. 'I want you inside me forever.'

He wanted to tell her then that she was inside him, too. Inside his head, his heart, his soul. But he couldn't form the words, he couldn't say what he wanted to say. All he could do was give her a little silver cup.

And then Cormack had taken it away.

Cormack. He could still see him in the cold yellow lamplight of that alley, slobbering over Tina. Defiling her.

He could still feel the brick cracking Cormack's skull, feel the blood splash onto his face, taste it on his lips. Feel that explosive urge to make Tina his again – only his. Pounding her into the wall, hearing her gasp, 'Oh God Sean, oh God Sean, oh God oh God, I love you I love you I love you.'

His heart was pounding, his breath rasped in his lungs. He felt like he'd been running for miles.

He remembered Tina in the bowling alley the night they saw Fitz on the telly. He heard her voice repeating what she'd said that night: *You want to go to prison? Go to prison, never see each other again – is that what you want? Then we stay calm, right, Sean? We stay calm.*

Calm, he told himself, slowing down to catch his breath. Calm.

Go to prison, never see each other again.

But how was he supposed to stay calm when bowling pins turned into dying men, when every time he closed his eyes he saw a room lined with black plastic, when his mouth tasted of salt and blood, when Tina was gone forever?

Never see each other again.

He couldn't live without her, didn't want to live.

If we're separated from each other, we'll die.

A car came out of nowhere, nearly hit him. It stopped just in time, only inches away. He slammed his fist down on the bonnet and kicked out one of the headlights.

The driver jumped out, shouting and waving a fist.

Sean could have killed him right then; he could have punched him once, hard. He could have smashed the guy's skull with just one blow.

We stay calm, Sean, Tina's voice urged him, *We stay calm*.

He kicked out the other headlight and ran, leaving the man standing aghast.

She'd told him they were one person, and she was right.

She was his mouth, his voice. And he was her strength, her curled fists ready to strike.

He was her vengeance.

TWENTY-SEVEN

'You wanted to see me?' Fitz asked, sticking his head round a door.

A man in his early thirties, dressed in a business suit and tie, looked up from the stack of papers on his desk. 'Oh, Fitz,' he said nervously. 'Yes. I mean, please sit down.' He gestured to the seat facing the desk.

Fitz sat down. 'So why did you want to see me? Is it about the annual company picnic? I've already ordered the burgers and the baps, and I was just about . . .'

'No, Fitz,' the man interrupted. 'It's not about the company picnic.'

'The office blood donor drive? I've given two pints already.'

'No, not the blood donor drive. It's . . .' He fingered the slim pile of papers in his out-tray, bending each sheet back at the corners. He suddenly became aware of what he was doing and stopped, folding his hands on top of the desk. 'I'm sorry, Fitz, I'm going to have to let you go.'

'*Upstairs, Downstairs,*' Fitz sighed.

'Sorry?'

'Oh, it's silly,' Fitz said. 'It's just that whenever they were going to sack one of the servants in *Upstairs, Downstairs* they always used to say, "I'm very sorry, we're going to have to let you go." You know, as if the servant was straining at the leash and poor old Hannah Gordon was hanging on for dear life, but she was knackered and she had to let them go.'

'Yeah, yeah,' the man said, nodding. 'My mother liked that one.'

'You're sacking me. Why don't you just say it?'

'I'm sacking you,' the man said. 'I'm sorry.'

'How sorry?' Fitz asked him. 'This sorry?' He held his index finger and thumb an inch apart. 'That sorry?' He held his hands about a foot apart, then he spread his arms out wide. 'Lose a night's sleep sorry? Go home and top yourself sorry? Divide up your salary and give me half sorry?'

'It's not a question of money,' the man said nervously. 'This job is no longer . . .' He paused, fumbling for words.

'No, no, you can pay me for doing nothing,' Fitz assured him. 'I'm not proud.'

The man shook his head. 'That's impossible, I'm afraid.'

Fitz changed tack. 'Why me?'

'Well, it's nothing personal, Fitz . . .'

'Are you married?' Fitz interrupted him.

'Yes.'

'Kids?'

'One,' the man said carefully, obviously unsure what this was leading to.

'That's nice,' Fitz told him. 'I've got two. Mortgaged up to the hilt. In debt up to the eyes. I owe more than the bloody third world. I've got Barclays worried sick; if I go, they go. And you think I'm just gonna creep home and say that I've been sacked. Well no sir, I will not do it.' He pulled a gun out from his pocket and held it against his temple. 'No, no. I'm gonna splatter my brains all over your nice clean office wall.'

The man reached for the gun, but Fitz was too fast for him. He pulled the gun away, then pointed it directly into the man's horror-stricken face. 'I'd like to take you with me,' Fitz said. 'You first, then me. But then you'd miss it. You wouldn't see, would you? You wouldn't see what you do to a forty-four-year-old man when you throw him on the scrapheap when there's three million people out of work, would you? Well, I'll show you.' He pointed the gun at his head. 'This is what happens! This!'

Fitz closed his eyes and screwed up his face, bracing

203

himself, then pulled the trigger. A little flag popped out, printed with the word: BANG.

Fitz rubbed his hands together and turned to the seminar audience. 'Comments?'

Several rows of people in business suits sat open-mouthed.

Fitz indicated the man sitting across the desk from him. 'He didn't handle that very well, really, did he?'

Tina sat sprawled in a chair turned sideways to face a blank white wall, leaning one elbow on the table, tapping a foot against the floor. Staring straight ahead without expression.

Bilborough and Penhaligon walked into the interview room, sitting across from her at the table. She didn't look at them, didn't acknowledge their presence in any way.

Penhaligon switched on the tape recorder, and Bilborough began. 'Interview commences 0900. Those present are DCI Bilborough, DS Penhaligon, WPC Hartley, PC Johnson, and the suspect Tina Brien, who has been cautioned.' He looked at Tina, smiling. 'We've got Sean.'

She finally turned her head slightly. 'Connery?'

Penhaligon chuckled silently to herself.

'Kerrigan,' Bilborough said.

Tina shrugged as if the name meant nothing to her. 'The person in the car park?'

'Yeah.'

'He got away.'

'We picked him up two hours ago,' Bilborough told her.

She smiled her congratulations. 'Well done.'

'You're not doing yourself much good here, Tina,' Penhaligon broke in. 'We're videoing this interview.'

Tina's expression hardened as she turned to face Penhaligon. She was still wearing her previous evening's make-up, but it didn't look so glamorous after a night in the cells. Powder had collected in the creases between her nose and mouth, red lipstick had smeared onto her chin, her black eye make-up had faded to a dirty grey smudge. 'I couldn't care less what you think.'

'It can be shown to a jury,' Penhaligon said.

'I couldn't care less what you think, right?'

'I don't think that they will be too impressed by your attitude,' Penhaligon said.

Tina looked away and started humming to herself.

'He's saying it was all your doing,' Bilborough told her.

She sighed and looked at Bilborough with the patient expression of a saint. 'Who?'

'Sean.'

She laughed, more a snort than a laugh. 'Who's Sean?'

'We know you spoke to Detective Sergeant Giggs,' Bilborough went on. 'We can prove he was murdered in your flat. We can prove you owed money to Cormack.'

Tina started humming to herself again.

'They're going to crucify you, Tina,' Penhaligon said. 'Sean, they will understand. A male – violence comes natural. But a woman?'

Tina threw her head back, laughing as if Penhaligon had just said something hilarious.

Penhaligon persisted, her voice earnest. 'They will crucify you because you're a woman and I don't think that's fair. I don't want to see that happen.'

'I appreciate your concern.'

'Come on, Tina,' Penhaligon said. 'Nothing you do or say now will make it any worse for Sean; he's going down for murder, no matter what. But you might just make it a little bit easier on yourself.' She sat back, watching Tina's reaction. She was thinking about it; she could see she was thinking. 'It was all Sean's doing, wasn't it?'

Tina leaned across the table, pursing her lips and opening her eyes wide in an exaggerated expression of bewilderment. 'Sean who?'

Sean peered out from the clump of bushes where he'd spent the night; no sign of anyone. He stood up and stretched, reaching into one of the bags for a biscuit. His hand came upon something solid and rectangular: Tina's photo album.

She'd told him to burn it, and it turned out to be one of the few things he'd saved from the burning car. He sat down in the grass, flicking through the pages.

Tina as a little girl, Tina in her early teens. Never photographed alone, always with someone else. Someone without a face, someone she'd scratched out again and again.

He imagined Tina's voice, urging him on: *Do it, Sean. Do it for me. Make it as if she'd never existed.*

He tore the pages from the album one by one, and tossed them into the canal.

A uniform came into the interview room and leaned down to speak to Bilborough.

'OK,' Bilborough said, standing up.

He found Fitz in the next room, watching Tina on a video monitor.

'Where the hell have you been all morning, Fitz?'

'Teaching corporate bastards how to dump people onto a scrapheap. I find it very fulfilling; they're paying me two-hundred quid an hour.' Fitz pointed to Tina's image on the monitor: leaning back with her arms folded across her chest, staring at the ceiling. 'Now, correct me if I'm wrong, but taking a quick glance at this young woman's body language I'd say that you haven't exactly won her trust and admiration, now have you?'

Bilborough stayed at the back of the room, near the door, leaning against the wall with his arms crossed. Penhaligon sat in a chair with her legs crossed, balancing a notepad on one knee. Tina slouched back in her seat, feigning sleep.

Fitz sat at the table, doodling on the back of a betting slip. He placed an open pack of cigarettes on the table in front of him. 'What age are you, Tina?' he asked her.

'Twenty,' she said, not bothering to open her eyes.

'Do I seem old to you?'

She laughed. 'Yeah.'

'When I was your age, anyone forty was ancient. Anyone fifty was decrepit. Anyone sixty should've been humanely gassed.'

She opened her eyes and rubbed the back of her neck. 'Yeah?' she said, unimpressed.

'If you're a good girl and you keep that gob of yours shut and you let the dykes in Holloway do what they want to you, and you never complain . . .' He made a show of counting on his fingers. 'You'll be six . . . seven . . . eight years older than I am now when you get out.'

She sneered at him. 'You'll be dead.'

Fitz turned to Penhaligon. 'She's terrified.'

'Get rid of her,' Tina said suddenly.

'Who, Panhandle?'

'Get rid of her.'

'Don't you like her?'

'Get rid of her.'

'Why don't you like her?'

Tina pointed at the cigarettes on the table. 'Can I have one?'

'Yeah.' He lit it for her. 'Is she a bit of a John Lennon to your Mark Chapman, is that it? A bit of talent and achievement that you'd like to blow away?'

'Ha!' Tina snorted in derision.

'She's a detective sergeant. Next year she'll be an inspector. That's an achievement. Believe me, for a woman in the police force, that is achievement. That's hard work, dedication, stamina, and ten years of sleeping with the right people. She's staying.' There was a long silence. Fitz eventually broke it. 'Where's Sean?'

'Under arrest.'

'You know he's not. Come on.' He wrote something on the betting slip. 'Do you think he'll kill again? Hypothetically speaking, of course.'

Tina regarded Fitz warily. 'Hypothetically speaking?'

'Yeah.'

She giggled. 'I don't even know this guy – I'm speaking hypothetically?'

Fitz nodded.

She frowned and bit her lip, making a big show of being deep in thought. 'Hmmm . . . yeah. Yeah, I think he just might kill again.'

'But you won't be there this time,' Fitz told her. 'Why let innocent people die when you won't be there to enjoy it? Tell me where Sean is.'

She stared straight ahead, smoking.

'What's your favourite bit of *Bonnie and Clyde*?'

'Never seen it.'

'Course you have,' he chided her.

'The part where they look at each other,' she said.

'Just before they die?' Fitz asked her excitedly.

'Yeah,' she said cautiously, not sure what to make of his latest change in behaviour.

Fitz leaned forward, eyes bright with enthusiasm, playing her along. 'Yeah, it was absolutely brilliant, wasn't it?'

Tina's face finally came to life; she finally smiled a genuine, spontaneous smile.

'After all they've been through,' Fitz went on dramatically, 'and they just look at each other and don't they relive every moment? And then they die in a hail of bullets. God, I cried. I did, really. I cried. Did you cry?'

'Yeah,' she said, nodding. Relaxing in the company of a kindred spirit.

'You did?' he asked her excitedly. 'You cried?'

'I cried.'

Fitz held up the betting slip to show her what he'd written: 'The bit where they look at each other before they die.'

Her mouth dropped open: how did he know that? 'And the birds take off,' she said wistfully.

'That's right. They know it's going to happen and then they die. God, I wept buckets. I wept buckets.'

Tina nodded. 'I know.'

Fitz's expression hardened, his voice became harsh and accusing. 'I thought it was one of the worst moments in the entire history of Hollywood.'

Tina froze, not sure what had just happened here.

'I wept buckets all right,' Fitz went on angrily. 'I wept buckets for all the victims and all the families of their victims. You see, I've been to their homes, Tina. I've *seen* it. I've seen what a violent death does in a family. I've seen the grief and the numbness and the bitterness. I've seen them trying to imagine what they went through in their last moments. I've seen that kind of grief, you stupid little bitch! And it's always caused by empty-headed, self-centred, sentimental little pieces of shit like you.'

Tina's lip was trembling; there were tears welling up in her eyes.

Fitz swiped a hand across her cheek. 'Don't you bloody dare.'

'You know nothing about me!' she screamed.

'Well tell me then,' Fitz said. 'Tell me everything there is to know. Tell me what makes you tick. I'm sure it'll take all of fifteen seconds.'

Tina sniffed and wiped her eyes, eventually composing herself. 'Do I think he's going to kill again? I *know* he's going to kill again. I know it.'

She looked at the fat man sitting across from her, his pink face glistening with sweat, and began to laugh.

TWENTY-EIGHT

'It was me,' Sean practised saying in his mind. 'Tina had nothing to do with it, do you hear? She had nothing to do with it, it was all down to me.'

There was a phone box up ahead, in the middle of a shopping precinct. He ran towards it, mentally rehearsing the words he had to say: *It was me, it was all down to me.*

He took a wrinkled betting slip from his pocket – Fitz had written down his phone number that night in the cell, told him to call if he ever wanted help. He'd meant help with the stutter, said he could put Sean in touch with a good therapist – not like the dickhead he'd seen when he was a kid. But Sean didn't care what kind of help he'd meant, the help he needed now was to get Tina out of trouble. He didn't care what happened to himself; he'd never cared about himself. Only Tina.

He heard the phone ringing. Heard the fat man's voice. 'Fitz.'

It was me, it was all down to me.

Sean could hear the words in his head; he could see them in front of him, like the titles on a movie screen. But he couldn't say them. He opened and closed his mouth, but no sound came out.

It was the phone – he could never talk into a telephone. 'Hello, hello. This is Fitz.'

Maybe he could sing it. He took a deep breath and opened his mouth wide – *It was me, it was all down to me* – but nothing happened. The only sound he made was a long hiss. It was the telephone; he couldn't even *sing* into a telephone.

And then Fitz hung up.

The bathroom door opened and Mark stumbled into the hall, clutching his side, his face contorted in agony. 'Dad!'

Fitz dropped the phone and ran towards him, reaching him just as he collapsed onto the floor. 'Oh my God!'

Sean dialled again. *It was me, come and get me, it was me, it wasn't Tina, nothing to do with Tina.* The line was engaged. 'Shit!'

He tried again a minute later. No answer.

Fitz placed one foot directly in front of the other, counting his steps as he paced from one side of the hospital corridor to the other. Earlier he had counted the plastic stacking chairs piled up in one corner, next to the linen closet; there were twenty-seven. Four stacks of six chairs each, plus three single chairs lined up in a row against the wall.

He heard heels clacking on the smooth, tiled floor, heard them speed up. Those weren't doctor's shoes, clacking away like that. Most doctors were too tired to move that quickly. And nurses always moved without a sound, padding endlessly up and down the wards in sensible footwear.

He looked up and saw Judith running towards him in printed leggings, a matching scarf draped across her shoulders. Her son's having emergency surgery and she still manages to look like something out of a magazine, he thought, wondering where she'd been when he phoned. She hadn't been home, all the old man would say was she'd gone out. But she was here now, he reminded himself, and that was all that mattered.

She was only inches away from him, he could smell her perfume, could remember waking every morning to the fragrance of honeysuckle lingering on the sheets of their bed.

She looked up at him questioningly, her beautiful face a mixture of worry and fear. 'What is it?'

'Appendix,' Fitz told her. 'He's all right.'

She sighed and collapsed into his arms. She realised what she was doing and tried to pull away.

'Don't,' Fitz said, holding her tightly.

She let him hold her a few moments longer before gently pushing his arms away and disentangling herself. 'Can we see him?'

'No, he's still in theatre. Where's Katie?'

'Asleep at Dad's. Last time I saw him, he was holding his side. I knew there was something wrong.'

Fitz tilted his head towards the stairs. 'There's a cafe down there.'

She shook her head distractedly. 'No, I don't want anything.'

'Well, I could do with a smoke.'

'I'll wait here.'

'I've told them we'll be there. They said they'll give us any news.'

'If you want a cigarette, go and have a cigarette.' She walked over to the twenty-seven plastic stacking chairs and planted herself on one of them. 'I'm waiting here.'

Fitz stayed where he was, defeated. 'This corridor is seventeen shoes by eighteen,' he said, resuming his slow pacing. 'Which means if I wanted to cover the whole floor, it would take six hundred and three pairs. If I wanted to stack 'em from floor to ceiling – and why wouldn't I? – it would take two thousand four hundred and twenty-eight pairs.' He stopped pacing. 'Come home.'

Judith narrowed her eyes. 'Don't you dare,' she threatened him.

'What?'

'Don't you dare take advantage of this.'

'I'm not,' he protested.

'I want to win one concession, one tiny concession!' She realised she was shouting and lowered her voice, remembering she was in a hospital. 'You do not gamble.'

'I'll try.'

'No. Forget *try*. You do not gamble.'

'You want me to tell lies, is that it? All right, I'll tell you lies.' He placed a hand over his heart. 'I promise I'll never gamble again, dear. Do you want me to go down on my knees?'

She shook her head, disgusted. 'I want you to mean it.'

He knelt down on the floor before her. 'There I am, I'm down on my knees. You want to hear the clichés? OK. Life has no meaning without you. I love you more than life itself.'

A nurse padded silently by; Judith looked away, embarrassed. Fitz stood up.

He moved to the centre of the corridor, resuming his pacing. 'We can head them off at the pass,' he said, briefly becoming John Wayne. 'The only good injun is a dead injun.'

He waited for Judith to say something, anything.

'It's quiet,' he said, 'too quiet.' He turned round, miming an arrow thudding into his back – complete with sound effects – then turned back to see Judith's reaction. She wasn't even looking.

He sighed and started counting the lights in the ceiling.

Sean used the same lead pipe he'd used to kill the copper. He broke the car window on the driver's side, then cleared away the glass and started the engine.

Three minutes later, he pulled up into the brightly-lit forecourt of a combination twenty-four-hour mini-mart and petrol station. He got out of the car and walked up to the counter, singing, '*I want twenty Benson and Hedges.*'

A man in a suit was ahead of him, paying for some petrol by credit card.

'*I want twenty Benson and Hedges,*' Sean sang again, loudly.

The cashier was about the same age as Sean, wearing a white shirt and a tie. 'Just a minute, mate,' he said. 'I'm busy.'

Sean slapped some money down on the counter. *'I want twenty Benson and Hedges and I want 'em now.'*

'I'll get them for you in a minute, Pavarotti. In a minute, all right?'

'I want twenty Benson and Hedges and I want 'em now!'

The other customer signed his credit card slip and hurried away, leaving the cashier on his own.

'Look, just slow down and ask.'

There was a flap in the counter. Sean reached down to lift it and walk through.

The cashier slammed his hand down on the flap. 'Leave it,' he warned Sean, 'or I'll call the police.'

Sean pulled the flap up and stepped behind the counter, reaching for the cigarettes.

'Hey, wait a minute,' the cashier said, stepping in front of him to block his way. 'Just ask, OK? Now leave it or I'm gonna call the police.'

Sean head-butted him and he fell to the ground, moaning.

Bastard! Sean kicked him hard in the ribs. Bastard! Kicked his head, his stomach, his balls. Bastard! Bent down to pummel him with his fists. Bastard! Brought a display cabinet crashing down on top of him.

The cashier lay unconscious, more dead than alive.

Sean reached up to take a pack of twenty cigarettes and a box of matches. Kicked the prone body one more time.

He walked back to the car, calmer now. He shifted into reverse and put his foot down, crashing backwards through the plate glass window.

He got out of the car, nonchalantly kicking several long shards of glass to one side. He picked up four large cans of petrol and put them in the boot. Then he walked over to a row of shelves beside the counter and took one small pack of notepaper, a rope and a pen.

Mark lay on a table in the recovery room, still groggy from the anaesthetic. He looked so pale and fragile, strands of

214

dark hair plastered to his forehead, mouth hanging slightly open, tubes in his arms. Judith sat down beside him, brushing the hair away from his face. 'How are you?'

'Better than an hour ago,' he answered weakly.

'Your appendix?' she said.

'They took it out.'

'Found a bibliography,' Fitz said, sitting down across from her.

Mark grimaced in pain. 'Don't make me laugh.'

'Last time I saw you, you had pains in your side,' she reminded Mark.

'They came and went, thought nothin' of it,' Mark said. 'Mum, do you think they'll give it me?'

Judith shrugged. 'You could ask them, I suppose.'

'Toby had his cartilage out, they gave him it to keep in a jar.'

She looked across at Fitz; he didn't see her. He was sitting with his head bent forward, shoulders heaving. Face buried in his hands, weeping silently.

'Doctor asked me if I'd had worms,' Mark said.

'Uh-huh,' Judith said, not really listening.

Fitz sat at a table in the hospital cafeteria, drinking bitter coffee and smoking cigarette after cigarette. Seeing Mark and Judith together like that brought back so many memories of how it used to be, in the early days. The good days, when they'd been a family.

He remembered how he and Judith used to tuck Mark in at night and give him a kiss, and how Mark always used to beg for a story before he went to sleep. The story was always Fitz's job. He'd sit by the bed and tell him about fairies and dragons and beautiful princesses, watching his son's eyes flutter closed. Mark always had a talent for sleeping, even as a baby. He never woke them in the night, always slept right through to morning.

He'd loved him so much then. Loved him so much it hurt.

215

And now he couldn't even talk to him. Judith was right; he couldn't talk to his own son, didn't know how any more. Didn't even know where it had all gone wrong.

Mark, Judith, Katie. He could feel them drifting away from him. He was on the verge of losing them. Of losing everything.

Peaks and troughs, he thought, mountains and valleys. I know about the lows, he'd told the walking dead at Gamblers Anonymous. I like the lows. The lows make the highs even higher.

But what if there aren't going to be any more highs, he asked himself. Peaks and troughs, bollocks. What if it's all one long trough from now on? What then?

He stubbed out his cigarette and stood up.

He took the lift up to the fourth floor. Walked down the hall to Sarah's ward, walked up to her bed. She wasn't there.

He walked back to the nurses' station, asked if Sarah Heller had been moved somewhere else. 'Sarah Heller?' the sister repeated. 'Just a moment, I'll check.' She flicked through some file cards. 'There's no patient with that name.'

'But she was here yesterday,' Fitz protested. 'I saw her.'

Another sister came to the desk, checked through a different set of files. 'Are you a relative?' she asked Fitz.

'No, just a friend.'

'I'm terribly sorry,' the sister told him gently, 'but I'm afraid she passed away early this morning.'

He took the lift back downstairs and went outside to get a taxi. Looks like it's going to be one long trough, he thought, heading back to his empty house.

TWENTY-NINE

Fitz turned the key in his front door lock and headed straight for the ringing phone. 'Fitz,' he answered, slightly out of breath.

'I've been phoning you every five minutes for the last two hours,' Penhaligon told him.

'I knew it was only a matter of time before we'd kiss and make up.'

'Fitz,' Penhaligon said, exasperated. 'Sean Kerrigan ram-raided a petrol station mini-mart a little over two hours ago, beat up the cashier pretty badly.'

'Have you got him?'

'No,' she said, 'but there's a witness; he identified Sean from a photo. Bilborough's there now, he wants you at the scene. I'll be round to get you in a minute.'

He was waiting at the kerb when her car pulled up. She reached over to open the passenger side door. 'Are you all right, Fitz?'

'Yeah, sure,' he said, getting in beside her.

'Your eyes are awfully red,' she persisted. 'And so's your nose. If I didn't know better, I'd think you'd been . . .'

'Touch of hay fever,' he interrupted. 'So tell me about the cashier.'

Penhaligon sighed. 'Ruptured spleen, fractured skull, every rib broken. He's lucky to be alive.'

'Bit of a hero, was he? Protecting the night's receipts?'

She shook her head. 'I don't know, Fitz. The place is a wreck – you'll see that when we get there – but as far as anyone can tell so far, there doesn't seem to be anything missing. The till is full of cash – it hasn't been touched.'

Fitz filled his cheeks with air and blew, thinking.

'Giggsy used to do that,' Penhaligon said.

'What?'

'Blow out his cheeks when he was thinking. Made him look like a chipmunk.'

'You must hate Tina Brien,' Fitz said. 'You think about what she did to Giggsy . . .'

'I have a job to think about, Fitz,' Penhaligon interrupted him. 'When I'm on duty, I think about the job.'

'Something to think about,' Fitz said. 'Something to focus on.'

'That's right,' Penhaligon said, pulling into the petrol station forecourt. 'Oh yeah, I meant to tell you,' she added as they got out of the car. 'Tina's known to Sheffield police. They're faxing some stuff. The boss wants you to have another go at her when it arrives.'

Bilborough stood in the middle of the brightly-lit shop, looking up at the formidable figure of the Chief Superintendent, a man with steel-grey hair, an immaculate uniform, and the well-honed body of an athlete.

Fitz and Penhaligon entered through the gaping hole that had once been a window, carefully stepping round the last remnants of shattered glass still scattered about the floor.

The Chief Superintendent didn't even glance in their direction. 'Aim?' he asked Bilborough, crossing his arms.

'To find him,' Bilborough said, stating what he believed to be the obvious.

'No,' the Chief Superintendent corrected him. 'To find him before he kills again. Method?'

'I've given out a name, a description and the fact that he stutters,' Bilborough said. 'Every time he's been spotted, I've followed it up. If there's anything else I can do, I'd like to hear about it, sir.'

'This girl,' the Chief Super said. 'This Tina.'

'Fitz is gonna have another go at her.'

The Chief Super uncrossed his arms and walked over to

Fitz. 'What do *you* aim to get out of her?'

Fitz looked up at the Chief Superintendent looking down at him – it was rare for Fitz to meet anyone taller than he was. He saw the kind of stern, no-nonsense face that automatically commanded respect. Fitz pulled his shoulders back and directed the same stern, no-nonsense look right back at him. 'How far did your wife go on your second date?'

'You'd better be good,' the Chief Superintendent said.

Penhaligon stepped in to intervene. 'There's a bond between them, sir. Fitz will try to break that bond. If he does, she might tell us where Sean is.'

'I'll speak to the media,' the Chief Super said, walking away.

'I could handle that, sir,' Bilborough volunteered, rushing after him.

Tina leaned against the plain white wall of the interview room, staring down at her feet. Without make-up, her face was pale and tired. She was still wearing the same black dress she'd been arrested in, looking more than a little bedraggled after two nights in a cell. Her black hair fell loosely from a side parting, exposing lighter brown roots in need of a retouch.

In the next room, Bilborough and the Chief Super sat watching her on the video monitor.

Penhaligon followed Fitz into Interview Room 1. She carried her usual notebook. Fitz carried four books and several torn-off sheets of thermal paper. They sat at the table, facing Tina. Fitz put his little stack of paper in the centre of the table, placing a book at each corner to keep it flat. 'Don't you hate it when you get a fax,' he asked Tina, 'the way it curls up at the edges?'

She shot him a look of contempt before turning her attention back to the floor.

'And how are we this morning, Tina?' Fitz asked her, all friendly bonhomie. 'Sleep well, did you?'

Tina didn't answer.

Fitz picked up the faxed pages and walked around to where Tina was standing. 'Christine Brien. Manchester. More juvenile convictions than the Artful Dodger. Sheffield. Three convictions for soliciting,' he said, looking down at the top sheet. 'Panhandle hates prostitutes.'

Penhaligon was careful to keep her expression neutral. She hated it when Fitz dropped her in it like that. But he'd always justify it later, always say something like, 'But I had to do it, Panhandle, you know I had to do it.'

'I'm not surprised,' Tina said, finally looking up from the floor. 'Who'd pay for that?'

Penhaligon gave Tina one of her biggest, brightest smiles; she figured Tina would hate that.

'Twenty quid a time, though, eh?' Fitz went on, taunting her. 'What's twenty quid, Tina, when you can have a man by the balls for the rest of his life? Half his income, half his house, half his life? She despises you because she thinks you sell it cheap.' He glanced at Penhaligon. 'Affirmative?'

'Affirmative,' Penhaligon agreed.

'Does Sean know?' Fitz asked Tina.

Tina glared at him. So Sean didn't know.

'First chance I get, I'm telling him,' Penhaligon said.

'Why?' Fitz asked her.

'Just for the thrill,' Penhaligon said.

'Is this some kind of a double act?' Tina said.

'Could be.' Fitz pointed to the books on the table. 'I wrote these.'

'Who's a clever boy, then?'

Fitz walked back to the table and sat down next to Penhaligon. 'I was wrong when I said you should be locked up and forgotten about,' he told Tina. 'I'd like to write a book about you.'

Tina's expression changed ever so slightly. She was trying to hide it, but Fitz had captured her attention.

'Immortality,' he said, 'that's what we all want. No shame in that.'

'What sort of book?' Tina asked carefully.

'A book about you. How you grew up. How you met Sean. How it felt to kill.'

Penhaligon could see the wheels turning inside Tina's head; she was relishing the idea of it. Mentally casting Julia Roberts to play her in the Hollywood film version.

'Tell me about Mummy and Daddy,' Fitz said.

Tina shook her head. 'No.'

'Brook Road, Hale. Nice middle-class house. Where did they go wrong?'

'I didn't ask to be born to them.'

'Did they ignore you?' Fitz asked her, voice dripping with mock sympathy.

She laughed. 'No. They talked. They never stopped bloody talking to me.'

Fitz was a little surprised by that; it wasn't the answer he'd expected. 'And you didn't like that?'

'No.'

'Where's Sean?' he asked suddenly, trying to catch her off guard.

'I've no idea.'

'Do you like yourself, Tina?'

She looked at him vaguely, as if the question had confused her.

'How many times is it you've tried to kill yourself now?'

Penhaligon leaned forward, resting her chin on her hands. She watched with some satisfaction as Tina began to squirm uncomfortably under her unflinching, expressionless gaze.

'Twenty pounds a time,' Fitz said. 'That's all your body's worth. You despise it. Your body, your soul, you despise. All those thoughts in your head, all those evil, twisted thoughts, you despise.'

Tina slumped back against the wall, slowly sliding down to the floor.

'And you despise Sean too, don't you?' Fitz went on, purposely tormenting her. 'What kind of man could love anybody so evil and twisted and worthless as you?'

Her shoulders jerked as if she was sobbing, but no sound came out.

'Why did you buy the camcorder?'

She hid her face behind her hands. 'What camcorder?' she said, her voice a barely audible croak.

'Did you film yourselves making love?'

'I've no idea what you're talking about!'

'Sex and death, that's what I'm talking about. You kill Giggs, you're hot, you're lustful, you do it right there and then. Not terribly romantic, really, is it? More a run-of-the-mill sex murder, I'd say. Did you shut that out of your mind? Did you and Sean discuss it?'

Tears rolled down her face, dripping onto her wrinkled dress.

'Did it bother you?' Fitz demanded.

Tina's face twisted in agony. 'Do you get off on this kind of crap?' she demanded, sobbing. The B-movie glamour was gone, the tough veneer was gone. All that was left was a figure of absolute wretchedness, huddled in an almost foetal position on the cold, uncarpeted floor.

'It did bother you. Just something more to despise about yourself.' He changed tone again, became friendly and comforting. 'Let me put your mind at ease,' he said. 'It's nature.'

He rose from the table, approaching her gently. 'Whenever we experience death at close quarters, nature sends all these little messages down our body. They say death is all around, death is rampant. Make more babies, make more babies.' He crouched down in front of her. 'Does that make you feel better?'

She raised her tear-streaked face, silently mouthing the word: 'Yes.'

'I understand these things,' he said, soothing her. 'I know how you feel. I can help you. Nobody's born like this. Things have happened to you that have made you like this. I won't let anyone judge you. They have not got the right; they have not been through the things that you've been through. I can help you. I can make you like yourself.'

Her eyes searched his face, pleading.

'Wouldn't that be nice,' he said, 'to like yourself?'

'Yes,' she whispered.

'But you have to trust me. You have to prove to me that you trust me. Tell me where Sean is.'

She began to shake all over, her mouth working as if she was trying to speak but couldn't find the words. Just like Sean.

'Where is he, Tina?'

She shook her head angrily, a new flood of tears rolling down her cheeks. 'I was born to be a dog,' she told him, sobbing.

THIRTY

Sean parked across the street, gazing up at the large detached house he'd never been allowed to enter. Well, he was going to enter it now.

He pulled his hood forward, almost completely obscuring his face, and jumped out of the car, feeling a rush of adrenaline as he crossed the street and ran past the open gates into the driveway. The house looked different in the daylight, not so big after all. Not so forbidding.

He stepped up to the door and rang the bell, lowering his head so that his face was completely hidden. The door opened and he pushed his way inside, pinning Tina's father against the wall.

But it wasn't Tina's father, it was a skinny old man with a shiny bald head and thick glasses. 'What do you think you're doing?' the bald old man demanded.

Sean let go of the man and ran into the living room; it was piled high with boxes. He ran into the kitchen; more boxes.

He ran back into the hall just as the bald man was picking up the phone. Sean ripped the phone from its socket and shoved the man back against the wall. Sean took a deep breath and opened his mouth wide. 'H-h-how l-long?' he said.

The man looked at him as if he thought he was crazy. 'What?'

Sean jerked his head forward and back, drawing out the words like that dickhead speech therapist had told him to: '*Hooww looonng haaave yoooou liiived heeere*?'

'Will you please get out of my house?' the man said.

A woman appeared at the end of the hall. 'What's going

on? What do you want?'

'Call the police! Use the phone in the lounge,' the bald man shouted at her.

Sean let go of the man and rushed towards the woman. 'How long have you lived here?' he demanded.

'We've only just moved in,' the woman said.

'Sh-shit!' he said, kicking the wall. 'Shit!'

He ran out the door and drove away.

The uniforms took Tina down to the cells; Fitz and Penhaligon walked into the adjoining room where Bilborough and the Chief Superintendent sat side by side with their arms crossed, staring at a video monitor which now displayed an empty white room.

'Why did you stop?' the Chief Super demanded.

'I stopped because I can't get anything more out of her,' Fitz told him. 'Not just now, at any rate. She's too upset, she needs time to calm down.'

'She's upset,' the Chief Super repeated. 'You want us to hold up an investigation into the murder of a police officer because the suspect is upset.'

Once again, Penhaligon stepped in. 'Fitz thinks that if he speaks to Tina's parents before continuing with her interview, they might be able to shed some light on whatever it is she's talking about. And then, armed with that understanding, it might be easier to get Tina to open up, to tell us where Sean might be.'

'All right,' the Chief Super said. 'Go.'

Tina had told him she didn't know her parents' address; the last time she saw them they'd been about to move, and they hadn't told her where.

Fitz waited while Penhaligon phoned the estate agents. 'They completed a couple of days ago,' Penhaligon said, putting down the phone. 'Moved to twenty-two Willow Way.'

'Know where that is?'

'I think I can find it,' Penhaligon told him drily.

He pushed the incident room door open and saw Judith walking towards him. 'Is it Mark?' he said, rushing forward to meet her.

'He's fine,' Judith said. 'I need to talk to you.'

Fitz indicated Penhaligon, walking towards them. 'We've got to go to Hale now.'

Judith looked at Penhaligon, a glimmer of recognition on her face. Penhaligon came to a stop beside Fitz and looked away, biting her lip.

'I really need to talk to you, Fitz,' Judith insisted.

Fitz turned to Penhaligon. 'Just give us a minute.'

'There's a room along here,' Penhaligon said, leading the way. She opened a glass door marked NO ENTRY, then closed it behind them.

Judith walked the length of the room, glancing at her surroundings. A couple of cluttered desks, a bulletin board covered with scribbled notes on index cards. An overflowing metal bin stuffed with crumpled papers, discarded tea bags and the contents of at least a dozen ashtrays.

She wrinkled her nose slightly; the room smelled like an ashtray. That was one good thing about living in her father's house; the air didn't reek of stale tobacco. She didn't notice it when she'd lived with Fitz, she'd become so used to it, but after a few days in her father's sterile house, she suddenly realised that every item in her wardrobe smelled of smoke.

She turned to look at Fitz, regarding her curiously. As always, lighting another cigarette. Beyond him, she saw the long reddish-brown hair of the woman from the restaurant – a policewoman, just a work colleague, she told herself – pressed flat against the glass. She was leaning her head back, probably staring blankly out into the corridor, waiting impatiently.

Judith could sense the other woman's tension, as if it was coming at her in waves. Maybe there was more than just work between them after all.

She felt a brief flash of jealousy, then suppressed it. She

226

had no right to feel jealous, she reminded herself. No right to feel angry. She was the one that had walked out, she was the one who'd told Fitz it was over, and she was the one who had . . .

No, she told herself angrily, no guilt. What's done is done. It was over in minutes. It meant nothing. Only served to make her remember what it had been like once, with the man she sometimes felt like she hated, but had never really stopped loving.

And then she'd seen him in the hospital. Despite all the bickering and carping between Fitz and Mark, the constant power struggle, she had seen how deeply Fitz loved him, seen how deeply he was hurting. She'd wanted to wrap her arms around him and tell him everything was going to be all right.

But she didn't want to make a scene. Not in front of Mark, the nurses, everyone. And then she'd gone home to her father's sterile house, and wished more than anything else in the world that she had made a scene, that she'd pressed Fitz's sobbing head to her chest and told him that no matter how hard she tried to stop herself loving him, she just couldn't do it.

'I want to come home, Fitz,' she said.

His face relaxed visibly; he looked so relieved.

'But there's something you should know.'

The look of relief vanished. 'About Graham?'

'Yes.'

'I don't want to know.'

'I'm not coming back under false pretences,' she told him. 'I want total honesty. Everything out in the open.'

'Don't give me that bullshit. You've done something to hurt me. OK, I know nothing about it. It can't hurt me. But it's eating away at your conscience; you need to get it off your conscience. You! Pure bloody selfishness. I am not listening.'

She shook her head in frustration. He always did this to her, always. 'You're doing it again. You're twisting everything I say, every single word.'

'You want honesty; I'll give you honesty. I do not want to know. OK?'

That didn't make sense to her, nothing he was saying made sense. He must have told her a hundred times there was nothing he despised more than hypocrisy, and now he wanted her to be a hypocrite. He'd said he wouldn't be a hypocrite for her, and now she was determined not to let herself become one for him. 'Graham and I . . .' she began.

Fitz drummed his fingers on the sides of a filing cabinet, singing loudly, '*Beautiful dreamer, wake unto me . . .*'

'We had sex.'

He covered his ears with his hands, still singing.

'Graham and I had sex, Fitz.'

Fitz dropped his hands; it was no good, he'd heard her say it. Of course he'd known all along what she was going to say, but until he actually heard the words, he could still pretend that maybe that wasn't it – maybe she'd only felt the need to confess some minor unimportant indiscretion. But there was no point in pretending now; she'd said it. *Why did you have to say it, Judith? There was no need, no need to say anything at all.* But she had to clear her conscience, didn't she?

He looked her up and down, searching for some outward sign of her betrayal. The logical side of his mind knew she looked exactly the same as before, but the emotional side told him she had changed irrevocably. The face, the eyes, were somehow different. This was some stranger he had never known. He moved behind one of the desks, keeping it between them.

'After the restaurant?' he asked the stranger standing opposite him.

'Yes.'

'At his place?'

The stranger gazed at him calmly, refusing to answer.

'Emotional masochism. The more you know, the more it hurts, but you can't stop; it's like picking a scab,' Fitz

228

explained, more to himself than to her. 'At his place?' he asked her again.

'Yes,' she said, clenching her fists.

'He played it just right, didn't he? Not one word of criticism about me all the way back. Left that to you. Am I right?'

'Yeah, that's about right.'

'Yeah,' Fitz said. 'Next: displacement.'

The stranger – Judith, he reminded himself, this was Judith – looked at him questioningly.

'First phase, emotional masochism,' he told her, 'second phase, displacement. The need to blame the man. I tell all my patients, "he didn't rape your wife, she did it willingly, you can't blame the man".'

'You can't,' she agreed. She saw his face, saw that she had hurt him. 'I'm sorry.'

'Phase three,' Fitz said. 'This is a killer. Sexual insecurity. Was he better than me?'

Judith couldn't believe what he was asking her. 'Fitz!'

'Did you reach orgasm?'

'Please stop this.' She cursed herself for coming here, cursed herself for opening her mouth. Why did nothing ever turn out the way she expected? Why couldn't it have turned out like the picture she'd had in her head of him joyfully enfolding her in his arms, whispering in her ear that he loved her and he understood? He was a psychologist, for Christ's sake! It was his job to understand, to wipe away the guilt. He could do it for total strangers, why couldn't he do it for his own wife?

'Come, Mrs Fitzgerald,' he said, putting on another voice, becoming a late night chat show interrogator, distancing himself even further. 'Don't be so coy. Tell the ladies and gentlemen, was he better than me?'

'No.'

'Did you reach orgasm?'

'No.'

'I don't believe you. Phase four: complete refusal to

229

believe anything your partner says or has said. You start scouring your memory for all the other times it might've happened.'

She could feel her throat tightening, her eyes starting to burn. He always had to push and push; he wouldn't stop until he had her in floods of tears. 'For God's sake, Fitz.'

'You look at your own children and wonder if they're really yours. Phase five: the thirst for revenge. Physical revenge against the man, sexual revenge against the woman.' He looked towards the glass door, saw Penhaligon standing in the corridor, looking at her watch. 'I've got to go to Hale.'

He started towards the door, then came to a sudden stop. 'Phase six,' he said, turning back to Judith, circling her slowly, his voice full of menace, spitting words at her like bullets. 'The need to rape! To claim her back, to brand her again as your own. Something Neanderthal and primitive.' He stood over her, scrutinising her body, mentally undressing her. A picture of Graham sprang unbidden into his mind. Graham naked in bed with Judith. 'God,' he said, 'I can't bear to look at you.'

He started towards the door once more, then stopped again, a final question he still had to ask. 'Did you sleep with him? As in spend the night?'

'No.'

'I don't believe you,' he said, reaching for the door handle. 'Can't believe you.'

'We had sex,' she said matter-of-factly. 'I got dressed. I went home.'

Fitz looked back at her one last time, hand still poised to open the door.

'You're right, Fitz,' she said, 'he played it perfectly. He was so bloody politically correct, so bloody smooth about it all I nearly didn't go through with it. But I'd made my mind up. In the restaurant. You know what we were to you, in that restaurant? Your audience. Well no, Fitz; I had a part to play as well.'

Fitz stormed out into the corridor, slamming the door behind him.

Penhaligon glanced back through the glass door; Judith was still in there, leaning against one of the desks, blowing her nose. She didn't look as if she was leaving.

Fitz was halfway down the stairs before Penhaligon caught up with him. 'What happened?' she asked him.

'We've got to go to Hale.'

THIRTY-ONE

PC Ronald Smith got out of a panda car and walked up the drive to a rather desirable detached suburban residence. 'Some day I'll have a house like this,' he told PC Holden, who'd been driving.

'On a copper's salary?' Holden asked him.

'It's nothing to do with salary,' PC Smith told him. 'It's to do with this in here.' He pointed to his head.

'What, empty space?'

'No, brains,' PC Smith said, ringing the doorbell. 'That's why I'm going right to the top.'

'Top of what?'

The door opened before PC Smith could answer his partner. 'I understand you've had a bit of trouble, sir,' he said to the bald-headed man standing in the doorway.

'Please come inside,' the man told them.

The two policemen listened as the man described what had happened. 'Terrified my wife,' he said.

'I wasn't terrified,' she protested. 'He was just a boy.'

'Looked quite young, did he?' PC Smith asked, turning towards the woman.

'That's right,' the bald man's wife said. 'Late teens, I'd say.'

'They're the ones you've got to watch,' her husband insisted.

PC Smith read them back his notes. 'Light brown hair, blue eyes, slim, about five foot ten, wearing a dark blue hooded jacket and jeans. That it?'

'No,' the woman said. 'He had a stutter. He wanted to know how long we'd lived here but he couldn't get the words out.'

'Had a girlfriend like that once,' PC Smith said. 'By the time she said no it . . .' PC Holden nudged him with his elbow. 'Ow!' Smith said, rubbing his side.

'How long have you lived here?' PC Holden asked the wife.

'We only moved in the day before yesterday.'

Fitz was quiet for the first half of the ride. The second half, he wasn't. 'I can't believe it,' he said over and over. 'I mean, you saw him, Panhandle. How could she?'

'Revenge, Fitz. The more repulsive the man, the greater the damage to your ego.'

'But he isn't even a man, Panhandle. He's a little piece of oozing slime. It's like going to bed with a Tory MP, how could any woman do it?'

'There you've got me, Fitz,' she admitted. 'But as for Judith and Graham . . . Can I say I told you so?'

'No, you can't. I tell you, I wanted to strangle her, Panhandle. I honestly felt like I wanted to kill her. Why did she have to tell me? Why did she have to say it?'

'If it's any consolation . . .' Penhaligon began.

'It isn't.'

They pulled up in front of a large detached house in the middle of a tree-lined street. A young woman was bent over some flowers in the front garden. A short distance behind her, a young man was mowing the lawn.

'Excuse me,' Penhaligon said, calling over the fence.

The young woman straightened up. She was in her early twenties, very attractive, with long dark hair tied into a ponytail. She was wearing a knee-length button-down dress, conservative in cut and style. A key hung from a small chain attached to her belt. 'Yes?'

'Are Mr and Mrs Brien here?'

'Yes,' she said, reaching out her hand.

The young man switched off the mower and moved over to join her, walking hand-in-hand with her towards the door of the house.

'Are you Tina's sister?' Fitz asked her, following Penhaligon through the gate.

The young woman stopped and turned around. 'Who are you?'

'I'm a police officer,' Penhaligon told her, holding out her ID.

The young man bent forward to look at it; the woman didn't budge.

'Doctor Fitzgerald here is a psychologist,' Penhaligon continued, gesturing towards Fitz.

'I'm Tina's sister, yes,' the young woman sighed, looking straight ahead. 'What's she done now?'

'I think it might be better if we discussed this inside,' Penhaligon said.

The young man led Tina's sister to the door. She felt for the key hanging from her belt with one hand. She used the other to find the lock.

Fitz and Penhaligon exchanged surprised glances. Tina never mentioned that her sister was blind.

'Come in,' she said, opening the door.

They followed her through an inner door into a long, carpeted hallway. Pictures had already been hung on the walls. An upholstered chair had been placed next to a small table at the foot of the stairs; the table held a lamp and a telephone.

A door on the left led into the lounge. Furniture all in place, books on shelves, no sign of a box or packing crate anywhere. Tina's sister ushered them into the room and told them to have a seat. 'I'll tell my parents that you're here.'

She turned and walked out of the room, leaving the young man – the boyfriend, Fitz surmised – standing uncomfortably in the doorway. Keeping an eye on the unlikely pair of intruders now ensconced on his future in-laws' sofa, politely enquiring whether they would like a cup of tea.

He hadn't been introduced as the blind girl's fiancé, but he didn't need to be. Fitz could tell by the way he behaved towards her, solicitous, yet proprietorial. By the way he took it upon himself to offer them refreshments, as if he already considered himself part of the family. Mummy and Daddy had accepted him without question, had welcomed him into their home.

No doubt about it, this man was marriage material. The perfect son-in-law in waiting. Polite, well-dressed, squeaky clean. Short, young-executive style haircut. Probably an accountant; Mummy and Daddy would like an accountant. Mummy and Daddy wouldn't like Sean Kerrigan, wouldn't even let him in the door.

And then Mummy and Daddy were standing before him. More solidly middle-class than he had ever imagined. He and Penhaligon stood up.

The father was almost as tall as Fitz, a large man with a neatly-trimmed beard. Wearing a tweed jacket with leather patches on the elbows. Looked like a pipe-smoking university lecturer, though Fitz doubted that was his job; more likely he worked in middle management somewhere.

That reminded Fitz he wanted a smoke. He reached into his pocket for a cigarette, then realised there was no ashtray on the coffee table in front of him. He looked around the room and saw to his dismay that there were no ashtrays anywhere.

Mummy and Daddy wouldn't approve of Tina's smoking; they'd call it a filthy habit. They wouldn't approve of his smoking, either.

He lit up anyway, enjoying the look of horror on the mother's face. The accountant-stroke-fiancé hurried out of the room and came back with a cut-glass ashtray which he placed on the table in front of Fitz without a word. Then he left the room again, in search of his fiancée; Tina's sister had not returned to the lounge with her parents.

Mrs Brien was a handsome woman, would have been quite a beauty when she was young. She had long dark hair like both her daughters, but pulled back into a severe bun at the nape of her neck. Her face creased with tension as

Penhaligon introduced herself and Fitz. Her face went white as Penhaligon explained why they were there. Her husband helped her over to a chair. 'We must go to her,' she said.

'I'll be happy to drive you,' Penhaligon said, 'but Doctor Fitzgerald would like to ask you a few questions first. If you don't mind.'

'What kind of questions?' Mrs Brien asked.

'I'm here because I want to help your daughter,' Fitz told her. 'I know this is a difficult time for you, but if you could just answer a few questions, it might help me to help her.'

Mr Brien stood beside his wife's chair, a hand on her trembling shoulder. 'What do you want to know?'

'What was she like as a child, did she do well in school, did she have friends . . . that sort of thing. Ideally, I'd like to see her old room, but I understand you've just moved.'

'Two days ago,' Mrs Brien said.

'Two days? The last time we moved house, it took three months of my wife's nagging before I even started to unpack.'

'We had to get things organised very quickly,' Mrs Brien said. 'For Sammy's sake.'

'That's your other daughter, the one that let us in?'

'Samantha, actually,' Mr Brien said.

'But we've always called her Sammy,' his wife added.

'She's older than Tina, isn't she?'

'Two-and-a-half years,' Mrs Brien said.

'Blind from birth?'

Mrs Brien nodded.

Guilt, Fitz thought. The child is born without sight; it must be the parents' fault. Something in the genes. 'It must have been a great relief to you, when your second daughter was born seeing.'

Mrs Brien nodded again. 'Oh yes.'

The second child becomes an instrument for assuaging the parents' guilt. The younger child can provide the older one with the one thing her parents believe they deprived her of: a pair of working eyes. The second child grows up with

236

her parents' guilt pushed onto her. Develops a guilt of her own: why should I be the one to see? The older one becomes the total focus of all attention, the younger feels lost and forgotten. 'Where's Sammy?' Fitz asked. 'I'd like to talk to her, if you don't mind.'

'In her room,' Mrs Brien said. 'But I think she'd rather not speak to you. To talk about Tina would only upset her.'

'And why is that?'

'They were very close once. They were always together, completely devoted to one another. Tina loved Sammy, she'd do anything for her. Everyone used to comment on it; they used to say how touching it was to see the two of them together. Tina was a very bright little girl; she used to describe things for her sister, so that Sammy always knew what was going on, always could appreciate her surroundings. We always made a point of taking the girls to beautiful places, so Tina would have something interesting to tell her sister.

'Then everything changed when Tina was about twelve or thirteen. She stopped spending time with her sister. Wouldn't even speak to her. Sammy was heartbroken, I can tell you. She didn't understand what she'd done to upset her little sister. She didn't know why she'd turned on her like that, suddenly acted as if she hated her.' Mrs Brien dabbed at her eyes with a tissue. 'And I couldn't give her an explanation, because I didn't know why myself.'

A picture came into Fitz's mind, of little Tina trotting along at Sammy's side, dutifully describing every object they came across. Loyal, trusty and devoted. Making sure it was safe for her to cross the road, steering her round obstructions and holes in the pavement. Acting out her parents' guilt. Acting as her sister's eyes. Until one fateful day, when she finally decided that she'd had enough. 'Do you have a dog, Mrs Brien?'

'We've got a Labrador.'

'A guide dog for Sammy,' Fitz said. 'When did you first get a dog?'

'When Sammy was in her early teens; we had to get one then.'

When Tina stopped co-operating, Fitz thought.

'It's in the kennel at the moment,' Mrs Brien went on. 'We thought it best to keep it out of the way while we were moving. We were supposed to pick it up this afternoon; I imagine the dog will have to wait now.'

'I imagine it will,' Fitz said.

THIRTY-TWO

Penhaligon followed Fitz into Interview Room 1. Tina sat slumped in a chair, her head on the wooden table. Fitz and Penhaligon sat in their usual positions, across from her. Fitz spread a series of glowing school reports across the table in front of him. 'Your parents are outside,' he said.

Tina stiffened, not looking up. 'Is *she* there?'

'Sammy?'

'Yeah.'

'You never told me she was blind,' Fitz said.

'Is she there?' Tina asked again, still refusing to lift her head.

'No,' Fitz said. 'She hates you.'

Tina finally looked up. 'Mutual.'

'What went wrong?' The sympathy in his voice was genuine this time.

'I didn't ask to be born. I was born because my sister was blind. They needed a guide dog.'

'They say they gave you every bit of love and affection that they gave Sammy . . .'

'Bollocks.'

'Can I show them in?'

Tina nodded towards one of the reports on the table. 'Third year report. The teacher wrote I had no personality. He was right. She got all my personality. She was blind; she got all the fuss, all the attention. She only had to twitch and I was there. I'd get a pat on the back. I'd hear them tell their friends how devoted I was to Sammy, what a good little doggy I was.'

'You were her eyes,' Fitz said.

239

'Yeah,' she said, putting her head back on the table.

'And you had to describe everything to her?'

'Yeah,' she said tiredly.

'And your parents expected this?'

'Yeah.'

'They thought it would do you good . . .'

'I know.'

'Expand your vocabulary, increase your powers of description . . .'

She lifted her head again, eyes shining with anger. 'I've heard these excuses.'

'Well up to the age of thirteen you were top of your English class. Maybe they were right.'

'They were wrong.'

'Then you turn thirteen, suddenly you're at the bottom. What happened?'

She shrugged. 'I got bored with it.'

Fitz shook his head. 'You got sick of it. You got sick to the very soul of it. It snows, you have to describe it to Sammy. The wind blows, you have to describe it. You're on a beach, in a forest, halfway up a mountain, anywhere of any interest, anything of any beauty, you've got to describe it. You begin to hate beauty.'

'Interest?' she snorted. 'Beauty? I remember a picnic when I was eight or nine. We drove in the car. I had to describe the leather seats, the steering wheel, the bloody windscreen wipers! You tell me, is that beauty? We finally stop. My dad says, isn't this a pretty spot? I know that's my cue, I have to tell Sammy *how* pretty it is. There are tall trees, I say. How tall? asks my dad. Taller than our house, I say. How much taller? At least three times, I say, with thick, rough barks and long branches that get narrower and narrower the higher up you go. That's good, my mum says, what else do you see? So I tell them I see a brilliant blue sky with white fluffy clouds that remind me of a pillow stuffed with feathers. But that isn't enough. My dad brings out the picnic hamper, says look at all the work your mum's gone to, and then I have to describe the food.'

'So you begin to pray for boredom,' Fitz said. 'Long stretches of nothingness.'

'But even that didn't help,' she said. 'A rainy, grey day, stuck inside the house – that's boredom, right? That's nothingness. So what do I have to do then? Lead Sammy from room to room, describing every object. The curtains, the wallpaper. The light fixtures in the ceiling. Sometimes dad would cut pictures out of magazines for me to describe.'

My God, Penhaligon thought as she sat listening to Tina, it must have been like living on the set of a quiz show, twenty-four hours a day. Mum points at a photograph on the wall: *Describe that in detail to your sister.* Dad points at a figurine on the mantelpiece: *Tell Sammy what that looks like.* They call you to the window to look at the sunset: *Make what you are seeing perfectly clear to someone who has no visual frame of reference.*

But none of that was Sammy's fault, Penhaligon thought. Sammy had nothing to do with it, she was only a child. So why blame Sammy?

Fitz leaned forwards across the table, speaking earnestly to Tina, answering Penhaligon's unspoken question. 'You felt guilty because you could see and Sammy couldn't. Then you felt guilty for abandoning her; you knew it wasn't her fault she was blind. The guilt you felt was eating you up inside, tearing you apart. You started to blame Sammy for the way you felt – if Sammy had never existed, you would never have had anything to feel guilty about, you would never have felt the way you do. The guilt turned to hatred; hatred was so much easier to deal with. But the guilt was still there, Tina, wasn't it? The guilt over abandoning someone who needed you, someone who was incomplete without you. So how do you deal with that guilt? You choose a man every bit as needy as the sister you turned your back on, a man with whom you can re-enact the previous relationship. Your sister can't see; you become her

241

eyes. Sean has a problem with speech, and you become his mouth. You're acting out the same relationship, Tina. Surely you can see that.'

Sean drove up and down the streets of Hale, searching for houses with estate agents' boards. They must have stayed in Hale; they'd lived there forever, since before Tina was born.

He was driving up the high street when he saw her, walking hand in hand with her nerd of a boyfriend. He'd never seen her up close – never seen any of them up close – but it had to be her. Wearing dark glasses, being led by the hand through the crowds, never glancing at anyone she passed.

He followed at a discreet distance, watching them turn down a tree-lined street, then enter a big brick house about halfway down.

He parked across the street and waited.

Tina got out of her chair and leaned back against the wall, swaying and singing at the top of her lungs, '*I just called to say I love you . . .*'

'Sit down, please,' the red-haired policewoman told her.

Tina ignored her; that plain stick of a woman who knew nothing about love, who no man would ever look twice at. '*I just called to say how much I care.*'

The policewoman got up and grabbed hold of her arm. Tina shook herself free, and sang right into the woman's astonished face: '*I just called to say I love you . . .*'

She stepped towards the fat psychologist, ignoring the woman gaping at her side. 'It fills the dance floor that one,' she said. 'My parents on holiday, all dressed up for the evening disco, dancing like a pair of stiff wooden dolls while I'd sit by the wall and cringe at the sight of all those dried-up old couples, pretending . . . Even a fat bastard like you gets up for that one – to sing it down your wife's ear: *To say how much I care . . .* Am I right?'

'Yeah.'

She took another step forward. 'Because you can't say it stone-cold sober,' she said, leaning across the table towards him, shoving her face up close to his. 'Because it's a lie. So you just lie to each other half-pissed on the dance floor. You sing it into her ear, not looking into her eyes. Forty-odd years old, twenty-odd years of marriage, bored stiff, not one drop of passion left. So you just lie to each other half-pissed on the dance floor. But I've got a man who's killed for me.'

She straightened up and walked away from the table, heading straight for the door. The policewoman ran up behind her, grabbing hold of both her arms.

'I'd like to see my parents now, please.'

The woman loosened her grip slightly, not quite letting go, and told one of the other coppers to open the door.

The redhead and the fat psychologist escorted her down the hall to the room where her parents were waiting. She paused in the doorway, saw them sitting behind a table, staring up at her expectantly. They'd dressed for the occasion – her father in a tweed jacket and tie, mother in a tasteful grey dress and little string of pearls. Come to visit her, had they? Come to see her in the kennel before they had her put down?

She bared her teeth and growled.

Her mother leapt back in her seat, startled. Her father looked down at his lap, embarrassed.

She growled again, deeper this time, threatening.

Her mother's face crumpled into a wrinkled mess, tears streaming down her cheeks, as Tina began to bark like the dog her parents had always wanted.

It was PC Smith's turn to do the driving. He brought the panda car to a stop outside an Indian take-away. 'You're not hungry again?' PC Holden asked him.

'I suppose that means you don't want anything.'

'You're going right to the top, all right,' Holden told him. 'Top of the scales.'

'You want something or not?'

PC Holden shrugged. 'Maybe I'll have a little something after all.'

'Like what?'

'Maybe a little chicken curry – make that a vindaloo – some pilau rice, a stuffed nan – make that two – cucumber raita and an order of dal.'

PC Smith rolled his eyes and went inside to order. There was a television set mounted on the wall behind the counter; the Chief Super was on the local news. 'The man is described as young – about twenty years old – with light brown hair and blue eyes. But probably the most striking characteristic of this man is a severe stutter.'

'Holy shit!' PC Smith shouted, running from the shop. He opened the car door and reached for the radio.

PC Holden looked up from his newspaper. 'Hey, what happened to the food?'

'Shut up,' Smith said. 'Oscar Romeo Two to Control . . .'

Fitz rubbed his forehead, a collection of polystyrene cups half-full of tepid coffee sitting on the table before him. Tina sat across from him, her hair tied back with an elastic band, no longer the *femme fatale* – just a lost little girl. 'I know what it's like to hold somebody you thought you'd lost,' he told her. 'Like nothing else on earth. I can arrange it for you. One hour. Somewhere private. Just tell me where he is right now.'

Tina glanced across at Penhaligon. 'Can he do that?'

'Yeah.'

Bilborough leaned towards the video monitor, waiting. She was going to tell them, he could feel it. Behind him, a phone started ringing. Damn, he thought, what timing. He reached around to pick up the receiver, never taking his eyes away from the screen. 'Bilborough.' He listened for a moment. 'Say that again,' he said, turning away from the monitor. He leapt to his feet, slamming down the phone. 'Jimmy!'

● ● ●

'Is anything more important than that?' Fitz asked her. 'To hold him again one more time – before you're separated forever?'

Tina shook her head. 'No.'

'Then tell me where he is.'

'You promise us an hour? You promise?'

'Yeah, I promise,' he said. '*Bonnie and Clyde*, just before the hail of bullets.'

'My sister,' she said finally. 'He's going to kill her.'

Bilborough raced into the room where Tina's parents were still waiting, Tina's mother still sniffling into a handkerchief. 'Mrs Brien, have you ever lived in Brook Road?'

She blew her nose. 'We've just moved.'

'What's your present address?'

'Twenty-two Willow Way, Hale.'

He turned to Beck. 'Get a car round there fast.'

Beck ran off down the hall; Bilborough turned to follow him.

'Wait,' Mrs Brien called after him, 'wait a moment!'

Bilborough swung around to face her.

'My daughter's there,' she said.

'Alone?'

She nodded. 'She's on her own.'

'Shit!' He stepped out into the hall and saw Penhaligon running towards him.

'We think he's going to be at twenty-two . . .' she began, gasping for breath.

'I know where he is,' Bilborough interrupted her. He saw Fitz come out into the hall behind her. 'Got there before you, Fitz,' he called back as he hurried away. 'Police procedure!'

'I won't lift a finger in future,' Fitz shouted after him.

Beck hurried past him, chasing after Bilborough. Fitz caught him by the arm. 'See how you'd manage on your own,' he threatened him.

'Do you mind?' Beck asked, breaking free.

'You bloody walking lobotomy,' Fitz shouted, following him down the hall. 'Sole surviving brain donor, you couldn't solve a crossword puzzle!'

By the time Fitz reached the end of the corridor, Beck and Bilborough were nowhere in sight. 'Ungrateful bastards!' he said, pounding a fist into his open hand. He walked back to where Penhaligon was still standing, outside the interview room. 'Ungrateful bastards!'

She threw her hands up in the air, completely at a loss.

THIRTY-THREE

The front door opened and closed; Sammy's nerd of a boy-friend headed off down the street, whistling. Sean waited until the man was out of sight, then got out of the car.

He transferred a single folded sheet of paper from his jacket pocket to his jeans, then carefully folded his jacket and put it in the boot. He picked up a can of petrol and emptied it over his head, saturating his hair and his black tee shirt. He slammed down the boot and walked towards the house, carrying the remaining three cans of petrol and a length of rope.

The telephone was ringing. Sammy left the kitchen and moved towards the source of the sound: the low table in front of the sofa. Everything had been arranged as much as possible like the old place, furniture in approximately the same positions, lots of open floorspace free of clutter. She'd been over every inch of the place in the last two days. Measured the steps from one room to another, located every switch, every socket, every window and door. Memorised the layout as a series of right and left turns.

From the kitchen doorway to the living room: turn right, walk three steps, turn left, walk twenty steps, turn right again. The ringing phone was directly in front of her. She took a few more steps forward, felt the edge of the table against her shin and reached down.

The doorbell started ringing. Whoever it was just kept ringing and ringing. It sounded as if they were leaning all their weight against the bell. She felt for the receiver and lifted it. 'Just a minute,' she said, then put the receiver down on the table.

'Sammy!' her mother screamed, 'Sammy, wait! Are you there? Are you all right? Sammy, for God's sake, pick up the phone!'

Turn right at the living room doorway, walk ten steps. The doorbell kept ringing and ringing. She opened the front door. 'Hi.'

A hand pushed her back into the hallway, knocking her off her feet. She screamed, and the hand pulled her up by the hair. There was an overwhelming smell of petrol. 'What do you want?' she said. 'Please, what do you want?'

She screamed again as the hand pulled her by the hair into the living room, throwing her onto the sofa.

She heard her mother shouting her name, distant and tinny. There was a grunt, then a splashing sound; something cold was being poured all over her, soaking her. The fumes were overwhelming: petrol. 'No! No! Please God no!' It splashed into her eyes, burning them. She rolled off the sofa onto the floor, screaming in terror and agony. She crawled across the floor, trying to get away. Another container of petrol was emptied over her back.

She bumped her head against a wall. The petrol fumes were making her nauseous and dizzy. She clung to the wall, weeping. 'Please don't hurt me, please.'

Bilborough sat across from Sammy's parents, frustrated and powerless. Listening to the girl's terrified screaming, not knowing what was being done to her, completely unable to stop it. Mrs Brien was nearly hysterical, and he couldn't blame her. He grabbed the phone from her, ripping it out of her hands. 'You keep your hands off her, you filthy bastard. You understand me. Get your dirty stinking hands off her. Pick up this phone! Pick up this phone!' There was no answer, just the sound of someone whimpering. 'Listen to me son, listen. You touch her and I'll cut your bollocks off! Now pick the phone up, Sean.'

● ● ●

Sean made his way round the room, splashing petrol over everything: the antique furniture, the leather-bound books, the fresh-cut flowers in a vase. There was an annoying whining sound coming from the phone: 'Come on son, talk to me. Don't touch her, listen to me, you don't touch her. You leave her alone.' He poured some petrol over it, then slammed down the receiver.

Sammy was huddled in a corner, quiet now. He crouched down beside her, shaking a box of matches next to her ear.

'Please,' she said. 'Please.'

'Sh-sh-sh . . .'

'Sean?' she said. 'Sean,' she repeated, knowing she was right.

'Yeah.' He grabbed her by the hair and pulled her, screaming and crying, out into the hall.

'Why are you doing this?' she gasped between sobs. 'Why?'

He threw her to the floor, then picked up another can of petrol, almost emptying it over the hall carpet, the walls, and the stairs, then splashing the remainder onto Sammy's face. 'For what you did to Tina, right? For what you did to Tina.'

She threw her hands over her eyes, screaming. 'I didn't do anything to Tina . . .'

'For what you did to Tina!'

'I didn't do anything to her!'

'You did!'

'She's lying.'

He grabbed her by the shoulders, shaking her so hard her head banged against the wall. 'You're lying . . .'

'She's lying,' Sammy insisted, 'she's lied all her life.'

'Shut your mouth. Right? Shut your mouth.'

'All she's ever done is tell a pack of lies, Sean . . .'

He pulled her to her feet and dragged her down the hall. 'Shut your mouth! Shut it!'

'I promise you, Sean. I promise whatever she's told you, it's a lie. I promise . . .'

He pushed her ahead of him into the kitchen. 'I'm not

listening so shut your lying mouth!'

'It's a lie!' she screamed. 'She's lying, Sean.'

'I told you to shut your lying mouth!' He shoved her head down on the hob and turned on the gas. There was the sound of an approaching siren, then the doorbell. He pulled her up from the hob, twisting an arm behind her back. 'You tell 'em to keep away, right? You tell 'em to keep away or you're dead!'

'You're hurting me!'

He pushed her down the hall towards the door, increasing the pressure on her twisted arm. 'You tell 'em to keep away!'

'Keep away!' Sammy screamed. 'He'll kill me if you don't keep away!'

Bilborough's car screeched to a halt at the end of the street. Mr and Mrs Brien leapt out of the car; Beck leapt out after them, putting a hand out to stop them from going any further. 'But my daughter,' Mrs Brien said, trembling.

'There's nothing you can do,' Beck told her.

The area had been roped off and several PCs were currently clearing the street of pedestrians. 'Jimmy,' Bilborough said, 'get them out quick. Make sure every house is empty and get an ambulance.'

Beck nodded and rushed up the street.

Bilborough took a mobile phone from his coat pocket. 'Can you tell me your phone number again please, Mrs Brien?'

'Six two five, five five seven one.'

'One more time.'

'Six two five, five five seven one. Call them up, please . . .'

The phone rang several times before someone finally picked it up. 'Sean?' Bilborough said.

'He won't come to the phone,' said a woman's voice. 'The only person he'll speak to is Tina. We're both soaked in petrol. The living room, too. And he's got matches.

Please help me . . .' The line went dead.

'Jimmy!' Bilborough called, walking away from the car. He found him a little way up the street, directing some local residents to the far end of the road. 'Get the Chief Super,' Bilborough told him. 'We're gonna need marksmen. Then the major incident unit. Then the council for a plan of the house.'

Beck nodded. 'Right.'

Bilborough walked back to his car, pressing the redial on his mobile phone.

Sammy sat on the living room floor, her hands bound with rope. Sean leaned back on the sofa behind her, absent-mindedly twirling her hair with one hand. The phone started ringing. He waited, letting it ring, then reached over to pick it up, sliding down onto the floor beside Sammy. He pulled her head close to his, placing the receiver between them so they both could hear.

'Sean?' said a man's voice, the same man as before.

Sammy was quiet; Sean tugged at her hair. 'Sammy,' she said.

'Everything's gonna be all right, Sammy,' the man's voice said. 'Will you put Sean on for me?'

'He won't talk on the phone.'

'Is he there? Can you hear me, Sean?'

She felt Sean push her head forward and back, as if she was nodding. 'He can hear you.'

'Sean, will you talk to me?'

Sean moved the receiver around to his other ear, so only he could hear. 'My name's David Bilborough. I'll come on my own, and I promise no tricks. We'll talk about Tina . . . Would you like that? Are you still there, Sean? No tricks, I promise.'

Sean shook his head, scowling. He didn't want to talk to some wanker he didn't know. There was only one person he might be able to talk to, one person who might understand. 'Fitz,' he said.

251

Bilborough ran up to meet the car as Penhaligon drove through the police cordon with Fitz at her side. The media were out in force once again, but this time they were firmly held back behind the lines of tape stretched across each end of the street. No cute researchers with notebooks to stroke Bilborough's ego this time, Fitz mused as the car pulled to a stop.

There were police cars everywhere, crackling radios everywhere, an ambulance and a couple of fire engines on stand-by, a bloody huge mobile incident unit. Armed officers with rifles and bulletproof vests scattered in every direction, taking up positions behind cars and trees and garden fences, climbing onto neighbouring rooftops. And of course there were the onlookers, always crowds of onlookers. Craning their necks, anxious lest they miss something.

'I've been onto my boss,' Bilborough told him, leaning into the passenger-side window. 'We're gonna get marksmen overlooking the house, back and front. If you're getting nowhere, just walk out. As soon as you walk out without the girl, we shoot the bastard.'

Fitz opened the door, pushing Bilborough out of the way, and climbed out of the car. 'I'm not going in there.'

'You've got to go in there,' Bilborough insisted, heading towards the mobile incident unit.

Fitz grabbed him by the arm. 'Rule one about hostage negotiation is you do not put yourself at risk.'

Bilborough calmly removed Fitz's hand from his arm. 'That's not rule number one.'

'It's my number one.' Fitz became aware of Penhaligon standing beside him, making no effort to hide her disapproval. 'Where's the telephone?'

'In here.' Bilborough said, leading him up the steps into a long caravan in which a crew of uniforms sat monitoring a row of screens. 'Down here, Fitz.' He gestured to a table down at the far end.

Mr and Mrs Brien sat on a padded bench facing a table on which two paper cups of coffee that had long since gone cold sat beside a couple of white telephones. They looked up at him expectantly, Mr Brien placing a protective arm around his wife. Fitz sat down beside them, lighting a cigarette. Then he picked up the nearest phone.

'Hello,' a woman's voice said, barely above a whisper.

'Hi Sammy. It's Fitz. I'm gonna get you out of there, I promise. I promise. Put Sean on, will you.'

'Fitz,' Sammy said.

Sean grabbed the receiver from her, holding it close to his ear. 'Yeah,' he said, wrapping an arm around Sammy's neck.

'What do you want, Sean?'

'I w-w-w . . .' He pulled Sammy's head down onto his lap, his grip on her throat tightening with every attempt to say the words in his head. 'W-w . . .'

'Want,' Fitz prompted him.

'I want,' he said, spitting out the words. 'I want . . .' The words failed him again, got stuck somewhere in the back of his throat, choking him. 'T-t-t . . .' He took a deep breath and tried again, squeezing Sammy's neck as he made a supreme effort to force the words out of his mouth. 'T-t-t-t-t-t-t . . .'

Sammy gasped for breath. 'You're hurting me.'

'Tina,' Fitz said.

'You're hurting me,' Sammy said again.

'T-t-t-t-t . . .'

'Breathe, Sean,' Fitz urged him. 'Nice and slow and nice and deep.'

253

Sean breathed; it didn't help. 'T-t . . .' He shook his head in frustration; his mouth wouldn't do what he wanted it to. He curled his lips back, baring his teeth. 'T-t-t . . .'

'Please, you're hurting me!'

'T-t-t-t-t-t . . .'

Fitz sighed and rubbed his forehead; this was like listening to machine-gun fire. 'To?' he suggested.

'To,' Sean blurted, before going on to the next word: 'G-g-g . . .'

Fitz turned to Bilborough, looming anxiously behind him. He placed the receiver against his chest so Sean wouldn't hear. 'It's going to be some bill,' he said.

'G-g-g . . .' Sean made a final attempt, then slammed down the phone in disgust.

'He can't talk on the phone,' Fitz sighed. 'You've got to let me go in there,' he said, putting on an American B-movie accent. 'I'm the only one he trusts.'

'But you can't, Fitz,' he protested in a high falsetto. 'It's too dangerous!'

'No, I'm going in,' he insisted in the first voice. 'Am I bollocks,' he added as himself.

'I'll go in,' Bilborough said.

'I'm no hero,' Fitz said. 'I know heroes. They're people who are too frightened to be cowards. Well, I'm not.' Bilborough and Penhaligon were staring at him coldly. 'Police procedure, you know,' he added, sarcastically. He became aware of someone crying; he turned and saw Mrs Brien collapse forward onto the table, shoulders convulsing. Her husband threw his arms around her, his red-rimmed eyes accusing. Penhaligon reached across to hold the woman's hand. All right, Fitz thought, I give up. You win, you all win.

He held up his cigarette. 'At least let me finish this? I don't think it'll be very safe to smoke in there somehow, do you?'

THIRTY-FIVE

Two officers armed with rifles crouched on the pavement outside the house, one either side of the front garden gate. 'Slightly better than gnomes, I suppose,' Fitz said.

He walked through the gate and up the path. The door opened before he could raise a hand to knock; Sean was waiting for him. Fitz stood in the small porch between the outer and inner doors, watching as Sean backed away, an arm round Sammy's neck. Her hands were bound tightly together in front of her; Fitz could see the rope digging into her flesh. Sean let go of her as he reached the entrance to the living room, pushing her roughly through the doorway and out of Fitz's line of sight. He planted himself in the centre of the hallway, holding a long wooden match in one hand, the matchbox in the other. 'Cl-cl-cl . . .'

'Close it?'

'Yeah.'

Fitz shut the door and immediately started coughing. The air in this house was pure poison. 'God,' he said, reaching into his pocket for a handkerchief. He held it over his nose, trying not to breathe. 'Are you OK, Sammy?' he called.

A voice called back weakly. 'Yeah.'

'Petrol,' Sean said, coughing. 'And gas. I've turned all the gas taps on.'

Fitz sank into the chair next to the hall table, wheezing. 'I gathered that.'

'I strike a match, the whole lot goes up. Right? The whole bloody lot! Me, her, the house, everything.'

'I think I've grasped the point you're making here, Sean.'

'I'm in,' Sean said, pacing up and down excitedly. 'I'm in now. I came with Tina and they wouldn't let me in. They treated me like crap. Made me wait outside, with the bloody dog barking at me through the door. Told Tina to get shot of me, treated me like I was nothing. Treated me like I was crap. Now I'm in, I'm gonna take the whole bloody place up with me.'

'What do you want, Sean?'

He stopped pacing, pointed a finger in Fitz's face. 'I want you to let Tina go. She had nothing to do with it, right? Sweet f.a.! Sweet f.a. to do with it, right? So you let her go, right?'

He shook his head. 'Can't do that, Sean.'

Sean pointed to a piece of paper sticking out from beneath the phone on the hall table, next to where Fitz was sitting. 'Then take that, right. And do one. That's my statement. Right? All down to me.' He started his pacing again. 'Everything was down to me. Tina had nothin' to do with it. I made her go along with it. I forced her into it. Right?'

Fitz reached over to pick up the paper, glanced at it, then nodded, stuffing it into his pocket. 'I know.'

Sean paced a couple more steps, then stopped. 'What do you mean, you know?'

'She told me everything. She blamed it all on you.'

'You're lyin',' he said, but Fitz could see the beginnings of doubt in his eyes; he wasn't so sure now.

'How do you think the cops got here so quickly?' Fitz demanded. 'Huh? I'll tell you how: she told them you were here.'

Fitz could see the panic rising: what if this was all for nothing? What if he was sacrificing himself for someone who had already betrayed him? What if it just wasn't worth it? *Come on, Sean*, Fitz urged him mentally, *give it up; you know it isn't worth it.*

'I d-d-d . . .' Sean was trying desperately, but the impetus just wasn't there now; the doubt had really set in, had begun

256

gnawing away at the anger.

'You don't believe me,' Fitz said sarcastically. 'How touching. All this for a slut like Tina.'

Sean gasped for breath, dizzy from the fumes. 'No!'

'She was on the game,' Fitz told him, his tone implying that everyone but Sean knew it all along.

Sean shook his head slowly, refusing to believe what he didn't want to hear.

'She screwed Giggs,' Fitz said. 'Remember, the policeman you killed?'

'I'm gonna strike this,' Sean threatened him. 'I'm gonna strike this match if . . .'

'She screwed Giggs in the afternoon and told him to come back and that's why he was so keen to come back. She screwed him in the afternoon.'

Sean shook his head, his lips curling into a ghoulish smile.

'She screwed him when you weren't there,' Fitz insisted.

'I was there,' Sean said, eyes gleaming with manic triumph. He laughed. 'You're sussed, right? I was there!'

Fitz coughed into his handkerchief, silently cursing himself for going too far. He'd had him, and then he'd blown it.

Sean waved the matchbox in the air. 'I'm gonna strike this if you don't shut your dirty lyin' mouth. I'm gonna strike it, right?'

The phone started ringing.

Sean froze, match poised in his hand, staring at the phone.

Fitz shrugged. 'It could be my stockbroker.' He picked up the receiver, keeping his eye on Sean the whole time. 'Fitz . . . Petrol fumes, gas . . . Really,' he said, glancing at his watch. 'Thanks.' He stood up and started to walk towards the kitchen. 'Sean, I'm just going to turn off the gas.'

Sean jumped in front of him, brandishing his matches. 'No. No. No.'

Fitz kept moving, forcing Sean to walk backwards. 'Go on, just the gas.'

Sean planted himself in the kitchen doorway, refusing to budge another inch.

'The thing is, Sean, when the central heating comes on, the house is going to blow up anyway.'

'Yeah?' Apparently he thought that was funny; he was giggling about it.

'If they had the same system they had at the last house, with a pilot light, you would have had the pleasure of blowing yourself to kingdom come quite some time ago, but apparently this house has some kind of electronic ignition. What time does it come on, Sammy?' Fitz called down the hall.

'Six,' she called back. 'What time's it now?'

'You'd better go then,' Sean told Fitz.

'What time is it now?' Sammy asked again.

He checked his watch. 'Three minutes to,' he yelled down the hall. He heard her in the next room, half coughing, half weeping. He looked down at Sean, still holding out his box of matches as if they meant something. 'You know,' he said. 'A day or two ago, I would've called your bluff. But I don't want to take chances right now. You see, I'm quite determined to live. Something to do with my wife and daughter. I won't bore you with the details.' He held up Sean's scribbled statement so that he could see it, then tore it into tiny pieces which he stuffed into his mouth and swallowed. 'There,' he said, gulping. 'I've eaten your words. Now I'm going to let Sammy go.' He turned and walked down the hall, towards the living room.

Sean followed him out into the hall, rattling his box of matches. 'You're not!'

Fitz found Sammy huddled on the living room floor. The knot in the rope around her wrists was too thick and complicated-looking to untie now; there just wasn't the time. He pulled her to her feet and walked her to the door.

'I'll strike this!' Sean shouted.

'You just don't get it, Sean, do you? You're not in control any more. Go on, light your bloody match. The whole place

258

is going to blow up anyway. Forget about Tina. Forget about your statement. Forget about taking the blame. Go on, light your match.'

Sean hesitated, his bluff called.

'Or come with us,' Fitz added, his voice pleading. 'Come with us.'

Sean seemed to shrink before him, becoming small and helpless and confused. He'd had all that power over all those people – the police, the fire brigade, the neighbours – and now it had been taken away from him. Nothing he could do now would make any difference. 'If you touch that door . . .'

Fitz turned the handle and gently pushed Sammy forward. 'Out the door, turn left, fast as you like . . .'

She stumbled forward down the path, weak and dizzy. Chest hurting, head pounding. She could hear voices calling her name, urging her on: 'Don't stop, keep going, this way, Sammy. This way! Run, Sammy, run!'

Her mother ran from behind the tape to meet her, pulling her the last few feet. The armed officers who'd been stationed by the front gate jumped up and ran back to the safety of the line. Everyone on the street was cheering and applauding.

Everyone except Jane Penhaligon; she stood perfectly still, eyes searching the street. There was no sign of Fitz. He was still in the house.

Fitz stood just inside the outer door, holding it open so he could breathe. 'It was nearly all lies, anyway, Sean. You know she wasn't on the game; you know she didn't screw Giggs. She did tell us where you were though, and you know why? Because I promised her one hour with you. Somewhere quiet. Just to say goodbye. Would you not like that, Sean? An hour with Tina.'

Sean sank to the floor, coughing. 'One lousy hour,' he said slowly, drawing out the syllables the way they'd taught him in speech therapy all those years ago. 'You expect meee to saay all I've got to saay in one lousy stinking hour? This,' he held up the matches, 'will say mooore. Riiight? This will say more than I could ever say in one lousy stinking hour.'

'Don't be daft, Sean. You don't really want to die. Come with me, please.'

Sean looked up at him from the floor, eyes glistening with tears. '*Sad, sweet dreamer,*' he began to sing, '*it's just one of those things you put down to experience. Sad, sweet dreamer, it's just one of those things you put down to experience.*'

Fitz glanced at his watch, there was no more time. He turned and left the house.

'*I was so happy when I found you,*' Sean closed his eyes and kept singing, '*but how was I to know that you would leave me walking down that road, all alone?*'

Fitz walked down the street towards the police line, slow enough for Sean to catch him. *Come on, Sean, come on, then we'll run together.*

'Fitz,' Penhaligon screamed. 'Run, you stupid bastard! Run! Fitz, run!'

There's still time, Sean. If you'll jump up and run, there's still time.

'Fitz!' Penhaligon screeched from behind the line of tape, 'Run, you lump of lard!'

Sean sat on the hall floor, tears running down his face. Tina appeared in front of him, holding out her arms. *Never see each other again, Sean, is that what you want?*

One hour. One final hour.

He got to his feet, and started to walk towards the door.

The central heating went on.

The pavement was showered with glass and bricks; flames leapt into the air, igniting trees and neighbouring roofs. The affluent suburban street resembled a war zone, black smoke rising up to obscure the grey Manchester sky, dozens of fires giving everything an eerie orange glow. Sirens wailed in the distance. Closer by, people were screaming. Fitz lay motionless, arms outstretched, face down on the pavement. Covered in brick dust and rubble.

Penhaligon ran along the street of burning houses, smoke burning her eyes and throat, glass crunching beneath her feet, shouting Fitz's name. She sank to her knees beside him, ignoring the pain as she cut both her legs on the scattered remnants of someone's window. 'Fitz!' she screamed, shaking him. 'Fitz!' She leaned forward, trying to listen for a heartbeat, and heard nothing. He's dead, she thought, the bastard went and got himself killed. She threw herself onto his back, sobbing hysterically. 'You stupid bastard. You stupid, stupid . . .'

He raised his head slightly. 'I think you'll find there's some activity further down.'

She hit him, simultaneously relieved and furious. 'You stupid bastard,' she said, still sobbing. 'Stupid bastard!' She hit him again and again, pounding her fists against his enormous back.

'I'm sorry,' he said, pulling himself up to his knees.

'You stupid,' she choked, still kneeling. Slapping at him harmlessly now. 'Stupid, stupid, stupid, stupid . . .' She collapsed into his arms, weeping. 'I thought I'd lost you, you belligerent, overbearing, obnoxious . . . fat bastard! Don't you ever do that to me again! Don't you ever . . .'

'I'm sorry,' he said, stroking her hair, gently rocking her back and forth as they knelt together in the middle of the road, oblivious to the screaming crowds and the flames.

'Stupid bastard,' she sobbed. 'You can't even see what's going on under your own nose, can you? Right under your own bloody nose, and you haven't got a clue! You haven't got a bloody clue!'

'I'm sorry,' he said, holding her tight. 'Panhandle, I'm sorry.'

'Bastard!' she said, hitting him again. 'Just once in your stupid life, I wish you'd call me Jane.'

The Cracker Writers

Jimmy McGovern

Jimmy McGovern's scriptwriting career began in the early 1980s with plays for Liverpool's Everyman and Playhouse theatres. His Merseyside association continued with scripts for over eighty episodes of Channel 4's soap opera *Brookside* between 1983 and 1989. During the 1990s he has written for over a dozen films and television series, including *EL CID*, *Backbeat* and, of course, *Cracker*.

Molly Brown

Molly Brown has been everything from an armed guard to a stand-up comic. She is author of a recently published science fiction thriller for young adults, *Virus*, and is currently working on a historical crime novel, *Invitation To A Funeral*.

The Cracker Stories

Series One

The first three Cracker stories, first broadcast on British television in 1993, were all written by Jimmy McGovern. Based on the original scripts, Virgin's Cracker novels add depth and detail to the televised stories.

The Mad Woman In The Attic
Adapted by Jim Mortimore

Dr Edward Fitzgerald, who insists that everyone call him Fitz, is a psychologist with an apparently conventional life. He teaches and practises psychology; he has an attractive wife, two children, and a big house in a pleasant suburb of Manchester. But he's also addicted to gambling, booze, cigarettes, and pushing his considerable bulk into any situation he finds intriguing. His wife Judith has had enough. She leaves him. Fitz's life is beginning to fall apart.

When one of his students is murdered, Fitz can't resist becoming involved. The police have a suspect; they are sure he's the serial killer, but he's claiming complete amnesia. The police reluctantly hire Fitz to get a confession.

As Fitz investigates, he finds that the police theory doesn't fit the facts. He discovers, in solving murder cases, a new focus for his life. And he meets Detective Sergeant Jane Penhaligon.

To Say I Love You
Adapted by Molly Brown

People do strange things for love.

Tina's parents had nothing but loving intentions when they turned her into a talking guide dog for her blind sister. Sean, full of bitterness and fury, is prepared to kill for the love of Tina. And Fitz, psychologist and occasional catcher of murderers, would do anything to win back the love of his wife Judith – if only he didn't find himself working so closely with DS Jane Penhaligon.

In this, the second Cracker thriller, Fitz can find a murderer, prevent a catastrophe, and still find time to flirt with a pretty policewoman. But he also knows only too well the motivations that drive Judith into another man's bed and that push him to the edge of self-destruction.

Compared to the complications of Fitz's own life, tracking down a team of cop-killers is simple.

One Day A Lemming Will Fly
Adapted by Liz Holliday

Everything's going to be all right. Judith is back home, Penhaligon's falling in love, and Fitz has a new problem to solve from the police.

It's an open and shut case. A schoolboy – a young, effeminate, scholarly and often bullied schoolboy – is found murdered. His English teacher – male, single, lives alone – tries to commit suicide. It's obvious: the teacher killed his pupil. The police think so. The boy's parents think so. Everyone in the family's neighbourhood thinks so. And Fitz thinks so. It's just a matter of obtaining a confession.

But the truth is as elusive as trust and honesty, and the case goes badly wrong.

In this, the third Cracker story, Fitz reaches the crisis in his personal drama. He has to choose between Judith and Jane. And that's the least of his problems.

The Cracker Stories

Series Two

Three new Cracker stories are appearing on television in the autumn of 1994. These will be adapted into novels which will be published in the spring of 1995.